The End of Loneliness

ABOUT THE AUTHOR

Benedict Wells was born in Munich in 1984. Starting at the age of six, he attended three different state boarding schools, then moved to Berlin on graduating in 2003. He decided against going to university, choosing instead to concentrate on his writing and earn a living doing a variety of jobs.

In 2016 Wells won the European Prize for Literature with his fourth novel, *The End of Loneliness*. It has been on the German bestseller list for over 18 months, and has been translated into 26 languages. After living in Barcelona for several years, Wells recently moved back to Berlin.

Benedict Wells

The End of Loneliness

TRANSLATED BY
CHARLOTTE COLLINS

SCEPTRE

First published in Great Britain in 2018 by Sceptre
An Imprint of Hodder & Stoughton
An Hachette UK company

I

Copyright © Benedict Wells 2018

Translation copyright © Charlotte Collins 2018

The right of Benedict Wells to be identified as the Author of the Work has been asserted
by him in accordance with the Copyright, Designs and Patents Act 1988.

First published in Germany in 2016 by Diogenes Verlag AG

A CIP catalogue record for this title is available from the British Library

Trade Paperback ISBN 978 1 47 365403 7
eBook ISBN 978 1 47 365405 1

Typeset in Sabon MT Std 11.75/14.75pt by
Palimpsest Book Production Limited, Falkirk, Stirlingshire

Printed and bound by CPI Group (UK) Ltd, Croydon, CR0 4YY

Hodder & Stoughton policy is to use papers that are natural,
renewable and recyclable products and made from wood grown in sustainable
forests. The logging and manufacturing processes are expected to conform
to the environmental regulations of the country of origin.

Hodder & Stoughton Ltd
Carmelite House
50 Victoria Embankment
London EC4Y 0DZ

www.sceptrebooks.co.uk

For my sister

Draw your chair up
close to the edge of the precipice
and I'll tell you a story.

F. Scott Fitzgerald

Part One

I've known Death a long time, but now Death knows me.

I open my eyes carefully, blink a few times. Slowly the darkness fades. A bare room, lit only by the green and red glow of small machines and the shaft of light falling through the half-closed door. The nocturnal silence of a hospital.

It feels as if I've woken from a dream that's been going on for several days. A dull, warm pain in my right leg, my stomach, my chest. In my head a faint buzzing, getting louder. Gradually I realise what must have happened.

I've survived.

Images start to surface. Riding the motorbike out of the city, accelerating, the curve up ahead. Wheels no longer gripping the road, seeing the tree coming towards me, trying in vain to swerve, closing my eyes . . .

What saved me?

I squint down at myself. A neck brace; my right leg immobilised, probably in plaster, my collarbone bandaged. Before the accident I was in good shape – very good, even, for my age. Perhaps that helped me.

Before the accident . . . Wasn't there something else, something entirely different? But I don't want to remember; I prefer to think of the day I taught the children how to make a stone skip across water. Of my brother's hands gesticulating when he argues with me. Of the trip to Italy with my wife, and how early one morning we walked a bay on the Amalfi coast while all around us it was starting to get light and the sea foamed gently against the rocks . . .

I doze off. In my dream we're standing on the balcony. She gives me a penetrating look, as though she's seen right through me. She tilts her chin towards the inner courtyard where our children are playing with the boys next door. Our daughter is boldly climbing onto a wall, while our son hangs back, watching the others.

'He gets that from you,' she says.

I hear her laugh, and reach for her hand . . .

Continuous beeping. A male nurse rigs up a new infusion bag. It's still the middle of the night. A calendar on the wall says *September 2014*. I try to sit up.

'What day is it today?' My voice sounds strange.

'Wednesday,' says the nurse. 'You were in a coma for two days.'

It's as if he were talking about someone else.

'How do you feel?'

I lie down again. 'A bit dizzy.'

'That's perfectly normal.'

'When can I see my children?'

'I'll let your family know first thing in the morning.' The nurse walks to the door and pauses briefly. 'If you need anything, ring the bell. The consultant will come and check on you again shortly.'

When I don't answer, he leaves the room.

What is it that makes a life into what it becomes?

In the silence I hear every thought, and suddenly I'm wide awake. I start going over all the different stages of my past. Faces I thought I'd forgotten swim towards me: I see myself as a boy on the sports field at boarding school, and the red light of my darkroom in Hamburg. At first the memories are blurred, but over the next few hours they start to come into focus. My thoughts roam further and further back in time, until at last they settle on the calamity that overshadowed my childhood.

Currents

(1980)

When I was seven, my family went on holiday to the south of France. My father, Stéphane Moreau, was from Berdillac, a village near Montpellier. One thousand eight hundred inhabitants, a baker's, a brasserie, two wineries, a carpentry workshop and a football team. We were visiting our grandmother, who in the past few years had not left the village.

As on all long drives, our father was wearing an old, pale-brown leather jacket, pipe stuck in the corner of his mouth. Our mother, who'd been dozing for most of the journey, put on a cassette of Beatles songs. She turned to me.

'For you, Jules.'

'Paperback Writer' – my favourite song, back then. I sat behind her, humming along. The music was drowned out by my siblings: my sister had twisted my brother's ear. Martin, whom we all called Marty, screamed and complained to our parents.

'Stupid snitch.' Liz pinched his ear again.

They fought harder until Mother turned and gave them both a look. That look was a masterpiece. It conveyed understanding for Marty, with his mean sister, as well as for Liz with her annoying brother, but above all it conveyed that fighting was utterly point-less; furthermore, it even contrived to indicate that there might be ice creams for good children at the next petrol station. My brother and sister instantly stopped scrapping.

'Why do we have to go to Granny's every year?' asked Marty. 'Why can't we go to Italy instead?'

'Because it's the done thing. And because your *mamie* loves it when you visit,' said Father, in French, not taking his eyes off the road.

'Not true. She doesn't like us at all.'

'And she smells so funny,' said Liz. 'Like old armchairs.'

'No, she smells like a mouldy cellar,' said my brother.

'Don't keep saying things like that about your *mamie*!' Our father steered the car round a roundabout.

I gazed out of the window. Thyme shrubs, garrigue and kermes oak stretched off into the distance. In the south of France the air was more fragrant, the colours more intense than at home. I put my hand in my pocket and played with the silver franc coins left over from last year.

We reached Berdillac towards evening. In retrospect, the place always reminded me of a grouchy but essentially lovable old man who dozed all day. As in many parts of Languedoc, the houses were made of sandstone; they had plain shutters and reddish, weathered roof tiles bathed in the soft light of the setting sun.

The gravel crunched beneath the wheels as our minibus came to a halt in front of the house at the end of the Rue Le Goff. There was something eerie about the building; its façade was overgrown with ivy, its roof dilapidated. It smelled of the past.

Our father got out first and bounced up to the door. Back then he must have been in what you would call his prime. In his mid-thirties, he still had thick, black hair and was friendly and polite to everyone he met. I would often see neighbours and colleagues standing round him when he spoke and listening, spellbound. The secret was his voice: soft, not too deep, not too high, with the merest hint of an accent, it encircled his listeners like an invisible lasso and drew them in. He was very highly thought of in his job as a chartered accountant, but the only thing that mattered to him was his family. Every Sunday he would cook for us all; he always had time for us children, and his boyish smile gave him an air of optimism. Later, though, looking at photos of him, I realised that something wasn't right even then. His eyes. There was a spark of pain in them, perhaps fear, too.

Our grandmother appeared at the door. She had a wry set to her mouth and barely looked at her son, as if she were ashamed of something. They hugged each other.

We children observed the scene from the car. Our grandmother was said to have been an excellent swimmer in her youth, and very well liked in the village. That must have been a hundred years ago. Her arms looked fragile, she had the wrinkled head of a tortoise and seemed scarcely able to bear the noise her grandchildren made. We were afraid of her, and of the sparsely furnished house with its old-fashioned wallpaper and iron beds. It was a mystery why our father wanted to come here every summer. Marty once said, later on, 'It was as if he had to return year after year to the scene of his greatest humiliation.'

But there was also . . . the smell of coffee in the morning. Sunbeams on the tiled floor of the parlour. Subdued clattering from the kitchen as my siblings fetched the cutlery for breakfast. My father immersed in the newspaper, my mother making plans for the day. Afterwards: cave tours, bike rides, or a game of pétanque in the park.

Finally, at the end of August: Berdillac's annual wine festival. A band played in the evenings, houses were decked with lanterns and garlands, and the streets were filled with the smell of grilled meat. My brother and sister and I sat on the big flight of steps in front of the town hall, watching the grown-ups dance in the village square. I was holding the camera my father had entrusted to me. A heavy, expensive Mamiya: I'd been tasked with taking pictures of the fête. I regarded this as an honour; our father never usually let us handle any of his cameras. Proudly, I took a few photos as he spun our mother elegantly across the dance floor.

'Papa's a good dancer,' said Liz, knowledgeably.

My sister was eleven, a tall girl with blonde, curly hair. Already she was infected with what my brother and I called 'theatre sickness'. Liz behaved at all times as though she were on stage. She beamed as if several spotlights were shining on her, and spoke so loudly and clearly that even the people at the back had no

7

difficulty hearing her. She liked to act precociously around strangers when in fact she had only just emerged from her princess phase. My sister drew and sang, liked to play outdoors with the neighbours' children, would often go days without taking a shower, wanted to be an inventor one day then dreamed of being an elf the next, and there always seemed to be a thousand things going on in her head at once.

Back then, most of the girls made fun of Liz. I often saw my mother sitting with her in her room, consoling her when her fellow pupils had been teasing her again or had hidden her satchel. Afterwards, I'd be allowed into Liz's room, too. She'd fling her arms around me, I'd feel her hot breath on my skin, and she would tell me everything she'd told our mother – probably more. I loved my sister to bits, and that didn't change when, years later, she deserted me.

After midnight it was still sultry and humid in the village. The men and women still on the dance floor – our parents among them – swapped partners after every song. I took another photo, although by this point I could barely hold the Mamiya.

'Give me the camera,' said my brother.

'No, Papa gave it to me. I'm supposed to look after it.'

'Just for a minute; I only want to take a photo. You don't know how to, anyway.'

Marty snatched the camera from me.

'Don't be so mean to him,' said Liz. 'He was so happy he was allowed to have it.'

'Yes, but his photos are rubbish, he doesn't know how to set the exposure.'

'You're such a know-all. No wonder you haven't got any friends.'

Marty took a few photos. He was the middle child. Ten years old, glasses, dark hair, pale, nondescript face. You could clearly see our parents in Liz and me, whereas in appearance he had nothing in common with them. Marty seemed to have materialised from some kind of non-place, an alien who had positioned himself between us. I didn't like him at all. In the films I saw, older brothers were always heroic boys who stood up for their younger siblings. My brother was a loner who spent the whole day sitting in his room playing with his ant colony or examining blood samples from dissected salamanders and mice; his supply of small dead creatures seemed inexhaustible. Not long ago Liz had called him a 'disgusting freak', which pretty much hit the nail on the head.

I have only a few, fragmented memories of that holiday in France, apart from the dramatic incident at the end. But I do remember the three of us at the fête, watching the French children playing football in the village square and being overcome by a sense of foreignness. We'd all been born in Munich, and we thought of ourselves as German. Apart from some special meals, hardly anything at home indicated our French roots, and we rarely spoke the language. Yet our parents had met in Montpellier. My father had moved there when he finished school because he wanted to escape his family. My mother had moved there because she loved France. (And because she wanted to escape her family.) When our parents talked about those days, they spoke of evenings when they'd gone to the cinema or Mother had played the guitar, of their first meeting at a mutual friend's student party, or of how the two of them – our mother by then already pregnant – had moved to Munich together. After hearing stories like these, my brother and sister and I always felt that we knew our parents. Later, when they were gone, we were forced to realise that we knew nothing about them, absolutely nothing.

We went for a walk, but when we set off our father didn't tell us where we were going, and he hardly said a word while we were walking, either. The five of us hiked up a hill and came to a little wood. My father stopped on the slope in front of a massive oak tree.

'Do you see what's carved there?' he asked. He seemed distracted.

'*L'arbre d'Eric*,' Liz read out. 'Eric's tree.'

We stared at the oak. 'Look, someone's lopped off a branch.' Marty pointed at the rough circle protruding from the tree.

'So they have,' murmured Father.

My brother and sister and I had never met our Uncle Eric. We'd been told he'd died many years ago.

'Why's the tree called that?' asked Liz.

My father's expression brightened. 'Because my brother used to seduce girls under this tree. He'd bring them up here, they'd sit on the bench, look down into the valley, he'd recite poems for them, and then he'd kiss them.'

'Poems?' queried Marty. 'And it worked?'

'Every time. And that's why some joker took a knife and carved those words into the bark.'

He gazed up at the cool blue morning sky. Our mother leaned against him. I looked at the tree and repeated silently: *L'arbre d'Eric.*

And then the holidays were nearly over: just one last trip. It had rained again in the night; fat dewdrops clung to the leaves, the fresh morning air wrapped itself round my skin. Whenever I got up early I had the wonderful sense that the day belonged to me. I'd met a girl from the village, Ludivine, a few days earlier, and was telling my mother about her. As always when we came to the end of our French holiday, my father was relieved to have got it out of the way for another year. Occasionally he stopped to take a photo, whistling as he did so. Liz wandered on ahead while Marty trotted behind us, bringing up the rear. We almost always had to wait for him.

In the wood we came to a river full of fallen rocks with a tree-trunk lying across it. We had to get to the other side anyway, so my brother and sister and I asked if we were allowed to balance our way across.

Father stepped up and tested the wood. 'Could be dangerous,' he said. 'I'm definitely not walking over that.'

We too jumped up onto the trunk. Only then did we realise

how high the drop was, how slippery the bark, how rocky and wide the river. It was almost ten metres across, and anyone who slipped and fell was sure to injure themselves.

'There's a bridge up ahead, anyway,' said Liz. Although she would usually try anything, this time she chickened out and walked on. My brother followed her. I was the only one who didn't move. In those days I didn't know the meaning of fear. Just a few months earlier I'd been the only one in my class who'd dared to cycle down a very steep slope. A few metres in I'd lost control, somersaulted and broken my arm. Yet scarcely had I got rid of the plaster, barely had the break healed, before I was looking for the next dangerous adventure.

I was still staring at the tree-trunk in front of me, and without thinking about it too hard I started to put one foot in front of the other.

'You're crazy,' Marty shouted, but I didn't listen. Once I almost slipped, and glancing down at the rock-filled river below made me dizzy, but I was already halfway across. My heart beat faster; I ran the last two metres, landed safely on the other side, and flung my arms up in relief. My family walked along the left bank of the river as far as the bridge, while I walked alone on the right; from time to time I looked across at them and grinned. I'd never been so proud in my life.

The river led out of the wood. It grew wider, the current faster; the water had risen after the last few days of rain. The bank was muddy and soft; a sign warned hikers not to step too close to the edge.

'If you fell in there, you'd drown.' Marty stared at the thundering water.

'Hopefully you'll splosh in, then we'll be rid of you at last,' said Liz.

He aimed a kick at her, but she dodged him neatly and linked arms with our mother as naturally and nonchalantly as only Liz could do.

'Have you been cheeky again?' asked Mother. 'Seems we'll have to leave you here with Granny.'

'No,' said Liz in half-feigned, half-genuine horror. 'Please don't.'

'I'm afraid you leave me no choice. Granny'll take good care of you.' She imitated our grandmother's reproving look, and Liz laughed.

Our mother was the undisputed star of the family, for us children, anyway. She was attractive and graceful, had friends all over Munich, and gave dinner parties attended by artists, musicians or actors she'd met God alone knows where. Incidentally, when I describe her as 'attractive' or 'graceful', it's a huge understatement. Such pathetic words can't even begin to convey our sense that we happened to have a mixture of Grace Kelly and Ingrid Bergman for a mother. When I was a child it seemed incomprehensible to me that she wasn't living the life of a famous actress; that she was just a teacher. She often went about her domestic tasks with an amused, affectionate smile, and it was only later that I realised how constrained she must have felt.

We stopped for a rest in a meadow by the river. Our father filled his pipe while we ate the ham baguettes we'd brought along. Later, Mother played a couple of Gilbert Bécaud songs on the guitar.

When she and Father started singing, Marty rolled his eyes. 'Please stop. This is so embarrassing.'

'But there's no one here,' our mother said.

'Yes there is – over there!'

My brother pointed to the opposite bank, where another family had just sat down. The children were about our age, and they had a young mongrel with them, romping in their midst.

It was midday: the sun was high in the sky. Marty and I took off our T-shirts and lay down on a blanket in the heat. Liz doodled in a sketchpad; little drawings, and her name, over and over again. Back then she would often try out different styles of handwriting to see which suited her signature best, and she'd write it everywhere – on papers, on the table, in folders, on napkins. *Liz, Liz, Liz.*

Our parents went for a stroll and disappeared off into the distance, snuggled up against each other. We children stayed behind in the meadow. The landscape was saturated with sun. Marty and Liz played cards; I tinkered about on the guitar and watched the family on the other bank. I kept hearing their laughter, overlaid with the barking of the dog. From time to time one of the children would throw a stick, which the mongrel would fetch immediately, until the boy clearly started to get bored and hid the stick under a blanket. The dog, however, wanted to go on playing; it kept running up to each member of the family in turn before eventually trotting a little further downstream. A fairly large branch was caught in the undergrowth on the riverbank. The dog clamped its jaws around it and tried to tug it out, but couldn't. The current was powerful and fast just there. I was the only one watching, and I felt the hairs stand up on the back of my neck.

The young dog tugged at the branch, and in its eagerness it came closer and closer to the water. I was about to attract the attention of the family on the other riverbank when I heard a yelp. A section of the bank had broken away, and the dog had fallen in the water. It was only clinging on by its front paws and teeth, which were still sunk into the branch. It whimpered, and tried to struggle back up the crumbling riverbank, but the current was too strong. Its whimpering grew louder.

'Oh my God,' said Liz.

'It's not going to make it,' said Marty. He sounded so categorical, as if passing judgement on the scene.

The family on the other side ran to the dog. They had just reached it when the branch broke free of the undergrowth and was swept away, taking the mongrel with it.

It kept its head above water for a little while, then vanished into the river. As the children opposite screamed and cried, I turned away and looked at my brother and sister. I've never forgotten the expressions on their faces.

*

That night, in bed, I could still hear the dog whimpering. Liz had been depressed all day; Marty had hardly said a word. The oddest thing, though, was that our parents weren't there when it happened. Of course they'd tried to comfort us when they got back, but it didn't alter the fact that my siblings and I had experienced something that was shattering only for us.

I tossed and turned half the night. I couldn't stop thinking about how the carefree happiness of the family on the other bank had been destroyed in the space of a few seconds. I remembered my Uncle Eric; how we'd been told that he had 'lost his life'. Up until then my life had been a sheltered one, but clearly there were invisible forces and currents that could change everything at a stroke. It seemed that there were families that were spared by Fate and others that attracted misfortune; and that night I wondered whether my family were one of these.

The Switching Point

(1983–1984)

Three and a half years later, in December 1983: the last Christmas with my parents. I was standing at my bedroom window early in the evening while the others decorated the living room. As every year, they would only call me when everything was all decked out, but how much longer was it going to take? Outside the door I heard my brother grumbling, my mother's bright, conciliatory laugh. I heard my sister and my father arguing about which tablecloth they should use. To distract myself, I stared down into the inner courtyard, at the bare winter trees, the swing and the treehouse. A lot of things had changed in the past few years, but never the view of our beloved courtyard.

There was a knock at the door. My father came in; he was wearing a navy-blue cashmere jersey and chewing on his pipe. He was nearly forty now. His black hair was thinning at the front; his boyish smile had disappeared. What had happened to him? A few years ago he'd still come across as cheerful and optimistic, and now here was this stooping figure standing in my room.

He and Mother seldom did anything as a couple any more. Instead, my father would often disappear for hours on end, taking photographs. He never showed us his photos, though, and even when I was playing with friends I could sense him and his sullen looks at my back. In his eyes, the world was a place of constant danger. Driving, for example, if my mother was at the wheel. ('That's much too fast, Lena, you're going to kill us all.') Or when I went to cross the river near Berdillac and ran across the tree-trunk, as I did every summer. ('Jules, I *really* can't watch this any more, if you fall down there you're going to break your neck!') Or when Liz wanted to go to a concert with friends from school. ('I forbid you – who knows what sort of people will be hanging around there!') If my father had written a self-help manual, the title would probably have been *Leave Well Alone*.

It was only when playing football in the park with friends that he was relaxed, and I admired him for the way he floated across the field with the ball, leaving his opponents standing. He'd played for an amateur team in Berdillac when he was young, and he still had an infallible feel for space, could intuit his opponents' passes and would dash into openings at exactly the right moment. As if he were the only one who truly understood the game.

My father came and stood beside me at the window. He smelled of tobacco and his tangy, mossy cologne. 'Are you looking forward to Christmas, Jules?'

I nodded, and he patted me on the shoulder. In the old days, we would often go for a stroll around Schwabing when he came home from work in the evening. The old corner pubs and stand-up cafés were still there then, the dirty yellow telephone boxes and the little grocery stores selling chocolate, woolly tights, or – my favourite – certified plots on the moon. The neighbourhood felt like an overgrown village where time passed a little more slowly. Sometimes we would eat ice creams in one of the parks, too, and my father would tell me about how, as a young man, he'd spent half a year working in Southampton, at the port, in order to finance his studies and learn English; or about the things his brother Eric had got up to when they were children, and these were the stories I liked best.

I particularly remember, though, the advice he gave me on our last walk together. I didn't really know what to make of it initially, but over the years his words became, for me, a kind of legacy.

My father said: 'The most important thing is that you find your *true* friend, Jules.' He realised that I didn't understand, and gave me a penetrating look. 'Your true friend is someone who's always there, who walks beside you all your life. You have to find them; it's more important than anything, even love. Because love doesn't always last.' He grabbed my shoulder. 'Are you listening?'

I'd been playing with a stick I'd found on the ground. I threw it away. 'Who's your true friend?' I asked.

My father just shook his head. 'I lost him' – pipe between his lips – 'isn't that strange? I just lost him.'

I didn't know what to make of all this, and perhaps I sensed, too, that these well-meaning words were an expression of his own disappointment. Nonetheless, I committed his advice to memory. I wish I hadn't.

'Heard you're going to be getting a really great present later on,' my father said, in French, as he headed out of the room again.

'Really? What?'

He smiled. 'You'll have to be patient for just a few more minutes.'

It was difficult. I could already hear piano music outside – 'Silent Night' and 'A la venue de Noël'. And then, finally, Liz and Marty came running down the corridor and flung open the door.

'Come on!'

The tree in the living room, which reached all the way to the ceiling, was decorated with colourful baubles, wooden figures and candles; the presents were piled up underneath, and there was a smell of wax and fir twigs. On the table were a large turkey with potato gratin, lamb ragout, roast beef, cranberry sauce, buttercream-filled cake and pies. There was always too much, so that over the next few days the leftovers were eaten as cold snacks straight from the fridge; I was particularly fond of this.

After the meal we sang Christmas carols, then came the final ritual before the big opening of the presents: our mother playing 'Moon River' on the guitar. She made the most of this every time.

'Do you really want to hear that song?' she would ask.

'Yes,' we'd all cry.

'Oh, I don't know. I think you're just being polite.'

'We do, we want to hear it!' we would cry, louder than before.

'Find me a new audience,' our mother would sigh, disappointed. 'This one's had enough, it doesn't want any more.'

We'd keep roaring louder and louder until at last she picked up the guitar.

For us, our mother was still the heart of the family. When she was around, my brother and sister's quarrels became silly battles of words, something to be laughed at, while crises at school turned into little setbacks we could easily overcome. She modelled for Liz's drawings, or let Marty show her the results of his research with the microscope. She taught me to cook, and even confided to me the secret recipe for her 'Irresistible Cake', a sticky choc-olate mush that was instantly addictive. And although she was a bit lazy (classic scene: our mother, lying on the sofa, directing us to the fridge to fetch her something), and a secret smoker, we all wanted to be like her.

At last she started playing, and her voice filled the room.

> *Moon River, wider than a mile,*
> *I'm crossing you in style some day.*
> *Oh, dream maker, you heartbreaker,*
> *wherever you're going I'm going your way.*

This was the moment in the year when everything was just perfect. Liz sat listening open-mouthed; my brother, clearly moved, fiddled with his glasses, and my father listened with sad eyes but a rapt expression. Next to him sat Aunt Helene, my mother's older sister, a large cheerful woman who lived alone in her apartment in the Glockenbach district and gave us massive presents every time. Apart from our grandmother far away in France, this was all the family we had left: a thin branch on the Moreau family tree.

When the presents were handed out, I snatched up the one from my father first. It was big and chunky. I ripped open the wrapping paper. An old Mamiya. My father looked at me expectantly. I thought the camera seemed familiar, but I hadn't taken any more photographs since the festival in Berdillac. Also, the Mamiya was used and covered in scratches, the lens looked like the colossal eye of a Cyclops, the dials clacked when you changed the setting. Disappointed, I set it aside and opened my other presents.

My mother had given me a red leather notebook and three novels: *Tom Sawyer*, *The Little Prince* and *Krabat & the Sorcerer's Mill*. She still read to me at night, but more and more often she would let me read to her, too, and praised me when I did it well. I'd written a story of my own for the first time not long before, about an enchanted dog. My mother had liked it a lot. I picked up the red notebook, and later, while the others were playing board games, I wrote down my thoughts.

Just before New Year we saw our father weep for the first and last time. That afternoon I was lying on my bed, writing a new short story. It was about a library where the books secretly talked to each other at night, boasting about their authors or complaining about their poor position in one of the farthest book stacks.

My sister walked into the room without knocking. She grinned conspiratorially and closed the door behind her.

'What is it?'

Actually, I could already narrow down her possible answers. Liz was fourteen by then, and interested in precisely three things: drawing, cheesy romantic films, and boys. She was now the prettiest girl in her class; she had blonde curls, a deep voice, and could wrap anyone round her little finger with her smile. You often saw her in the school playground surrounded by an entourage of girls, telling them which boys she had kissed where, and how boring or at best mediocre it had been. It was *never* good, and they were *always* older boys from town; the boys in her class, by contrast, didn't stand a chance. Sometimes they would try their luck anyway, but Liz paid them no attention.

She sat on my bed and nudged me. 'Traitor.'

I was still writing my story and not really listening. 'Why?'

'You kissed a girl.'

My cheeks burned. 'How do you know that?'

'A friend of mine saw you. She said it was right here, outside our building, and you stuck your tongue down the girl's throat. Like a pair of Labradors, she said.'

Liz laughed. At the same time she took the notebook out of my hand and started sketching figures in it and writing her name everywhere. *Liz, Liz, Liz.*

It was true about the kiss. I could talk to girls as if they were boys, and every now and then I would get love letters passed to me under the desk. Life seemed to be full of such promises, and my self-confidence grew. Despite being the class representative, I would often interrupt in lessons, or put my feet on the desk with a nonchalant grin until the teacher told me off. Later I thought my behaviour had been arrogant, but at the time I enjoyed calling the tune in front of my friends and being the centre of attention. I started hanging around with older boys, and often got into fights. For example, if someone in my new group of friends shot his mouth off about me, I'd immediately jump on him. It was never really serious, but it was never just a joke, either. A couple of the older boys were already smoking dope and drinking alcohol, but I still hesitated whenever they offered me anything; and I didn't tell them I liked reading or making up stories, either. I knew they would have made fun of me, and that I had to keep this side of myself well hidden.

'So what was the kissing like?' Liz tossed the notebook into my lap.

'None of your business.'

'Come on, tell. We tell each other everything else.'

'Yes, but I don't want to now.'

I got up and went into our father's study, which always smelled faintly of dusty files and old paper. When I heard my sister follow me, I pretended to be busy and rummaged around in the drawers of the desk. Most had nothing in them but spectacles cases, ink bottles and pages of yellowed notes. In the bottom one, though, I came across a Leica. Black body, silver lens. It was in its original packaging; I'd never seen my father use it. There was also a letter in the drawer, written in French. I didn't recognise the handwriting.

Dear Stéphane, this camera is for you. It's to remind you of who you are, and of what life must never be allowed to destroy. Please try to understand me.

Who was this letter from? I put it back in the drawer and examined the camera, opening the film spool and fiddling with the lens. Dust danced in the light falling through the window.

Liz had caught sight of herself in a little mirror. Delighted by what she saw, she studied herself from all angles, then turned back to me.

'And what if I've never kissed anyone yet?'

'What?'

My sister chewed her lip and said nothing.

'But you're always telling us about all the people you've been snogging.' The camera dangled from my hand. 'You never talk about anything else.'

'My first kiss ought to be something special; I . . .'

There was a creak. Our brother, who had an infallible instinct for when and where in the apartment secrets were being exchanged, appeared in the doorway. His devilish grin indicated that he had been eavesdropping.

Marty was thirteen, a swotty loner with metal-rimmed glasses, pale and thin as a stick of chalk. A child who hated children, who hung around with adults and otherwise preferred to be on his own. He'd always been in his sister's shadow; she provoked him whenever she could, ignored him at school and made fun of him because he hardly had any friends. And now, secret information – manna from Heaven! – had fallen into his hands, information that could ruin our sister's reputation at school in seconds.

'Interesting,' he said. 'Is that why you always give all the boys the brush-off: because you're scared shitless? Because you're a little kid who'd rather do kitschy drawings and cuddle her mama?'

It took Liz a moment to regain her composure.

'If you tell anyone, I'll . . .'

'You'll what?' Marty laughed and made exaggerated kissing noises.

Liz threw herself at him. They yanked each other's hair and lashed out, kicking. I tried to separate them, and didn't see which of them knocked the camera out of my hand; I only saw it fly lens-first across the room to land . . . Damn.

A sudden silence fell. I picked up the Leica. The lens was cracked.

We deliberated for a while over what to do.

'Let's just put it back in the drawer,' said Liz. 'Maybe he won't even notice.'

And, as always, our sister had the last word.

That day, our father came home surprisingly early. He seemed agitated, and immediately vanished into his study.

'Come on!' ordered Liz.

The three of us watched through the gap in the door as our father restlessly paced the room for a while, running his hands repeatedly through his hair. Then he picked up the receiver of the old green telephone and dialled.

'It's me again,' he said, with his slight accent, 'Stéphane. I wanted to say that you're making a mistake. You can't just—'

The person he was talking to seemed to fob him off straight away. Our father visibly crumpled. He kept inserting a 'But you—' or 'No, that's—' into the conversation, once even an imploring 'Please', but scarcely managed to get another word in edgeways.

'You could at least have indicated,' our father said at last. 'After twelve years. I could—'

Again he was cut off. Then he just hung up.

He walked to the middle of the room and just stood there, motionless, as if someone had pulled the plug. Scary.

At last he seemed to come back to life. He went over to the desk, and I knew immediately which drawer he would open. First he read the letter, then he took the Leica out of the packaging. When our father noticed the broken lens, he flinched. He put the camera and the letter back in the drawer and went over to the window. And then he wept. We couldn't tell whether it was because of the phone call or because of the Leica, or perhaps because of the heaviness that had come over him in the past few years. We only knew that we didn't want to see it, and we silently went back to our rooms.

After New Year our parents decided to go away for the weekend. A spur-of-the-moment trip that seemed to be connected to our father's redundancy, but our mother just told us they'd be visiting friends in Montpellier and we couldn't come along. Our aunt would look after us.

'But we don't need a babysitter,' said Liz. 'I'm fourteen now.'

Our mother kissed her on the forehead. 'It's more for your male companions.'

'Thanks, I heard that,' said Marty, without looking up from his newspaper.

Nine other tenants lived in our house in Munich, including Marleen Jacobi, a young, remarkably pretty widow who only wore dark clothes. Whenever you saw her she was always alone, and it was inconceivable to me how anyone could live such a solitary life. Liz, on the other hand, admired her greatly; every time she met her on the stairs or in the street she would get excited and pinch my arm or nudge me.

'She's just so beautiful!' she would say, breathlessly.

Her fascination led me and Marty to start teasing our sister. 'Mrs Jacobi was just here,' we told her that afternoon. 'You only missed her by a second or two. She looked more *beautiful* than ever.'

'Yeah, right,' said Liz, with exaggerated boredom. 'I don't believe a word.'

'She was – she asked after you,' we said. 'She wants to marry you.'

'You're both childish idiots,' answered Liz, sprawled on the living-room sofa with our mother. 'Mama,' she said, grinning at me, 'guess who just kissed a girl for the first time?'

My mother immediately looked in my direction. 'Is that true?' she asked, and I think she said it approvingly.

I can no longer recall what we talked about after that, but I do know that my mother suddenly got up from the sofa and put on a song: 'Via Con Me' by Paolo Conte. She stretched out her hand to me.

'Remember, Jules,' she said as we danced, 'if you want to get a girl, dance to this song with her. You're bound to win her over with this song.'

My mother laughed. It was only years later that I realised this was the only time she spoke to me as an equal.

Just before my parents set off that evening I had another little dispute with my father, and it's probably best if I recount it as I remembered it for a long time.

I happened to walk past the bedroom where my father was in the midst of packing. He seemed stressed.

'Good that you're here,' he said. 'I need to talk to you.'

I stopped, leaning against the door. 'What is it?'

He didn't come out with it straight away; instead, he used the pretext of his perennial misgivings: he didn't like my older friends; I was 'keeping bad company'. Then he started talking about his Christmas present, the camera.

'It's still sitting in the corner. You haven't taken a single photo with it, have you? You haven't even looked at it properly.'

I suddenly felt sorry for my father, and looked away.

'It's worth a lot, you know. At your age I'd have been really pleased with it.'

'I don't know how I'm supposed to use it. It's so heavy and old.'

At that, my father straightened up and came over to me. He was surprisingly tall, a lanky man. 'It's a classic, you understand?' For a moment there was something boyish about his face again. 'Better than the new cameras. It has a *soul*. When we get back I'll show you how to take photos with it and develop them. Deal?'

I nodded hesitantly.

'You've got a good eye, Jules. I'd be happy if you got into

photography later on,' said my father; and I never forgot those words, either.

What else do I remember from that evening? I definitely remember my mother kissing me goodbye on the forehead. Throughout my life I must have thought a thousand times about this last kiss and her last hug, her smell and her soothing voice. I've thought about it so often I'm no longer sure that it's true.

My brother and sister and I spent the weekend at home. We played Barricade with my aunt (as always, Liz's sole aim was to wall Marty in with the little white pieces), and in the evening I made everyone mushroom omelettes, using a recipe Mother had taught me.

On Saturday Liz and I went to the cinema, so Marty was the only one around when our father called from their holiday. Our parents had spontaneously decided to extend the trip by a couple of days. They'd rented a car so they could make a detour to Berdillac.

I didn't mind: mainly, I just looked forward to the little presents and cheese they'd bring back from the south of France.

And then came the eighth of January, a Sunday. In the years that followed I often tried to credit myself with having had some vague premonition, but that was probably nonsense. Towards evening the phone rang. When my aunt picked up the receiver I instantly sensed the change in the atmosphere, and sat down. Marty froze, too. All other details escape me, though. I don't know what I was doing that morning, what I did after the call, or why my sister wasn't there that evening.

All I was left with from that day was one last memory, the significance of which, however, I only came to believe in much later.

That afternoon I had run into the living room in high spirits. Liz was in the middle of drawing a picture story; my brother was sitting next to her, writing, in his tiny, spidery hand, to Gunnar Nordahl. This was his penfriend in Norway, but Liz and I always used to say Gunnar Nordahl didn't exist and Marty had just made him up.

I planted myself in front of my brother and struck a boxing pose. I was in my Muhammad Ali phase and considered myself an excellent impersonator; his loud-mouthed challenges in particular appealed to me.

'Hey,' I said to Marty. 'You're in for it today, you rat. You're just an Uncle Tom.'

'Jules, you're being a pain. You don't even know what "Uncle Tom" means, anyway.'

I tapped him on the shoulder. When he didn't react, I tapped him again. My brother lashed out at me, but I sprang back and started shadow-boxing. 'Float like a butterfly, sting like a bee.'

I wasn't actually a brilliant Ali imitator, but I was really good at the Ali shuffle, that rapid skipping on the spot.

Liz watched us expectantly.

I gave Marty another tap. 'In the second round you are *done for,*' I roared, wide-eyed. 'I done wrestled with an alligator, I done tussled with a whale, I done handcuffed lightning and thrown thunder in jail. Just last week I murdered a rock, injured a stone, hospitalised a brick. I'm so mean I make medicine sick. But you're so ugly I don't know how you can get any uglier.'

'Stop bugging me.'

'Yeah, stop bugging him,' said Liz mockingly. 'He's writing to his imaginary Norwegian friend again.'

'Oh, you two are boring,' said Marty.

This time I smacked him on the back of the head, so hard that his pen slipped. My brother suddenly jumped up and ran after me. We tussled: at first it felt serious, but when I kept squealing and yelling that I was the greatest, Marty had to laugh in spite of himself, and we let each other go.

At approximately the same time, my parents were getting into their rented Renault to go and visit our grandmother in Berdillac. Meanwhile, a young lawyer was getting into her Toyota. She had a dinner date in Montpellier and wanted to be there in good time. Her car skidded on the wet road and veered into the opposite lane, where it collided with my parents' Renault. Two people died on the spot.

The young lawyer only just survived.

Crystallisation

(1984–1987)

What follows is hazy bewilderment, and a thick fog illuminated only here and there by a few brief memories. Standing in my room in Munich looking out of the window at the inner courtyard with the swing and the treehouse, at the morning light catching in the branches of the trees. It's the last day in our apartment, which is now completely empty. I hear Marty calling me.

'Jules, are you coming?'

Reluctantly, I turn away. It occurs to me that I will never look down again on our beloved yard, but I feel nothing, not even that my childhood is over.

Shortly afterwards: the first night at the boarding school, when we arrive very late and I am separated from my brother and sister. Carrying my suitcase, I walk beside a teacher down a bare, linoleum-lined corridor that smells of vinegar. He's going too fast; I fall a little behind. Finally he opens a door. A room with three beds, two already occupied. The other children blink sleepily. I turn off the light and get undressed in the dark so as not to disturb them further. Hide a soft toy under my pillow. Lying in my new bed, I think of my parents, and of my brother and sister, close by yet very far away, and I don't cry, not for a second.

I remember a day in winter, too, a few weeks later. A gusty wind is whipping over the hilly, snow-covered landscape. I zip up my anorak, hold my hand in front of my face and trudge on. My nose is dripping; my shoes compress the fresh snow, which creaks with every step. The cold is a shock to my lungs. After an hour I sit on an icy bench and look down into the valley. It seems silent and unfamiliar. I imagine jumping down, the air catching me only metres above the glittering snow-crust, a heart-stopping moment. I see myself swiftly gain height, shoot upwards, accelerate, the wind in my face, before flying with outstretched arms towards the horizon, just flying away. I turn my gaze back to the school, so pleasantly far off, and picture what they're doing right now without me. I see them ice-skating, talking about girls, messing around and winding each other up, sometimes going too far, until a moment later it's all forgotten again. The first lights start to emerge from the gathering dusk, and I think of my old life in Munich, curtailed by chance; but the homesickness is now just a fading scar.

When I get back to the boarding house, later, it's already night and the sky is black. I open the door to the main entrance. Cheerful voices drift across from the dining hall, and my nostrils are invaded by an intense smell of food, sweat and deodorant. The air thick with expectations, laughter, and suppressed fear. I walk down the corridor and see a boy I don't know coming towards me. He looks suspiciously at me, the newbie. I instinctively draw myself up, trying to look grown-up and not make any mistakes. The boy passes me without a word.

I reach my room, sit on my bed and brush the snow from my hair. I am merely present: a ghost, a tiny creature, eleven years old. I sit in my room, numb and empty, while all the others are at dinner. Later I'll be punished for my absence. I stare out into the darkness.

The boarding school where my brother and sister and I ended up after the death of our parents was not one of those elite institutions with tennis courts, hockey fields and pottery work-shops, which was perhaps how we had pictured it. Instead, it was a cheap, state-run, provincial children's home, consisting of two grey buildings and a dining hall alongside the local secondary school. In the mornings we had classes with the local children; afternoons and evenings were spent in our rooms, by the lake, or on the football pitch. You got used to this barracks life, but even if you'd been there for years it could still be depressing when the day pupils went home to their families after school and you stayed on site like a prisoner, feeling that there must be something wrong with you. You shared a spartan room with strangers who sometimes became friends. After a year you had to move again. Difficult to have to live your entire life in so little time and space; there were a lot of arguments, but also conversations that went on all night. Very occasionally we would speak about really important things, things we would never have repeated in daylight, but for the most part we just talked about teachers or girls. 'Did she look over at me again at lunch today?' Or: 'What, don't you know her? Jesus, Moreau, she's the prettiest girl in the whole damn school!'

Many of the boarders had already come to the attention of the police at home, or else had failed their exams. Some had taken drugs. From time to time particularly criminal specimens would wash up like flotsam at the school, which, as a state institution, was obliged to take pretty much anyone. The village youth were forced to watch, aghast, as the maniacs from the city invaded their rural idyll. 'Are you from the *home* as well?' they would ask you then, meaning not so much boarding school as lunatic asylum. At meals we gobbled everything; there was never enough. The hunger in us could never wholly be stilled. There was a constant background of rumour, though: people noticed exactly who spoke to whom, who was making friends with whom, and who was popular with the girls. Not every change was condoned. There were new clothes, proudly paraded at first by their owners, that quickly disappeared back into the wardrobe because they hadn't been well received. Some boarders would try to reinvent themselves over the summer holidays; they would return to school full of new-found confidence, but within a few days most would be back to their old selves again. You were and remained whoever the others thought you were.

Up until then I had always had an inner sense of security, but now there were moments when I would see the faint light of evening shining into a gloomy corridor, or trees spreading ghostly shadows over the landscape at dusk, and something inside me would suddenly clench. The fact that I was on a planet hurtling through space at phenomenal speed seemed just as terrifying to me as the new, disturbing thought that death was inevitable. My fears grew like a crack slowly spreading in all directions. I began to be afraid of the dark, of death, of eternity. These thoughts drove thorns into my world, and the more often I contemplated them, the bigger the gulf between me and my often carefree, cheerful fellow students. I was alone. And then I met Alva.

In my first few days at the new school, I made a joke during a lesson. My old class had expected such things of me, but as I was leading up to the punchline I realised that wouldn't work here any more. I looked into the unfamiliar faces of my fellow pupils and sensed that my confidence had evaporated. No one laughed at the end, and with that my role was sealed. I was the weird new boy who paid no attention to what he put on in the mornings and who started twisting words out of nervousness: 'par cark' instead of 'car park', for example. I didn't want to become the laughing-stock of the class, so I more or less stopped saying anything at all and ended up sitting isolated at the back. Until, after a few weeks, a girl came and sat beside me.

Alva had copper-coloured hair and horn-rimmed glasses. The first impression was of a graceful, shy country girl who copied things off the blackboard into her exercise books using different-coloured pens. But there was something else about her as well. Some days Alva seemed to deliberately avoid the other children. She would stare gloomily out of the window, completely lost in thought. I didn't know why she wanted to sit next to me; we didn't exchange a single word. Her friends giggled whenever they looked over at us, and two weeks later I was alone in the corner again. As unexpectedly as she had come, Alva had moved away.

After that I often glanced at her in class. When she was called up to answer questions at the blackboard, I watched her standing uncertainly in front of the class, hands folded behind her back. I listened to her soft voice and stared at her red hair, her glasses, her white skin and her pale, pretty face. Most of all, though, I liked her front teeth, one of which was slightly crooked. Alva tried not to open her mouth too wide when she spoke, so that no one would see, and when she laughed she covered her mouth with her hand. Sometimes, though, if she wasn't paying attention, she would smile and you'd see her crooked incisor, and I really loved that. My whole life consisted of gazing at her from a few desks away, and if at last she glanced back I would look away, embarrassed, and be happy.

However, a few months later, something happened. It was a humid summer's day and in the last lesson we were allowed to watch a video, the film of a novel by Erich Kästner. In the middle of the film, Alva began to cry. She was hunched up in her seat; her shoulders shook, and eventually she let out a sob, at which the other pupils noticed her as well. Hastily, the teacher paused the video – a scene in a holiday camp – and went over to her. As the two of them left the classroom I caught a glimpse of Alva's reddened face. I think we were all shocked, but hardly anyone spoke. Only one person said that Alva's father never came to parents' day and was generally a bit odd; perhaps it had something to do with that. I often thought of that remark, but I never asked Alva about it. Whatever it was, her suffering must have been taking place in secret, and from then on she guarded it well.

A few days later, after school, I was walking back to the home on my own.

'Jules, wait!'

Alva tugged at my shirt until I turned round. She accompanied me to the entrance of the boarding house.

'What are you going to do now?' she asked, as we hesitated outside the door. She always spoke very quietly; you had to lean in towards her. Although she was a day pupil and lived at home, she didn't seem to want to go back.

I looked at the sky, which was overcast. 'Don't know . . . Listen to music, probably.'

She blushed, but didn't look at me.

'Do you want to listen with me?' I asked, and she nodded.

To my relief, my room-mates weren't around. I'd inherited my mother's record player, and her collection, almost a hundred albums by Marvin Gaye, Eartha Kitt, Fleetwood Mac or John Coltrane.

I put on *Pink Moon* by Nick Drake, one of my mother's favourites. I used to have very little interest in music; now every time the needle crackled onto the vinyl was a moment of happiness.

Alva was concentrating hard; her expression hardly changed as she listened. 'I like it a lot,' she said. Oddly, she had sat down not on a chair but on my desk. She took a book from her backpack and, without saying anything, began to read, as if she were at home in my room. I liked it that she felt so comfortable around me. The afternoon sun broke through the clouds and bathed the room in brandy-coloured light.

'What are you reading?' I asked after a while. 'Is it good?'

'Mm-hm.' Alva nodded and showed me the title: *To Kill a Mockingbird* by Harper Lee. Like me, she was eleven. I watched her immerse herself in the text again. Her eyes raced along the lines, left to right and back again, without stopping.

Eventually she snapped the book shut and inspected my things. A strange creature that had happened to wander into my room and was curiously studying the Spider-Man comics and cameras on my shelf. First she picked up the Mamiya, then the newer models my father had often used in his final years. She touched each object deliberately, as if wanting to make sure they were actually real.

'I've never seen you take photos.'

I shrugged. Alva picked up a photo of my family with my mother and father in it.

'Your parents are dead.'

This sentence took me by surprise. I think I even turned off

the music for a moment. Since I'd arrived at the school I hadn't
told anyone about it.

'What makes you think that?' I said.

'I asked a teacher.'

'Why?'

She didn't answer.

'Yes, they died six months ago.' It felt like I was ramming a
spade into a frozen field for every word.

Alva nodded, and for a long time – an unusually long time –
she looked into my eyes, and I'll never forget how in doing so
we were able to glimpse each other's inner worlds. For one brief
moment I saw the pain that hid behind her words and gestures,
and in exchange she sensed what I held deep inside. But we went
no further. We both stopped on the threshold of the other, and
we asked each other no questions.

Almost three years later, by the end of 1986, Alva and I were the
best of friends. We listened to music together several times a week.
From time to time she would tell me something about herself:
that she admired sportsmen, that her parents were doctors, or
that after school she wanted to go to Russia, the homeland of her
favourite authors. But we never talked about what really mattered
to us, or why she had cried in class that time when we were
watching the film.

We were about to turn fourteen, and there was a deep divide
in our Year Nine class. On one side were Alva and those of our
classmates who already looked several years older, who seemed
somehow coarser and louder. On the other were the late bloomers,
the clumsy, underdeveloped outsiders, of which I was one. I hadn't
grown in years, and while in my childhood I'd shown some signs
of ability, this phase of my youth was characterised by a persistent lack of talent. I'd always had a tendency to daydream, but
I'd had another, wilder side as well. Now that it had disappeared
I was increasingly retreating into myself, and I sometimes secretly
hated myself for what I had become.

One autumn evening I went to visit my brother. West wing, second floor; a danger zone for younger boarders like me, still unarmed by puberty. On this floor, which only housed sixteen- and seventeen-year-olds, you sensed that peculiar *unease*. That moment when one is overcome by the sudden urge to wrestle, tussle, punch or roar, out of an excess of energy and boredom. I saw some of the older boys prowling restlessly along the corridor; others sat in their rooms with the doors open, staring at the wall as if concocting a plan; some of them observed me with displeasure, like predators whose territory had been invaded. I exaggerate only slightly.

My brother lived right at the end of the corridor. Unlike my sister or me, the last few years hadn't really got to Marty; but he'd also had least to lose. He was like an ant carrying on undaunted after a nuclear war. He was now six foot two, a lanky giant with angular movements and long hair tied back in a ponytail. It was as if Woody Allen had been forced to go through a second puberty. These days he wore only black clothes and a black leather coat, was constantly spouting intellectual allusions that none of us under- stood, and with his hooked nose and glasses he looked like an existentialist scarecrow. He had no luck with the girls, but at sixteen he had become the leader of a gang of misfits and weirdos. Marty's shadow army comprised all the foreign boarders plus nerds and smart-alecks of all stripes, as well as his room-mate of two years' standing, Toni Brenner. Toni was the only Austrian at the school, where the internal positioning system had banished him to the fringes on account of his strong Viennese accent.

I was almost at Marty's door when two boys blocked my path. One was skinny, with bad skin; with his hoarse laugh and spiky hair he resembled a hyena. The other was a hulking great thug whose appearance I no longer recall.

'Hey, Moreau!' said the skinny one, and grabbed me. 'Not so fast.' They both grinned disdainfully.

How ridiculous, I thought. Who exactly do you think you are, you stupid pair of clowns! For a moment anger flared in me, the way it used to when I picked a fight. But then I gave in. Who was I trying to kid? My voice hadn't even broken yet. I was a bloody joke.

I called to my brother as loudly as I could; his door was just one metre away. He didn't respond. I called out to him again – 'Help me, Marty, please!' I shouted and shouted, but his door remained closed.

The two boys holding me grinned again, then dragged me off to the showers. Several jeering pupils joined them on the way; by the end I was being carried by five of them. I struggled and thrashed, but I didn't stand a chance. They held me under the shower, fully clothed, until I was soaked to the skin. There was a smell of cheap shampoo and mildew; I closed my eyes, heard the others laughing. Then one of them said it would be funny to strip me and leave me stranded on the girls' floor. They grabbed me again, to a chorus of noisy cheers.

'I hate you!' I had to press my lips together to hold back the tears.

'Hey! Cut the crap!'

A boy with sandy-blond hair had entered the room: Toni, my brother's room-mate. My heart leaped. He was a talented skier; not tall, but very muscular; he worked out in the gym almost every day. Toni went over to the skinny hyena and flung him across the bathroom with such force that the others shrank away. Then he came over to me.

'You okay?'

I was still shivering; the water in the shower had been ice cold. Toni put his hand on my shoulder and brought me to my brother's room. He was limping slightly after a second knee operation. It wasn't clear whether he'd have to abandon his plans for a professional skiing career.

Suddenly he grinned at me. 'Has she replied to the letter yet?'

He was trying to cheer me up. Like so many others, Toni was hopelessly in love with my sister. A few months ago I'd had to pass on a love letter to Liz from him, but she'd never replied.

Since then Toni was always asking me, jokingly, whether Liz had finally read the letter.

In my brother's room I continued to drip all over the floor. Marty, who had developed an impressive computer addiction in recent years, looked up from his PC. 'What's up with you?'

I ignored him and looked outside: the brightly lit windows of the neighbouring building, the nocturnal outline of the forest in the distance. Marty went on tapping at the keys of his second-hand Commodore, but his feigned activity couldn't disguise his guilty conscience.

'You didn't help me,' I said. 'I shouted for you.'

'I didn't hear you.'

'You heard me. I was right outside your door.'

'Honestly, Jules, I didn't hear you.'

I glared at him. 'If you'd just opened the door they would have let me go. All you had to do was come out.'

My brother wouldn't budge, though, so in the end I said, 'At least admit that you heard me. Then I'll forgive you.'

When Marty still hadn't answered several seconds later, I left the room. In those days, whenever I thought of my brother, the image that came to mind was a closed door.

We went down to the lake. I wanted to show Alva something. It was an icy, pale day, and for the first time in years I'd taken one of my father's cameras with me. Whereas I was well wrapped up in anorak, scarf and hat, I noticed how casually Alva was dressed. Thin jeans and a faded cardigan. Like a neglected child, a runaway from a sect, but although she must have been freezing she didn't let it show.

Dusk was already falling when we reached the lake. Some of the kids from the home were skating on the ice.

'Come with me.' I led Alva to a point a little way off. The others' voices were scarcely audible any more; we were standing alone on the frozen lake.

Alva screamed. She'd spotted the fox. You could see its stiff muzzle through the ice, and part of its body was still sticking up out of the frozen lake, shaggy fur strewn with glittering crystals. As if it had been in motion when it was suddenly frozen solid.

'What a terrible death!' Alva's breath came in clouds. 'Why are you showing me this?'

I ran my gloves over the ice and wiped away the snow so I could see the fox's dead eyes more clearly.

'I saw a dog drown once. But this is different. I thought it might interest you. It looks so peaceful – so *eternal*.'

'I think it's horrible.' Alva turned away.

'You think it's horrible now, but I bet you'll still remember the frozen fox in twenty years' time.' I couldn't help laughing. 'Even on your deathbed you'll still be thinking about the frozen fox.'

'Don't be silly, Jules.'

I took a few photos, then we walked back to the village. The last colours were fading on the horizon, and all around the landscape was disappearing into the darkness. It grew colder; I clenched my fists in my pockets. At last we reached the café.

Inside, Alva rubbed her hands together. She'd recently started varnishing her nails, and I stared suspiciously at her bright-red fingertips: a sign of change, of new departures. We drank cocoa and talked about my sister, who'd been in trouble again for sneaking out secretly at night.

'I've heard she's going to be expelled soon,' I said. 'She just doesn't take anything seriously.'

'I like your sister,' was all Alva said. She and Liz had met once, briefly, in my room. 'And I think she's very beautiful. I'd like to have a beautiful older sister like her.'

I didn't know what to say to that. Then I saw the Hyena walk past our window. I glared after him, furious. Alva, though, was looking at me in a way that bothered me. In an unguarded moment I'd told her about my humiliating experience in the shower room, and now I was afraid she might think I was a weakling.

'I should've punched him,' I bragged, sipping my cocoa. 'Before, I would've just . . . I don't know why I didn't do anything.'

Alva laughed. 'Jules, I think it's good you didn't do anything. He's much bigger than you.' She raised an eyebrow. 'How small are you, actually?'

'Five foot three.'

'Oh, come on, you can't be as tall as all that. Stand next to me.'

We both got up and stood beside the table. Alva towered over me by a couple of embarrassing inches. We stayed like that for several seconds, nose to nose; I could smell her too-sweet new perfume. Then she sat down again.

'You've got a chocolate moustache, by the way,' she said.

'Do you know what I sometimes think?' I wiped my top lip and looked at her belligerently. 'All this is like a seed. The school, boarding, what happened to my parents. All this has been sown in me, but I can't see what it's making of me. The harvest only comes when I'm grown-up, and then it's too late.'

I waited for Alva's reaction. To my surprise, she smiled.

At first I didn't understand. Then I turned and saw, behind me, a tall boy from the middle school who must have been about sixteen. He was walking towards us with the confident smile of an actor. Alva was looking at him in a way she'd never looked at me, and as the boy talked to her I felt an ashen sense of inferiority that would never fully leave me in the years that followed.

I came across my sister outside the dining hall. She was sitting on a bench like a queen, surrounded by her classmates, smoking. Liz was seventeen; she was wearing an olive-green hooded parka and Chucks, and her blonde hair hung over her face. She was unusually tall for a woman, at least five foot eleven; she still preferred to run rather than walk, often mistook admiration for affection, and did whatever she felt like doing. Liz had a playful curiosity about the male body. If she liked someone, she didn't hesitate or play games, she just pounced. In the holidays she often went off with older acquaintances, and twice – not without pride – she'd been brought home by the police.

She was talking about a disco in Munich, and her classmates were listening eagerly. Just then a student teacher approached her.

'Liz, will you come in, please? Your detention's already started.'

'I'm just finishing my cigarette,' said my sister. 'I don't see why I should have to do bloody detention again, anyway.'

Liz had a deep voice that could be quite intimidating. She also still spoke a little too loudly all the time, as if she were on stage. And, in a way, she was.

She started to argue with the teacher in front of everyone; she kept yelling angrily, 'I'm not doing that shit, forget it!' She always spoke to the student teachers as if they were her peers. 'Anyway, I don't feel well' – fag in corner of mouth – 'I'm sick.'

Then even she couldn't help laughing. She took another heavy drag on the cigarette and sighed. 'All right, I'll be there in five minutes.'

'Three,' said the young teacher.

'Five,' said Liz. She grinned at him, so sassy and charming that he had to avoid her eye.

All this happened just before Christmas. Wreaths hung on the landing doors; at dinner there were *lebkuchen*, mandarins, nuts and punch. A collective sense of anticipation descended on the boarding house like a bell jar; but I didn't like the holidays. Within the confines of the boarding school there were no parents, and I had that in common with the others. But when I was at my aunt's in Munich while my classmates had gone home to their families it pained me, every time.

Our aunt was in her early fifties then, gentle and affectionate; in the evenings she always had a glass of wine in her hand and a crossword puzzle on her lap. Losing her younger sister had driven the cheerfulness from her face; these last few years she had put on weight, and was like someone watching a game whose rules they no longer understood. Nonetheless, our aunt always managed to light up her face with a smile whenever we needed cheering up. She took us bowling and to the cinema, and told us stories about our parents; she also seemed to be the only person who could make sense of Marty's complicated character. At night the two of them would often sit together in the kitchen, drinking tea and talking. When he was around her my brother's voice lost its clever-clever undertone; sometimes, when he was telling her about his lack of success with girls, he even let our aunt give him a hug.

In the Christmas holidays we camped on mattresses on her living-room floor. Liz, who flung everything in a heap. And Marty, who arranged his things neatly and smoothed his bed down so meticulously that you hardly dared sit on it. Strange to be so close to my brother and sister again. We hardly did anything together any more; there were too many parallel worlds at the school for that. If you sat just one table away at lunch you might as well have been in a different country. Now, though, the three of us lay in front of the television watching a documentary about the Egyptian Pharaoh Ramses II. Ramses, it said, believed he was powerful not just since birth but in his mother's womb. He called it 'strong in the egg'. My brother and sister and I seized on the image. 'Are you strong in the egg?' we'd ask each other, and laugh. And if we were talking about someone who'd messed something up, we'd say, 'Well, what can you do, he wasn't strong in the egg.'

On Christmas morning I was looking for candles when I found my sister in the storeroom. She quickly shut the door behind me.

'Merry Christmas, kiddo.' Liz hugged me, then went on rolling her joint. Fascinated, I watched her lick the filter paper, closing her eyes as she did so.

'What exactly's going on between you and Alva?' She took a drag and puffed out the smoke in little rings. 'She'd be a good one for you.'

'Nothing; we're just friends.'

My sister nodded in commiseration, then nudged me. 'Have you even kissed a girl yet?'

'No, no one since . . . Don't you *remember*?'

Liz shook her head. She'd always seemed to only ever live in the present, and forgot a lot of things, whereas I liked to spend a long time contemplating my experiences and thinking about how to classify them.

'No wonder you don't have a girlfriend.' She looked at my clothes, which I'd bought at Woolworth's with my aunt. 'You dress like a bloody eight-year-old. We need to go clothes shopping together, urgently.'

'So I need to be cooler?'

Liz looked down at me thoughtfully. 'Listen. What I'm about to tell you is very important; you must never forget it.'

I gazed at her eagerly. I knew that I would believe every word she said.

'You are not cool,' she told me. 'That's just how it is, I'm afraid. And you'll never be able to change it, either, so don't even try. But what you can do is at least look the part.'

I nodded. 'Is it true you're going to be expelled soon?'

Liz gave a sniff. 'What? Who's been saying that?'

'No idea, it's just what I heard. What if they catch you one day with some kind of drugs? I don't mean hash, I mean the . . . other stuff.'

'They won't. I'm strong in the egg.'

I'd expected her to add, 'And anyway, I don't do stuff like that,' but she didn't do me that favour. 'You know' – a hard laugh – 'a lot's happened in the last few weeks. Sometimes I really think I just . . .' She struggled for words.

'What do you think? What's happened?'

Clearly it amused her to see me staring at her like that, wide-eyed; in any case, Liz just shook her head. 'Ah, nothing, kiddo, forget it. I'm not going to be expelled, okay?' She winked at me. 'More likely I'll fail my exams.'

Later we decorated the living room with our aunt, and there were *chansons* on the radio, and for a moment it was like before, except that two people were missing. It was like before, except that nothing was like before any longer.

*

The situation had escalated on Christmas Eve. That year, for the first time, Liz didn't give us something she'd drawn; instead, she accompanied us on the guitar while we sang. I often saw her at school sitting on steps, benches or the running track, practising intently. But although she also had a lovely voice, she refused to sing 'Moon River', as our mother used to do.

'I'll drop dead before I'll play that bloody song.' Liz studied her fingernails. 'I used to hate it so much.'

'You loved it,' said Marty quietly. 'We all loved it.'

After dinner we played Barricade. For a long time it looked as if Marty was going to win, until my sister and I ganged up on him and walled him in with the little white pieces. He howled and cursed us, especially when Liz went on to win and crowed triumphantly.

As we were putting the game away, my sister slipped one of the white counters into her trouser pocket.

'Lucky charm,' she whispered to me.

This, for me, was the most beautiful moment of that Christmas. The evening seemed to be heading towards a peaceful conclusion until our aunt asked us about boarding school.

While I kept silent, and Marty came out with a stream of complaints (even back then he could have started an argument in an empty room), Liz spoke with provocative openness about evenings by the lake, parties and boys. Gleefully she analysed the teachers' weaknesses or her admirers' clumsy behaviour, and kept bursting into dirty laughter as she did so.

Marty made a face. 'Liz, do you *always* have to show off with your stories? I don't mean to interrupt you, but it's annoying.' A typical Marty sentence. He always said, 'I don't mean to . . .', then did the exact opposite.

Liz waved dismissively. 'You're just pissed off because you still don't have a girlfriend. Do you know what they call your room at school? The masturbation cell.'

'The what?' asked our aunt.

'Oh, shut up.' Marty played with the collar of his leather coat, which he didn't take off even in heated rooms. His face was the colour of old paper, his long hair was greasy, and he'd recently started to grow a goatee as well. A grubby small-time crook from Philly, who might rob a supermarket at any moment and flee with five dollars and a carton of milk.

'You should be worrying about what they say at school about *you*,' he said.

'Why, what do they say?' asked Liz.

'Oh – nothing,' said Marty, obviously realising he'd made a mistake.

Liz looked first at him, then at me. 'Do you know what he's getting at?'

I didn't answer. Of course I knew what my brother was getting at. The stories people told about our sister had reached my ears as well. They had to be lies – rumours started by disappointed boys or jealous girls. But what did I really know about my sister?

'What do they say at school?' Now our aunt was asking, too.

'That she's a . . . *slut*,' said Marty. Even he was shocked by the destructive power of his words. I could clearly see that he didn't want to go on, but he seemed to be under some sort of inner compulsion. 'That she sleeps with men for drugs,' he continued. 'That one of them even got her pregnant.'

There was a loud clatter. Liz had thrown her dessert spoon onto her plate. She jumped up and left the room. Seconds later we heard the apartment door slam. I ran to the window and saw my sister walking swiftly away, disappearing into the dark.

She came back the next morning, but a few weeks after Christmas Liz dropped out of school and vanished from my life for years. She told a classmate that graduating from school wasn't for her, that she wanted to explore the world. That she had to do it. Back then I spent a long time trying to work out *why*. Every day I waited for a sign from Liz, for a letter of explanation, a card or a call. Like a castaway tirelessly turning the dials of a wireless, hoping finally to chance upon a voice. But all I heard from my sister was years and years of static.

Chemical Reactions

(1992)

I waited in the school car park, watching the shining vapour trails of planes on the reddening horizon. As often happened when one of nature's spectacles combined with my longings and memories, I sensed a slight tugging at my insides. At nineteen, I was about to take my school-leaving exam. The future was spread out before me, and I felt the deceptive elation of a young person who has not yet made any big mistakes in life.

A quarter of an hour later the red Fiat finally drove onto the school grounds. I climbed into the passenger seat and kissed Alva on the cheek.

'Late, as ever,' I said.

'I like it when you have to wait.'

She released the clutch and accelerated quickly.

'How was it at home?' she asked. 'Any womanising I need to know about?'

'Well, as you know, I'm not exactly a child of sorrow . . .'

'Jules, you're a child of terrible sorrow.'

Alva wouldn't let it go. She asked me about a particular girl from our class; it wouldn't be right to name her here. 'What happened with her? Did you see her in the holidays?'

'The accused invokes his right to remain silent.'

'Come on, tell me. How did it go?'

I sighed. 'We didn't see each other.'

'Dear oh dear, Monsieur Moreau, I expected more of you.'

'Very funny. I don't think she's interested in me, anyway.'

'Do you know how good-looking you are? Of course she's interested in you.'

Alva gave a big smile. She loved to boost my confidence and match-make me with various girls.

At this point I should mention that I had shot up over the past few years. My hair was as black as my father's; I'd inherited his strong beard, too, and only shaved sporadically. It astonished me how grown-up, how rugged and furtive I looked.

Over the last couple of years at school I'd had two short relationships, but I hadn't really been emotionally involved. At the time I was much more interested in photography. I learned all about the chemical reactions required to expose a negative; we had an empty room in the cellar of the boarding house that I was allowed to use as a darkroom.

I often went out into the countryside; I could sit for hours with my father's camera on the shore of the lake, or wander through fields and woods before returning late in the evening with my spoils. Through the lens of the Mamiya things came to life: tree bark suddenly acquired faces, the structure of water made sense. People too seemed suddenly different; sometimes I only understood their expressions when I saw them through the viewfinder.

'As of now, I don't want to hear any more excuses,' insisted Alva, beside me. 'You can't always just be shy, you've only got a few more weeks.' Cajolingly: 'Do you want to leave school without anything ever happening with her?'

I looked out of the window and said nothing. The landscape was darkening, as if a first layer of primer were being applied as foundation for the night.

After a while Alva nudged me. 'What are you thinking about when you look like that?'

'Why, how do I look?'

Alva gave a pretty good imitation of someone brooding, lost in a dream world and looking a bit daft.

'What are you thinking about?' she asked again; but I didn't answer.

Since I'd arrived at the boarding school we had seen each other almost every day. Alva had become my surrogate family, and in many ways I was closer to her than to my siblings or my aunt. But in the past few years she had changed. There were still moments when I was able to coax a rare, light-hearted laugh out of her, or when we'd be listening to music and would look at each other and just *know* what the other was thinking. But there was a second Alva now as well; one who increasingly withdrew from me, who sat on a bench, smoking and full of self-loathing, and said things like that it might have been better if she'd never been born.

Her red hair and pale skin had attracted several admirers, but she didn't have her first boyfriend until she was almost seventeen. After that, she had tentatively started relationships with one or two of the seniors. But whereas Liz, from what I could tell, just loved sex and could see something special in any man, with Alva it was more as if she were using her body as a weapon against herself. And as soon as someone developed feelings for her, she quickly rejected him. As if something inside her had shattered, and anyone who got too close to her cut themselves on the shards.

Then, at seventeen, she completely backed away from men. Any sort of approach seemed to absolutely disgust her, prompting rumours that she was more interested in women. Or was just *weird*. Alva didn't care. Instead, she studied obsessively and read books on philosophy: Sartre, and a great deal of Kierkegaard. Recently she'd started seeing someone again, but we never talked about this.

That evening we drove to a pub. Alva had to call her mother from a phone box *en route*. 'With Jules,' I heard her say. 'No, you don't know him, that was someone else.' Her voice kept getting louder. Finally she shouted, 'I'll come when I feel like it,' and slammed down the receiver.

Her mother kept track of her daughter's whereabouts with

spiteful vigilance, and more than once Alva had threatened that after her final exam she would just disappear and never come back. But I didn't know what exactly had happened between the two of them. Alva had always kept me away from her family and refused to answer any questions about her parents. I'd picked her up from home a couple of times, but she'd always already been waiting for me outside the door so I wouldn't come into the house.

'Everything okay?' I asked, as she got back into the car.

She nodded and started the engine, but it was still eating away at her, and it seemed to me that her eyes were a shade darker. Alva generally drove far too fast, but this time she was really racing into the bends. She opened the window and her hair whipped about in the wind. It was one of those moments when I had an inkling that she could – I can't put it any other way – be somehow *dangerous* for me. Alva had been playing this game with me for months now. She knew perfectly well that I was frightened when she drove too fast, and she also knew that I didn't want to admit it in front of her. So she drove the red Fiat faster and faster round the bends; it seemed to amuse her that I would squirm in my seat but remain obstinately silent. Each time she went a little bit further. And on this particular night, when I realised she would never stop, that she was prepared to take things to the limit, I gave in.

'Slow down,' I said, as she approached another bend too fast.

'Are you afraid?'

'Yes, damn it. Please slow down.'

Alva immediately took her foot off the accelerator and gave me a triumphant and strangely inscrutable smile.

She parked the red Fiat outside the grimy village pub, the Jackpot. Sixth-form hangout. The jukebox was usually playing old rock; the billiard table was threadbare. At the back, beside the dartboard, were two slot machines that exerted a mysterious attraction on every loser for miles around.

Instead of going into the pub, we stayed sitting in the car for a while. Alva turned the radio down and opened a can of beer. Then she gave me a meaningful look.

'Open the glove compartment.'

Inside, I found a rectangular present wrapped in colourful paper. 'For me?'

She nodded, and I tore open the wrapping. A memento album of photos from our time at school, each labelled with an affectionate little poem. She must have spent hours on it.

I was so moved that for a moment I couldn't say a word. 'Why did you do this?'

She said, rather casually, 'Oh, I just thought you'd like it.'

I looked at the photos. They showed us at the lake, on joint trips to concerts and festivals, at a street festival in Munich, or in my boarding-house room. I hugged Alva, and when she saw how happy I was she blushed.

As she often did, she talked about her favourite book, *The Heart is a Lonely Hunter* by Carson McCullers. 'You really must read it,' she said.

'Yes, I know, I will.'

'Please, Jules. I want to know what you think of it. The way the characters wander around alone at night, so restless. Eventually they all end up in this café, the only one that's also open at night.' She always got excited when she talked about books. 'I'd like to be a literary character like that. One who wanders around the city alone in the dark and goes to a café after midnight.'

Alva's voice was quiet but her eyes were sparkling; I liked that a lot.

I told her about my holidays in Munich, and how I'd gone to look for the house where I grew up. 'It's all been renovated. Even the swing and the treehouse in the courtyard have gone; they have flowers there now. It looks so different, so unfamiliar. When I was there it felt as if I were being watched, like a thief.'

Unlike me, Alva hardly ever talked about her childhood. Only once had she confided that, as a child, on particularly nice days with her family, she had always also felt pain because the moment would pass. And the more I thought about it, the more I recognised myself in this brief observation.

I watched two classmates coming out of the Jackpot.

'Do you want to?' asked Alva.

I didn't know how to answer this, but felt it was important I sit up first. Then I saw she was rolling a joint. I'd never taken drugs before.

'Yeah, sure,' I said. 'Where'd you get that?'

'I'm the boss of a drug cartel, did I never say?'

'The boss? Have you had anyone bumped off yet?'

'A couple of times it just had to be done.' She glowered at me most convincingly.

Alva had actually been very restrained up until then as far as drugs were concerned. When she finished rolling the joint she took a puff, then passed it to me.

'You have to take a deep breath and keep the smoke inside.'

I nodded, coughed to begin with, then after a while got the hang of it. My head swam. I stretched out in the passenger seat and thought again about the apartment I'd had to leave as a child. To my horror I had difficulty conjuring up precise images of it; I could hardly remember any more what the individual rooms had looked like. Where had the clock hung in the kitchen? What had been the last pictures I'd had on the wall?

As I pondered this, a taxi surfaced in my memory, turning a corner at night in the lamplight. I kept seeing this scene in my mind's eyes. I wanted to shout something after the taxi, but it had already vanished. I knew that this image was very important for me, but at the same time it felt as if the memory wasn't yet ripe, like a photo still lying in the developing bath.

'What's the matter?' asked Alva.

'Nothing, why?'

'You're trembling.'

I realised that I was, and took a few deep breaths in and out. Eventually I calmed down, and the thought of the departing taxi faded away.

'What's the situation with your brother and sister?' she asked. 'How often do you see them now?'

I drew deeply on the joint and wondered whether I should tell her about how my brother and sister and I had become strangers to one another. But I just shrugged my shoulders. 'My sister's living in London at the moment, I think. And my brother's in Vienna.'

'So you don't often see them any more?'

'No . . . Hardly at all, actually.'

Alva took the joint out of my hand and pulled on it, making it glow. She turned up the radio and closed her eyes. For a while she just sat there, motionless. Then, still with her eyes closed, she reached for my hand. She didn't do anything else, didn't move closer, just held it firmly. I squeezed once. So did she. Then she withdrew her hand.

That weekend, for the first time in ages, Marty paid me an unexpected visit. After he'd inspected my room we went out to his car, a second-hand Mercedes. I never really understood what it was my brother was doing alongside his computer science degree, but he obviously had fingers in a lot of successful pies. Some time earlier he had founded a company with his former room-mate, Toni, and a rich fellow student: it had to do with the (to me) abstract concepts of 'networking' and 'information'. The unhappy years at school seemed to have honed his resolve: Marty had turned past, present and future into a three-runged ladder taking him directly upwards.

'Do you think it'll work out with your company?' I asked.

'Everyone will want us.' My brother grinned. 'We're strong in the egg!'

We reached the car. I was pleased to see that Toni had come, too. Still as muscular as he'd been at school, he was leaning casually against the driver's door, munching an apple.

'Moreau, Jules,' he said.

'Brenner, Anton,' I said.

We hugged each other. A few years earlier, when I'd joined the athletics team, Toni and I had often pumped iron together in the school gym. Every now and then we'd go for a beer afterwards. He'd taught me a few card and magic tricks, and raved about Liz. Later, when he was invalided out of sport after a second knee operation, he'd claimed the right to marry my sister as consolation.

When I mentioned this to him, he just made a face. 'Has she replied to my love letter yet?'

We went down to the lake together. As Marty, in a moment of genius, predicted the Internet ('There's going to be a new world, Jules, do you understand? The old world has been mapped and measured, but soon all of us can be pioneers again'), I stared at his outfit: side parting, rimless glasses, suit and plaited leather shoes. A diligent, academic high-flyer had emerged from the cocoon of the black-clad nerd. Although my brother didn't have a particularly attractive face, with his long nose and thin mouth ('a face like a scribbled pencil sketch by Sempé', Liz had once said), he looked ten times better than in his schooldays, and was blazing with energy.

'Your brother's going to be a first-class manager; I always knew it,' said Toni. 'I'm just tagging along behind him.'

Marty still had his tics, though: he felt compelled to walk through the middle of every puddle on our way. Even at school he'd never been able to leave the room without pushing down the door handle several times. Sometimes just four times, then twelve, then another eight. With the scientific precision of a madman he seemed to have developed a system that had its own internal logic, but although I always counted along I never managed to work it out.

The two of them interrogated me about life at the home. What was I supposed to say? After nine years I had so completely mastered the role of the cheerful, sociable boarding-school kid that sometimes, for a few moments, I even believed I really was that carefree. But I still never spoke about my parents. My dearest wish was just to be normal, not to be a bloody orphan any more.

I kept the memories of my parents securely bound and sealed, leaving them to gather dust in a corner of my consciousness, and although I often used to visit their grave in Munich, I hadn't been there for a long time now.

'By the way, I don't want to worry you,' said Marty, 'but Liz is in a bad way. She came to see me in Vienna recently and she looked exhausted. She takes too much crap.'

'But she always has.'

'I'm talking really hard drugs. I think she regrets it now, dropping out of school.'

'What makes you think that?'

'She seemed sad when she came with me to the university. And I just *know* she regrets it.'

I couldn't think of anything to say. For years I'd heard almost nothing from Liz; at least now we were vaguely in touch again. The last time I'd seen her had been a few months earlier, in Munich. A perfunctory meeting, as always.

To change the subject, my brother told me about his girlfriend Elena, whom he'd met at university. When I asked him if he loved her, Marty dismissed the question. 'Love,' he said. 'It's a stupid, literary concept, Jules. It's just chemical reactions.'

I sprinted along the hundred-metre track at top speed. Alva lay on the grass, reading. The sandy lawn and the running track were in miserable condition; nonetheless, the sports ground was something like the soul of the school. All sorts of cliques would meet here in the afternoons to discuss their plans for the evening, to read, or just to kill time.

I was a good runner; I didn't break any records, but I'd already won a couple of races for our athletics team in sports tournaments. Panting, I came to a halt in front of Alva. She was holding a little Reclam book in her hand. Whenever she was reading, something about her changed. Her face relaxed, her mouth slightly opened and she seemed suddenly unassailable, protected.

I caught a glimpse of two lines of a poem, and read aloud:

Before us great Death stands
Our fate held close within his quiet hands . . .

'Very comforting,' I said. 'How does it go on?'

Alva snapped the little book shut. 'Go on, do another lap!' she said merrily.

After training I had a shower, changed, and went back to her with my camera. I took a couple of photos of her, then lay down beside her in the grass. I think it was Alva who first started talking about how she definitely wanted children later on.

'How many?' I asked.

'I'd like two girls. One is very independent and contradicts me a lot, the other is very devoted and always comes to me whenever she needs advice. She also writes poems that never make sense.'

'And what if both girls are completely screwed up or weird?'

'Well, they're allowed to be a little bit weird.' Alva smiled. The small wrinkle in the middle of her forehead vanished.

Then she said seriously, 'I have to warn you, Jules, if I get to thirty and don't have any children, and you don't have any either, I'd like to have some with you. You'd be a good father, I'm absolutely sure of it.'

'That'd mean we'd have to sleep together first, though.'

'I would accept that necessary evil.'

'Yeah, maybe you would. Who says I'd be willing to?'

She raised an eyebrow. 'Wouldn't you?'

The conversation faltered for a moment.

Embarrassed, I glanced over at the boarding house. The hot cement of the car park glittered like splintered glass in the sunlight.

'Yeah, that sounds good,' I said. 'I don't want to be an old father. Thirty's my limit, too. I would therefore be willing to impregnate you then if necessary.'

'But what if we don't know each other any more when we're thirty?'

'That can never happen.'

She gave me a long look. 'Things like that can always happen.'

53

Alva's cat's eyes were green; not faded and dark like a dollar bill, but bright as grass. The green was a fascinating contrast with the red of her hair, but there was often something unfriendly about them, almost cool. They were not the eyes of a nineteen-year-old but of a woman, indifferent and no longer young. Yet when she said, 'Things like that can always happen,' something in her eyes altered; all the coldness was gone.

A drop fell on her arm. We looked up. Heavy clouds had covered the sun; a massive thunderclap came as if out of nowhere. Seconds later it was bucketing down.

We packed up our things and fled to my room. Alva found the gin Toni had brought me on his last visit. She kept refilling our glasses, and without really noticing we gradually emptied the bottle. The alcohol made me feel elated. Alva, however, was tense.

'He finished with me,' she said suddenly.

Her boyfriend was in his mid-twenties, a rather boorish car dealer from town: I didn't like him. Alva shook her head. 'But I was probably shitty to him. I deserved it.'

'No you didn't. You were too good for that idiot, anyway.'

'Believe me, I deserved to be left by him.' Almost mocking: 'Jules, you always see this person in me that isn't who I am.'

'No – other way round. You are the person you don't see.'

She shrugged, finished her glass and immediately refilled it. By now she was swaying slightly. *Thank you, Toni*, I thought. *No idea why you brought me the gin, but I owe you one.*

I remembered how she'd taken my hand in the Fiat.

'Do you remember when you sat next to me in Year Six?'

'What made you think of that?'

'Just because . . . Why did you?'

'You were new, and you dressed oddly; blue and red socks, nothing matched. And you looked so sad and forlorn, and everyone made jokes about you.'

'Did they? I never realised.'

'They also laughed because you were always getting words

back to front. "Freep deeze", I remember that one. Or "Prot's your woblem" instead of "What's your problem".' Alva picked up the weighted vest I always sprinted in and studied it. 'That's why I sat next to you: so you wouldn't be so alone. But then when they all started teasing me and saying I was in love with you, I moved away again.'

'That was pretty feeble of you.'

'Yes, it was.'

We looked at each other for a long time.

'Alva, you're drunk,' I said.

'No, Jules, you're drunk. Since when do you drink gin, anyway?'

'Always; a bottle a day before class.' I stepped closer and took the weighted vest out of her hands. 'There's so much you don't know about me.'

She fixed her eyes on me. 'Oh? Like what?'

There was a silence. The longer the question went unanswered the more it shifted, from playful to serious. I laughed briefly, but it was more like a gasp.

As Alva didn't want to take the lead in this scene, I followed my instincts and put on some music: 'Via Con Me' by Paolo Conte, the song my mother played me shortly before she died.

I looked at Alva, her damp hair still hanging over her face. Her dress seemed to be sticking to her; she carefully pulled it back down over her bare legs. At that moment I began to move to the music. My knees were trembling.

'You dance really well,' she said, sounding surprised.

Instead of answering, I asked her to dance with me. I even held out my hand when she waved me away. 'Come on,' I said. 'Just this one song . . . Come on!' I impersonated a gesticulating Italian, mouthing the lyrics theatrically:

> *It's wonderful, it's wonderful, it's wonderful*
> *Good luck my baby*
> *It's wonderful, it's wonderful, it's wonderful*
> *I dream of you . . .*

Alva gave a short laugh. Then her face darkened, and I sensed that her thoughts were suddenly elsewhere. Her body went limp; at one point she even shook her head. The disappointment took my breath away. I pressed my lips together, and for a while I danced on alone, a courageous fool. In the end, though, I turned the music off, and shortly afterwards Alva gathered up her things and left.

The 1992 Whitsun break slipped past uneventfully, until one day I found my aunt in the kitchen, lost in thought, with a strange light in her eyes. I realised with a shock that she had grown old. And then I understood. This would have been my mother's birthday. I was ashamed that I had completely forgotten. Nonetheless, I only agreed out of politeness when my aunt wanted to sit on the sofa with me and look at family photos.

I saw my mother as a little girl, as a teenager, and as a young woman with fashionably short hair and a miniskirt in the middle of a group of students. Her admiring gaze was directed at the good-looking man beside her. He was wearing a white shirt and a short tie; his sleeves were rolled up, he had a pipe in his mouth, and his eyes were shining as he talked to the others.

'Your father could be so fascinating, so clever,' said my aunt. 'He loved to discuss things for hours on end.'

In the next photo I saw my French grandmother, who already had that hard set to her mouth. There was little Marty, too, with his ant colony. Liz in her princess dress with the pink bow in her hair, and me in the background, staring at her open-mouthed. In another picture I was in the kitchen, aged nine, bent over a saucepan in concentration. Familiar food smells immediately filled my nose. I hadn't cooked anything in years; but hadn't I once loved cooking? Or was I just imagining it now because of the photos? I racked my brains and found more memories that became increasingly clear.

Another photo showed me grinning my former, confident grin, standing in front of a climbing frame surrounded by several boys and girls.

'You always wanted to be the centre of attention,' said my aunt. 'A real go-getter. Heaven forbid someone didn't dance to your tune; then you'd get cross. And nothing was ever dangerous enough for you.'

I felt as if she were talking about someone else.

'Really?' I asked.

'You were a special child,' she said. 'Marty was always the clever one, Liz the glamorous one, but you were quite distinct – much more refined than most other children.' She smiled. 'Even if you did chatter constantly.'

Finally we came to a photo of my mother, gazing at me dreamily while I wrote something in my red notebook.

My aunt stopped turning the pages and paused at this photo. 'She loved you so much,' she said. 'You were her darling.'

I stared at the picture with my mother. When I was a child she used to call me 'little snail', because outdoors I would often stretch up like a snail, taking in everything around me. Whenever I was unsure of anything I would ask her for advice. She was my compass. I observed the look she was giving me, her familiar face, her hand resting on my shoulder.

To my surprise, I realised that my eyes were full of tears.

'That's . . .' I began.

My aunt clasped my head and hugged me. I felt her warmth, and couldn't help myself: I started crying as I hadn't cried in years.

'I miss her so much,' I said, over and over again, as my aunt ran her hands consolingly over my back.

The party was in a mountain cabin with no electricity or running water. All the written exams were over; the iron grip of the school system was loosening; there were just the oral exams left to go. My fellow pupils had decided to celebrate together one last time beforehand. Music blasted from a portable CD player; we were laughing louder than necessary and making silly comments. Finishing our exams felt as if we'd robbed a bank and now only needed to think about what to do with the money.

Suddenly Alva seemed to have disappeared. She would frequently go off on her own, but an hour later, when she still hadn't returned, I went to look for her. I found her a few hundred metres from the cabin. She was standing on a spur of rock, staring into the depths.

I kicked a stone with my foot. Alva turned.

'What's going on?'

'Nothing,' she said.

We sat beside each other, dangling our feet over the abyss. The moon shone brightly on the valley below us.

'I read your stories yesterday,' she said. 'I liked them a lot. Really a *lot*.'

Over the past few weeks I'd started writing again. It was as if the door to my childhood had sprung open; I'd realised that I enjoyed telling stories just as much as I had when I was ten. My short stories were modelled on 'An Indomitable Heart' by A. N. Romanov, whom Alva worshipped almost as much as Tolstoy or McCullers.

'You're really talented, Jules,' she said. 'You must keep writing; you're bound to be an author one day.'

'I don't know. Photos are more precise, more true.'

'Sometimes lies are better.'

I had to do my compulsory civilian service in Munich, and that evening I asked her if she would share an apartment with me, perhaps with one other person. Alva wasn't sure. She'd often talked about how the first thing she wanted to do was travel, or go and live somewhere far away. 'There's hardly anything keeping me here, really,' she'd said once, and then laughed. 'I'd have to fall madly in love or something to make me stay.'

I felt I needed to do something to bind her closer to me. At the same time I was dragging up all my fears, as if from the bottom of a deep and dirty well: that up till now Alva had pushed away every man who'd got too close to her. That she hadn't wanted to dance with me, and there could only be one reason for this refusal. *What should I do?* I kept thinking. *What should I do now?*

'Do you know what my father said to me before he died?' I fidgeted nervously with my fingers. 'He said it was important to have a *true* friend – a soulmate. Someone you'd never lose, who would always be there for you. He said that was much more important than love.'

Alva turned to me. Her lips glistened in the moonlight. 'Why do you say that?'

'Sometimes I think that's who you are for me, or me for you. I can imagine us being friends all our lives, and I'm just so infinitely glad we got to know each other here. I don't think there's anyone who means more to me.'

I put my hand on her shoulder, and as I did I realised how seldom I touched her. 'What I'm trying to say is: please come with me to Munich.'

She considered. 'Let's talk about it all tomorrow evening. I'll have decided by then whether we'll do the apartment thing. Okay?'

'Okay. I'll cook something, too, if you like.'

'You'll cook? Do you know how?' She was amused. 'Yeah, that sounds good. Pick me up at mine around seven?'

I nodded. I sensed that she wanted to be by herself again for a moment, so I went back in on my own. I'm sure I danced with the others in the cabin and had a good time, but I hardly remember anything about that. Rather, it was the second conversation I had with Alva that was to preoccupy me for years.

When we all went to lie down the few beds were soon occupied, so the rest of us lay scattered about the cabin on mats and in sleeping bags. It was a chilly night, and I was cold. I'd drunk too much and couldn't get to sleep; if I closed my eyes everything started spinning. Alva was right beside me; I kept hearing her fast-forwarding and rewinding her Walkman. Finally she put it down.

Silence . . . Silence.

For me, this was when the real work of the night began. Like a detective attending the scene of a crime, I returned to specific events of the day, and they were all still there. Every one of Alva's gestures, which I tried to interpret retrospectively; every conversation we'd had. Like when we'd talked about our fellow pupils, most of whom seemed not to have a care in the world. 'Sometimes I think there are people who don't actually know they're going to die.' That really bothered me. Why had Alva said such a thing? She was lying right next to me, and yet I longed for her. I imagined what it would be like to live with her in Munich. Thought about dinner the next day, when we were going to discuss everything.

I was just drifting off to sleep when she nudged me. 'Jules. Are you still awake?'

'Yes. What is it?'

'The Walkman battery's flat,' she whispered, 'and I can't get to sleep if I'm not listening to something. I always have to distract myself, otherwise . . .'

I waited for her to finish the sentence, but she didn't.

'Shall I tell you a story?'

She laughed quietly. 'No, I just wanted to ask if I could come over to you. If there's someone lying beside me it's not so bad.'

I nodded, and she slipped into my sleeping bag. There wasn't enough room for us to lie side by side, so she lay half on top of me, and I was surprised how cool, heavy and above all how soft her legs, her whole body felt. She too was cold, but my coldness mingled with hers and we warmed up. At regular intervals I felt Alva's breath on my neck, tickling me. Conscious of her unaccustomed proximity – her breasts at my shoulder, her knees on my leg – I got an erection. I didn't know whether she'd noticed. I lay there for a moment without moving, then put my arm around her.

'I keep thinking about my sister, all the time. It just never stops.'

Alva's voice sounded brittle. I lifted my head in surprise. Until then she'd never told me she had a sister.

I asked, carefully, 'What's with your sister?'

'I don't know . . . She was a year older than me, we were inseparable, we did everything together. Our parents said we were like twins. And then, a few years ago . . . she disappeared.'

I listened, stunned. I had the feeling the others were watching us, and I craned my neck. Alva, however, seemed to have momentarily forgotten me. 'Her name was Josephine,' she said, more to herself. 'But we always called her Phine.'

'What happened?'

'Nobody knows . . . One day she just didn't come back from ballet.' Alva's voice was shaky and staccato. 'The police looked for her, of course. They turned over every stone in the whole area . . . There were canine units, and search operations that went on for months . . . But apart from her jacket they didn't find anything. Not even her body . . .'

She turned her face away. I sensed the despair behind her words and didn't know what to do: I could only be here, right beside her. I remembered the time she had left the classroom when we were watching the film.

'Why are you only telling me now?'

She didn't answer. The first light of morning filtered into the cabin and the outlines of our sleeping schoolmates materialised out of the darkness.

'I'm too tired,' she said. 'Let's talk about it this evening.'

She snuggled up to me. 'You're not allowed to go to sleep before I do,' she whispered, so close to my ear that it gave me goosebumps. 'That's very important, Jules. Very important.'

'I promise.' I stroked a lock of hair out of her face. Alva's hand stroked my chest briefly, then rested again; and as her breath grew slower, more even, I kissed her temple and whispered, 'I'm here for you.'

Later that day I went into town to buy food for dinner. I reserved the pupils' kitchen in the boarding house, and took the bus to the village where Alva lived. To my surprise I saw that she wasn't waiting outside the house for me this time, as she usually did. I rang the doorbell. Nothing moved. The garden was painstakingly well tended; the setting sun was reflected in the spotless glass of the windows. I couldn't help thinking about Alva's sister; then I rang the bell again.

Finally there was a buzz and I stepped inside.

The light in the hallway was dim. Alva's mother stood there in the dark, her face split by shadows. She held a cigarette in one hand and the telephone receiver in the other; her voice sounded loud and stressed. Alva herself was still nowhere to be seen. A strong smell of bolognese sauce wafted from the kitchen. Sudden, loud barking; two big Dalmatians came running towards me. They looked absolutely identical, right down to the smallest black spot, and they eyed me, bristling.

'I expect you want to see Alva,' said her mother, when she'd hung up. Her face had a strangely despondent expression.

I nodded and followed her into the kitchen, the dogs trotting behind me.

'Do you want a juice or a cola first?' she asked, already heading for the fridge.

'No, thank you,' I said, and she stopped. 'I'm having dinner with Alva; I just wanted to pick her up. Is she upstairs?'

Maybe there was something in my voice, something hopeful, that irritated her mother. She stared at me for a long time. 'God, you're young.' Still appraising me, she exhaled a cloud of smoke. I felt uncomfortable.

'Yes, she's upstairs,' she said. 'No point in knocking, she's listening to loud music again.'

I went up the stairs, took the last few steps in one, already I was outside Alva's door, I opened it – and froze, no, was catapulted out of the scene. Even before I'd closed the door again, my world had fallen apart.

I ran downstairs. Images whirled around my head: the empty beer cans, the maths book and the pullover on the floor. The bed. The naked man, lying on his back. Straddling him, also naked: Alva. The red, sweaty strands of hair; her neck, a little flushed with exertion; her movements, slowing only for a moment; her slightly open mouth. The noises they were making; and, above all, the brief but piercing look Alva gave me.

A look more forceful than any answer: silent yet aggressive, accusing and, at the same time, regretful. In that moment I saw in her something that she was and did not want to be. Above all, though, I saw myself through her eyes: what I'd become, and what I had not. And whatever had been between us all those years, a single look was enough to undo it all.

As I ran down the stairs I felt the most tremendous rage. I didn't want to be just a boy any more, I wanted to shake off all traces of youthfulness, I would have thrashed them out of myself if I could. Alva's mother was standing at the bottom of the stairs with the two dogs. She tried to say something but I ran away, out of the village and straight across the adjoining fields without looking back.

The Harvest
(1997–1998)

In my memory I see myself at my sister's engagement party. Unfortunately, I'm not the elegant, besuited charmer making everyone around him laugh. Nor am I the coked-up guy jiggling his Air Jordans in Charleston rhythm and flirting with a student. No: that unprepossessing twenty-four-year-old over there at the bar who's clearly uncomfortable among all these strangers, *c'est moi*. As I break the back of a quartered lemon and squeeze the juice into my drink, I think about the birthday celebrations and parties of my childhood, when I was always the centre of attention. And had such tremendous energy. When exactly did I lose all that? I've ditched my law degree, and I'm not having any success as a photographer, either. Rightly so, I think; because a glowing coal of self-loathing has burned inside me for a long time now.

The only man in the room who looks as lost as I do is Liz's fiancé, Robert Schwan. A successful jazz pianist, but Liz doesn't like jazz. All in all, he's a puzzling choice. My sister always had a weakness for good-looking, interesting men, and took what she wanted with a voraciousness I often admired. Her fiancé, however, is a bony, black-haired man in his mid-forties with intense Paul Auster eyes and an absurd moustache that makes him look rather shifty.

'What a bore,' says a man's voice beside me. 'I just talked to him for ten minutes. No idea what she sees in him.'

My brother has joined me, with his girlfriend. Elena is small, black-haired, rather stocky, with watchful eyes that take everything in. She hugs me shyly and picks a bit of fluff off my jacket.

Embarrassed, I greet Marty as well. The last time I saw him was at our aunt's funeral, where we parted on bad terms.

'Congratulations,' I say. '*Dr* Moreau.'

'Not bad, eh? Never thought I'd get a PhD one day.' A hint of a grin flickers across Marty's face. 'Although, actually, I did always think it.'

We watch our sister. She's twenty-seven; tonight, she's wearing a blue dress, her blonde hair is pinned up, and in her high heels she towers over everything and everyone. Liz sees her beauty reflected in the eyes of all those present and allows them all to fall in love with her. She makes effusive speeches and kisses her fiancé tenderly; then she buzzes like a bee from one guest to the next, scattering her charm in all directions. She keeps bursting into laughter, and her laughter is captivating, just as anything my sister does is captivating. Yet it always feels as if Liz is merely fulfilling the instructions of an invisible cameraman. *Another dazzling smile, perfect, now a little pout, a quick, flirty look . . .* When she turns her gaze on you it's as if she's shining a spotlight on your very self, and the only thing you want to do any more is to please her. Even me.

And how long ago they seem, all of a sudden, those days when, as a child, I would sneak into her room at night. Often, Liz would still be reading or drawing her comics and would let me slip under the blankets. I was always fascinated by how warm her legs were; they seemed to glow. Usually she would tell me about boys from her class, how sweet this one was, how cheeky another. I would listen breathlessly to these rhapsodies, proud that my older sister confided all this to me. Sometimes, though, I would just lie beside her in bed while she read and listened to music. I loved those moments. My mother and father at the end of the corridor, Marty next door, everything so secure and cosy; I would cuddle up to Liz as she calmly turned the pages beside me, then simply fall asleep . . .

The next memory is of a different, darker hue.

Four months after my sister's engagement party, a terrible

phone call rouses me from sleep. There's no time to stop and think. I'm living in Hamburg, in a shabby bedsit near the port, and I immediately catch a train to Berlin to see Liz. In contrast to my last visit, her apartment is oppressively silent. Yet silence never suited my sister. The morning light shines dimly through the windows in the hall; in the kitchen, a mountain of dirty crockery looms up out of the sink; I almost stumble over a smashed guitar on my way in.

The bedroom smells of joss sticks and vomit. Liz is sitting on the floor, eyes half-closed. A few people are with her, clearly friends of hers, I don't know most of them. No sign of her fiancé.

'What's the matter with her?'

I kneel down beside Liz. She's wearing only knickers and a sweater, and has ashen rings around her eyes. She doesn't seem to recognise me, and mumbles something about an amplifier in her brain that can regulate the city.

'She had a breakdown,' says one of her friends, a woman I recognise from the engagement party. 'She was standing out in the street half-naked, shouting at people.'

I stroke my sister's damp hair back from her face. 'What's she taken?'

'Dunno. Coke, Ecstasy, a couple of downers, and mescaline – something like that.'

'Where's her fiancé?'

'Don't you know? Robert split up with her ages ago.'

For a moment I'm speechless. Then I call Marty at his office in Vienna.

'Don't take her to hospital, whatever you do,' he keeps saying. 'I'll send a doctor round, a friend of mine, and I'll come as soon as I can.'

Suddenly, Liz is cheerful again. She stretches out her hand to me and talks to me as if I were a child.

'Oh, *my baby brother*, what are you doing here?'

Then she laughs in my face. A shrill, crazy laugh, looking straight at me the whole time. But this isn't her sisterly look, the

U-certificate version; it's the hard, amused, infinitely superior look all men, all women, have struggled with for years, the look only Robert Schwan was able to withstand. She keeps on laughing madly, and it makes my skin crawl. Liz's eyes are black and unfathomable. The eyes of someone falling, falling, falling.

And she loves the fall.

'When will you be here?' I ask Marty.

'I'll catch the next plane.' He sounds harried; I hear him running down the steps and opening a door. As always, he pushes the handle down several times. Eight loud rattles. 'It's going to be okay, you hear me?'

Just then Liz signals to me to come closer so she can whisper something in my ear. She seems excited now, like a child who's just remembered something important. I lean over, the phone still in my hand, and when I'm right up close my sister murmurs, 'Sdedikildit.'

'What?' I ask.

'It's dead, I killed it,' she repeats.

In the summer of 1998 I went back to Berdillac with my brother and sister for the first time since our childhood. It was Marty's idea. We'd inherited the house from our grandmother, and he'd had it renovated. He said he could work from France as well; Elena would follow on a few days later. We talked about all this as if it were a holiday we'd been planning for ages, but the real reason for the trip was that we were worried about Liz. She still hadn't really got back on her feet after the abortion and break-down.

In France a storm awaited us; the windscreen wipers whipped back and forth. My brother steered the Mercedes along the country roads while Liz slept. I looked out of the window and recognised a lot of things: strangely familiar castles, the bright colours of the fields. I thought of the silver franc coins I used to play with as a child. My father, sitting at the wheel; my mother, listening to her Beatles cassette.

In Berdillac the rain had stopped; the air was fresh and pleasantly cool. Marty got out first and walked up to the front door. For a brief moment I thought of our father: how he too – in his leather jacket, pipe in the corner of his mouth – was always the first to go to the door. Coming back here after all these years was like seeing an old black-and-white film in colour for the first time. On the outside, the house at the end of the street looked unchanged. The front was covered in ivy; chairs and a picnic table stood on the stone veranda in the garden; the reddish, tiled roof was dirty, the dark-green paint still peeling off the front door. Inside, though, it was unrecognisable. The wall between kitchen and living room had been knocked through. A big room, cosily furnished with bookshelves, a corner sofa and fireplace at the front, oven, sink and wooden dining table at the back.

'The house is in tip-top condition now.' Marty showed us round. 'Bathroom completely refurbished, floors upstairs freshly tiled, and the hideous wallpaper's been stripped. The only things I kept were Grandpa's chests of drawers, tables and wardrobes.'

He strutted ahead of us. He and Toni had been among the first to correctly assess the potential of the Internet. Their company had set up an elite website where managers, lawyers, bankers, politicians or journalists could create a profile and network with each other. Their start-up had grown quickly. During our drive Marty had told us Microsoft wanted to buy it for a seven-figure sum. *Not bad*, I thought; *maybe I can borrow a bit off him.*

At dinner the conversation didn't really flow, and eventually we stopped talking altogether. I thought of the loud, cheerful dinners of our childhood, when my brother and sister would argue or we'd all laugh together about something that had happened. And now here we were, sitting at the table like three actors meeting again after a long time who can no longer remember the script of their most famous play.

At some point I couldn't stand the silence any longer. I took a portfolio of pictures out of my bag. 'I've offered them to a gallery.'

It was my new project: a series about *Unobtrusive Beauty*. One photo showed a valley covered in fog, a thick, white haze with only the black tips of the trees poking through; others showed a cottage in a wood, overgrown with moss and abandoned to decay, or a boy who'd just tied his shoelaces and was now running after his friends with an elated expression. I'd pressed the shutter just before he reached them.

My sister grabbed the pictures. 'I really like them,' she said, yet I couldn't help feeling that she didn't study the photos closely enough to see the depth and detail.

Marty, on the other hand, examined them carefully. 'They're not bad at all. You imitate the style of Salgado or Cartier-Bresson pretty well . . .'

'But?' I asked.

'But I still don't see how you plan to make a living doing this.'

I don't know what reaction I'd been hoping for from him, but an 'I believe in you' would have been nice. My sister didn't look as if she was going to come to my aid. Her financial situation was also tricky, albeit more stable than mine. Sometimes she earned her money by modelling; sometimes she gave guitar lessons or worked at an advertising agency for a few months.

'What's it to you?' I said quietly.

Marty sighed. 'I don't mean to interfere in your life, but I don't think you should have abandoned your degree.'

'I hated it,' I said. 'If I regret anything, it's that I ever started.'

'But it would have given you security. I know it's never easy in the beginning; you have to persevere with these things. Maybe you would have enjoyed it by the end.'

'Sorry, but how would you know what I enjoy? You know absolutely nothing about me, so stop acting like my father all the time.'

I took back the photos, annoyed. I'd had this conversation with Marty a lot in recent years, and it made me feel like a stroppy teenager every time. Not least because my brother wouldn't let me escape the role.

That night I couldn't sleep. I stared at the full moon for a while, shining like a perfectly round porthole in the black sky, then I got up and knocked on my sister's door. Liz opened it in her pyjamas. On her bed was an old children's book she'd obviously found here, and a packet of wine gums.

'Are you still angry?' she asked, chewing. 'Don't worry about earlier. Marty's just getting more and more like Papa. Every bit as critical. Not such a loser, though. He's like Papa would have been if he'd been successful.'

I nodded, but it hurt to hear her call our father a loser.

'Did it work out with the Kunsthaus exhibition?'

I just shook my head.

'Jules, can I ask you something?' Liz gave me a motherly look. 'How long have you been trying now to make it as a photographer – three years? Are you doing all this because of *him*? Because you feel guilty?'

I remember clearly that this question made me very uneasy, and it's possible that I raised my voice when I answered.

'Why should I feel guilty? I don't owe Papa anything. I know he was disappointed because I didn't use the camera before he died, but we settled that back then.'

'I didn't mean to—'

'I don't take photos because of Papa, I take them because it interests me. You sound just like Marty.'

Irritated, I looked away. On the wall was a framed drawing; it showed a man with eagle wings flying through the air, and the outlines of a castle in the distance. Beside it, in childish handwriting: *He has to free the princess who has been locked up in a dark tower* . . . Incredible that this drawing had survived! It was from the weeks after our parents' death. We'd been here in France with our grandmother, and it was the period when we still secretly believed our parents would walk through the door any minute and it would all turn out to have been a big misunderstanding. To cheer me and Marty up, Liz had thought of a game called Dream Department. She was the dedicated editor-in-chief and illustrator, and together we had to think up absurd or beautiful dreams which we then drew and wrote texts for. Then we'd burn the pages, and according to Liz the smoke blew away and was breathed in by others who, that night, would dream whatever it was we'd thought up.

'What if we'd grown up here in Montpellier?' I asked Liz. 'I often imagined what you'd have been like as a typical French girl. I think it would have suited you. You'd have finished school here and then gone on to study.'

'And what would I have studied?'

'Something arty, for sure. Painting maybe, or literature. Or you'd have become a teacher like Mama, that's also possible.'

Liz stared at me. 'Go on,' she said quietly.

'Well, in any case, you'd always have had a book in your hand; you'd have loved reading and drawing. Mama would have helped you sometimes, if she'd still been alive; you'd have talked a lot on the phone. After school you'd have gone to university in Paris, you see. You'd have had a few admirers, but you'd also have thought a lot about your high-school sweetheart, a guy called Jean or Sébastien who you went out with for years. Your first boyfriend. But he went abroad to study, so you split up. You were sad, but it was a beautiful kind of sadness, the only good kind. And somehow you knew you'd see him again some day. *He's just not for now; he's for later*, you'd have told us. You'd have dressed beautifully, like Mama. You'd have partied at weekends, of course, but you'd have been much more restrained than in Germany. You'd have had a few friends who always took good care of you. Then in the holidays you'd have come to us in Montpellier, and I'd have quizzed you on what it was like at university, whether there were lots of pretty girls. Marty, on the other hand, would have got a scholarship to Harvard, where he'd have studied biology, dissected his beetles and snails, and we'd all have teased him. Then, just before your finals, you'd have . . . oh, I don't know, help me out . . .'

I'd been smiling as I talked and had thought it would amuse

Liz as well. Now I looked at her and realised she had tears in her eyes.

'Sorry. I keep having these silly moments.' She wiped her face with her hand. 'I don't even know if it was a boy or a girl. It doesn't matter. I just miss it.'

I sat down beside her on the bed. 'We would have been there for you. All you had to do was tell us. I didn't even know the two of you had split up.'

'I find it hard to trust other people.'

'You can trust your brothers, though,' I said, and immediately wondered whether such a claim was justified.

'Do you regret it?'

Liz shrugged. 'Sometimes yes, sometimes no.' Suddenly she was like a ten-year-old. 'I know Robert wasn't the right man for me. It's just that I keep thinking what Mama would have been like as a grandma. I wish I could have phoned her; she'd have known what was the right thing to do.'

She went over to her jacket, which was hanging on a chair, took out a cigarette and lit it. Then she abruptly flung her arms around me and gave me three quick, fierce kisses on the cheek. I stroked her hair, and the smell of smoke mingled with the honey scent of her shampoo.

I remembered how her fiancé had hardly uttered a single sentence at our last meeting, often staring indifferently into space or tapping at his pager. Being bored for fear of being boring.

'What did you love about him?' I asked. 'He had nothing going for him.'

'That was it, I think. He was so empty, so wonderfully empty. I could turn him into whatever I liked. And he didn't have a single vulnerability. Nothing could hurt him. That fascinated me.'

The morning shimmered bleak and grey, but we drove to the seaside anyway. Liz wore a black bikini and sunglasses. She was lying on the beach, reading; already the milky sun had tinged her skin red. I dug my toes in the sand and watched my brother swimming in the icy sea. Marty was flailing clumsily at the water; he seemed to be on edge all day. Later, he told us that he had blood tests done several times a year and was still waiting for the results of the last ones.

'Why do you go to all that hassle?' asked Liz.

He shrugged.

'"*Dogs, do you want to live forever?*"' she asked scornfully. She waved her hand dismissively. 'I'm going to die young, but I don't care.' After the difficulties of the last few months this was precisely what we didn't want to hear.

'No, you're not.'

'I am, I *know* it.' Our sister stretched provocatively on her towel and lit herself a cigarette. 'I'll die young; it'll be just when I'm finally happy. Then something'll happen, and all of a sudden I'll be dead.' She looked at each of us in turn. 'But that's okay. I've been practically everywhere, I've seen so much: the morning mist in Manhattan, or the jungle in Ecuador; I've been skydiving, I've had lots of lovers and a wild, difficult time, but before that I had a happy, sheltered one, too; and I've really learned a lot about death. It doesn't matter if I die young, because I can still say that I've lived.'

Marty just shook his head. 'How arrogant does someone have to be to talk like that?'

'How inhibited does someone have to be to call that arrogant?'

As the two of them went on arguing, I strolled along the beach on my own. Liz was right, I thought. She loved unconditionally, wasted herself unconditionally, failed unconditionally.

And me?

An ice-cream salesman was approaching from a distance, pushing his little cart in front of him. He had a transistor radio that was blasting out music. I took a deep breath and felt the salty air in my lungs. In front of me the silver-speckled sea. The ice-cream salesman passed me by, and now I heard what song was playing.

> *It's wonderful, it's wonderful, it's wonderful*
> *Good luck my baby*
> *It's wonderful, it's wonderful, it's wonderful*
> *I dream of you . . .*

These last few years I'd thought of Alva repeatedly. Missed her, and maligned her. Lain awake at night reminding myself of how she'd written little comments in my books, or run her fingers through my hair and said, laughing, that I had tiny ears . . .

Never had the courage to win her, only ever the fear of losing her.

I wouldn't have admitted it at the time, but ultimately all my relationships since school had failed because I couldn't forget Alva. I often asked myself what she might be doing right now. Mobile phones were still an unusual sight back then, the Internet in its infancy: there was hardly a trace of her. At some point I'd heard that she was living in Russia, but I didn't know the details. I just felt that, with her, everything would have been different. The years after boarding school; studying law, a mistake no one had counselled me against; finally, my move, no, *flight* from Munich to Hamburg. Alva was nowhere to be seen in any of these pictures, and without her there was nothing else to save me from loneliness.

After a few days I managed to persuade Marty to go jogging with me. Every morning we ran through the village, past the church tower and up the hill to the tree with the lopped-off branch. Our turning point. Satisfied, we'd rest on the bench, looking down at the valley and the broad fields bathed in summer-morning mist, then run back to the house where our sister and Elena, who'd also arrived, were already sitting on the terrace.

'Women, we hungry,' we told them as we approached the veranda, panting. 'Ugg, ugg, women, bring us food.'

I beat my chest like a gorilla and Marty made monkey noises. I think he really enjoyed being able to fool around for once.

'You two can jog right on,' said Liz. 'If you can still talk like that, you haven't been running long enough.'

To my astonishment it was almost always my brother who entertained us during the breakfasts that followed in the garden. Marty didn't like novels, but he was a passionate reader of biographies and newspapers. Not someone who had an intuitive understanding of life, he'd had to acquire his wisdom painstakingly, by reading. He was a good storyteller, though: as we ate, he would often give a vivid account of an unusual new exhibition, a master art forger from England, or a momentous discovery in the field of prime numbers.

After breakfast he usually retired to his room to work for a few hours. Liz, who always had to be doing something, would go for a walk, play badminton with me or go into town on her own. I liked to get a book and sit with Elena on the terrace while she worked on her psychology dissertation. We got on well, even without talking much.

The fight came completely out of the blue.

That evening Elena had gone to Marseilles to see a university friend. My brother and sister and I paid a visit to the little cemetery in Berdillac. It was dark and deserted; Liz lit two candles. Their flickering light illuminated the names of our grandparents and our Uncle Eric. I stared at the gravestones. These three dead people had always been strangers to me. Uncle Eric had died years before we were born; he was only twenty-one. We'd always been kept in the dark about the precise circumstances of his death. Nor did we know much about our grandfather, who was a joiner. Only once had Aunt Helene hinted that he must have had quite a temper, and that apparently he'd drunk himself to death. 'He died just a few months after Eric,' said my brother, as if he'd guessed what I was thinking.

I was glad when we left the cemetery again.

Back at the house the feeling was one of relief. We drank three, four bottles of Corbières and told anecdotes about the old days. Liz talked about her ex-boyfriends ('They were all far too good-looking, like a beautifully wrapped present. When you opened it, it was nothing but an old shoe'), and at some point the conversation came round to Marty's Norwegian penpal Gunnar Nordahl, whose existence we'd never quite believed in.

'So was there really a Gunnar, or did you just make him up?' we asked.

'Of course there was a Gunnar,' said our brother. Then he stared at his wine glass. 'Okay, no, there wasn't.' He shook his head. 'I just wrote letters, for years, to some Norwegian I found in the phone book. I often wondered whether he ever read them.'

'Oh my God, I knew it!' crowed Liz. Marty took it calmly, like one who feels he is at heart unassailable.

Later on, Liz paraded a yellow miniskirt in front of us. 'Look, I got this from a shop by the uni that was full of nineteen-year-old girls.' She grinned. 'We're going out later, and guess what I'm going to wear.'

'I'm definitely not going out again.' Marty fidgeted with his glasses. 'And I don't mean to disappoint you, but I'm afraid you're not nineteen any more.'

'Oh yeah? Says *who*?'

She struck silly poses in front of him until he laughed and drove us into town after all. He left his last, full, glass of wine on the table; our sister, however, swiftly knocked hers back.

The three of us danced till dawn in a club in Montpellier, and the main thing I remember about it is how comfortable Liz was amid all those strangers on the dance floor. Not only because she was so self-assured, but because she simply felt welcome wherever she went.

It was already seven a.m. and I'd just gone to bed when I heard raised voices down below. I went to the top of the stairs and peered cautiously into the living area. Liz was standing in the middle of the room; Marty sat, slightly hunched, on the sofa. They didn't notice me.

'Yes, that I would like to know,' Liz was saying. 'Here you are, acting like bloody King Babar and playing the concerned brother, but where were you when we needed you?'

'I'm sorry, but if anybody round here did a runner, it was you,' said Marty calmly. 'And someone in our family had to earn some money for once.'

'Money's the only thing that interests you any more, isn't it? Market rates, property pages, your Internet portal, all that shit.'

'Stop talking like a bolshy adolescent,' said Marty. 'You sound awful. The truth is that you simply weren't there back then.'

'When?'

'When Mama and Papa died. You abandoned us – you just hung around with your friends getting off your face, you weren't interested in us any more. I don't know what it was like for you, but we were having a horrible time back then, we hardly had any friends, nothing. And you want to know why? Because we hadn't learned to have friends, because we'd always had the three of us. And then you just vanished from our lives, even though you'd promised to look after us. Can you maybe tell me *now* why you did that, why you just buggered off?'

Liz seemed stung by the question. She took a peach from the fruit basket on the dining table and fiddled with it.

'I was still much more of a child than you back then,' she said. 'Of course I was always talking about boys, and acting the mature older sister. But really I just loved being a child. I loved talking nonsense, cuddling Mama, sitting in my room for hours drawing. I didn't want to grow up; certainly not that fast. And then everything was gone. From one second to another. Jules was too young for any of it, and you were this black-clad freak who'd turned his back on everything, don't you remember?'

Marty shrugged, reluctantly admitting she was right.

'We were all hurting back then,' she said, 'and we all reacted differently. I made sure nothing was ever calm again, that my mind never had a chance to be still. I threw myself into life the way I did because whenever I sat alone in my room and thought about things, all I wanted to do was cry my eyes out.'

'But why did you abandon us like that?'

'If I could have looked after you both, I would have. But I didn't have the strength. Do you know what my first time was like? Do you?'

'You were with this older boy and—'

'No, that was a lie. Do you know what my first time was really like?'

Marty was getting quieter and quieter. 'No.'

'I don't even know his name.' Liz's voice was shaking. 'We'd only been at the home a few weeks, and the girls on my floor used to make fun of me – my soft toys, my childish comics, my uncool clothes. So I wanted to prove that I was harder than them. I was willing to inflict more wounds on myself than any other girl. That's why I was the only one who went when we were offered something or other in a club. I don't know what it was; I hardly saw or felt anything after that. And then this guy came along. He was in his early twenties, and there was something about him, something cold and fucked-up, that I didn't understand. He suddenly pulled me off the dance floor, and when we were far enough away he undid his trousers. I didn't want to, but I didn't have the strength to resist. Everything in my head was still fuddled by the drug. I thought about Munich and Mama and Papa and the two of you, and how far away all that was all of a sudden. And while I was doing that he just went ahead and fucked me.'

Marty bit his lip and said nothing.

'Suddenly I was someone I never wanted to be. And the more time went by, the more impossible it was for me to get back to you. You didn't know what it was like to throw up on speed at seven in the morning on the dance floor of some provincial club, or sleep with someone when you're tripping, or wake up next to someone you only clapped eyes on for the first time a few hours earlier. You never knew what it felt like to lose yourself in everything so completely. You were just immersed in your school-books and computer games, and Jules in his dream world. There's so much separating us. Still.'

They both stared at the floor and were silent. The scene was like a chess game with two opposing pieces left that can't attack each other, like two bishops on different colours.

'And what if we do it together?' I asked from the stairs.

They looked up, but weren't too surprised to see me.

'You're right,' I told Liz. 'We know nothing of what you know. You've had experiences we simply haven't had. The drugs alone. You've seen and felt things Marty and I can't even imagine. You've often told me how incredible LSD is, for example. So why don't we take it together? Then at least we'll be able to join in the conversation.'

Liz considered, then shook her head. 'You don't do drugs, you're just not—'

'You see,' I interrupted, 'that's exactly what I mean. "You're just not like me." That's what you were going to say, isn't it? And we can't be, if you won't let us. The fact is that we hardly have anything in common any more. We haven't for years. So will you finally let us be part of your life?'

Liz thought about it. 'Even if I did, where would we get acid, anyway?'

'That wouldn't be the problem,' said Marty, rather surprisingly. 'I could arrange it; I know enough people, here too. The only question is what can go wrong.'

We discussed the pros and cons and decided we wouldn't take the trip until Elena was back and could look after us. When she heard about our plan she wasn't exactly over the moon, but eventually let herself be persuaded.

Three days later a grey van stopped outside our house. Marty chatted with the friendly driver and returned with a plastic bag. Shortly afterwards the three of us were sitting next to each other on the sofa holding brightly coloured bits of paper in our hands. Liz explained that we just had to swallow them and that was it. I stared at mine. It was pale blue, and tasted of nothing.

We waited quite a while for it to have an effect. Marty fetched *Le Figaro* and read. Liz leaned back and closed her eyes. I looked at Elena, who was sitting opposite us; she looked back. Then I swallowed, and for a moment the stale taste of youth was in my mouth: a mixture of smoke, canteen food, cheap beer, and the moment when Alva took my hand. I drank a glass of water and the distant, synaesthetic echo on my tongue disappeared.

My brother seemed to be the next to notice something. He stared, fascinated, at the newspaper, murmured that the letters were running into each other, then went over to Elena and put his head in her lap.

At that moment a wave of memories swept over me; it was as if someone were leafing through my life. Back a few chapters: our aunt's funeral. She'd died of a stroke the previous year, plucked from the midst of life. On the way to the service Marty had seemed detached, almost emotionless, although he'd loved our aunt dearly. He drove to the cemetery in silence while Liz and I talked about how Fate had betrayed us yet again.

'Rubbish,' Marty had said suddenly. 'There's no Fate, just like there's no God. There's nothing; or just us humans, which comes to much the same thing. So it's completely absurd to wrestle with it. Death is a statistic, and it seems to be against us at the moment. But one day, when everyone around us, including us, is dead, it'll have balanced out again, just like that.' Half an hour later, though, at the funeral, as we sat staring at the coffin that contained our aunt, my brother – to my surprise – had wept bitterly. His sobs were heartbreaking: everyone in the chapel had looked at Marty as he leaned against Liz's shoulder and let her hug him.

Then my mind leafed back even further, and I saw myself as a child standing in the living room and hearing from my aunt that my parents were dead. Marty stood beside me, pale and motionless, but he might as well have been a thousand miles away. The words slowly started to take their terrible effect; they seeped everywhere, into the ground, which suddenly seemed uneven, into my eyes, where my vision was now blurred, into my legs, making me reel across the room. Later on the blast wave reached Liz as well, when she came in through the front door of the apartment and looked at me, instantly apprehensive. 'What is it?' she asked; but I couldn't tell her, and I didn't want to, as if that could protect her from the truth.

'I'm seeing the same thing,' said Liz, beside me. At least, I thought she did.

I wanted to tell her how different everything had become, how different *I* had become, but I couldn't. My heart beat faster; images flooded my mind. My father throwing me a ball. Liz, pocketing a little white Barricade piece as a lucky charm. My mother calling me *little snail* and reading aloud to me. Me sieving flour for her 'Irresistible Cake'. All mixed up, all so close, so beautiful, so fast, that I could hardly bear it.

I took a deep breath in, deep breath out, deep breath in, deep breath out.

'It's too much,' I kept saying. 'I can't take any more. Please stop.'

Liz took my hand. 'Relax,' she said. 'Everything's okay.'

Tears were running down my cheeks, the colours in the room were glowing, I could see every tiny indentation in my hand. My breath was racing, my chest constricting. Then in an instant everything was free and I could breathe normally again. The relief made me burst out laughing. I kept glancing at Elena, who was watching me, keeping the whole room under control by staying calm.

'I know now what picture I would have liked to paint when I was twelve.' Liz leaned against me. 'I'd forgotten these past few years, but now it's come back to me. I would have painted four dogs playing ball on the beach like humans. They'd have had funny names and worn old-fashioned clothes.'

I nodded, happy to be so close to her.

Now everything was merging together as my consciousness broke free of its moorings and travelled back in time.

I was . . . suddenly I *am* Marty, as a child, building a petrol-powered toy car. The wonderful precision of the individual parts engaging; the moment of joy when the engine starts and, at a stroke, the technology beneath the bodywork makes sense.

I am Liz, painting something in bright colours on a piece of paper, and suddenly living creatures appear that I myself have created, and it's so incredible that I lose myself in it. And in my head there are other radiant pictures, so many that it hurts sometimes, and I can't tell or show anyone, so every now and then I have to go wild and run madly round the room to get rid of all this energy and shake it off.

I am my mother, watching her children play and grow older, and I hope I'll get to keep them with me a little longer. And I'm content that I gave up my freedom for this life, even if I do sometimes miss it.

And I am my father, who's driving to work in his car and would like more than anything to turn around right now and drive home to his family, but, as with so much else, can't do it. I ask myself when things started to go wrong, or whether they were never right, from the very beginning. And I think about how just before I died I gave my younger son Jules an old camera for Christmas that he doesn't use. Because of that we have our final row, and . . .

'I remember,' I say. I see my father before me in sharp focus, pipe in hand, crestfallen, staring at me in shock. My guilt. My accursed guilt.

'Oh my God, now I remember it all.'

My eyes are still closed. Now I'm myself, running across a meadow, seeing incredible shades of green. My nose is filled with the fragrant scent of hay, resin and damp moss; my senses are filled to the brim. It's raining, and I reach a forest, soaked to the skin. Within seconds day slips into night. Suddenly it's dark and cold, and I sense that danger is lurking here. I have to pass through impenetrable undergrowth. Sharp black branches pierce my skin; I'm bleeding.

'Something's wrong,' I say. 'Something's very wrong. It won't stop.'

I can feel someone shaking me, but I keep my eyes tightly shut, keep on running. I know this forest. I haven't left it since my childhood. It's become my home. And if I'm not careful, this forest is where I will die.

I plunge on into the interior, and see an image clearly before me: our life, when our parents died, approaching a set of points, switching to the wrong track; ever since, we've been leading another life – the wrong one. An unrectifiable system error.

On my way into the interior I stumble and spear myself on a branch lying on the ground. The branch stabs me in the heart. I bleed to death on the spot; everything becomes warm and bright, which is both very pleasant and the bleakest feeling I've ever had, because I have to let go of everything, and am losing everything . . .

My eyes flew open; I was soaking wet.

'I don't want to die,' I cried. 'I DON'T WANT TO DIE!'

To have to take leave of yourself. All your thoughts, hopes and memories erased. A black screen for all eternity.

I curled up on the floor and wept. 'I don't want to die,' I kept mumbling. Liz lay down beside me; Marty and Elena held my hands. I sensed the others' proximity, and how warm and cosy it was in our house. But that all seemed very far away, because I was deep inside myself and the only thing there was cold fear.

On the last day of our holiday I sat on the beach with my brother. It was cool, and the refreshing wind blew through our hair. A fishing boat drifted past close to the shore, painting its outline on the surface of the water.

'Hey,' said Marty.

'Yes?'

'I'm sorry we saw so little of each other.' He took off his glasses and pinched the bridge of his nose firmly between thumb and forefinger. 'I probably wasn't a very good brother these last few years.'

'You were a smart-arse.'

'Yes, perhaps.'

'A smart-arse and a total jerk.'

'Thanks, I've got the message.'

We looked at each other. My brother patted me on the shoulder, and I thought he suddenly seemed youthful. 'I'll make up for it.'

That afternoon, while my siblings were packing for the return journey, Elena and I went for a last walk round the village.

'What's happened to Marty's tics?' I asked. 'Locking the door five times, pushing the handle down again and again according to some secret pattern, not treading on the cracks in the paving stones . . . Where's it all gone?'

Elena lowered her eyes. 'It got worse and worse,' she said. 'By the end he was going for cancer screenings five times a year, and he couldn't use escalators or lifts because he thought they brought bad luck.'

'Excuse me?'

Elena couldn't help laughing. 'Yes, escalators and lifts were *evil*. He kept it all a secret from me to begin with; he even joked about it if I noticed something. But it got to a point where the compulsions were governing his whole life. He's been having therapy for a few months now.'

We were approaching the house. From a distance I could see Marty already loading up the boot, whistling a melody from *Carmen* as he did so.

'So has he got rid of his tics now?' I asked.

'I wish. I think it's got better, but sometimes I have the feeling that the tics are still there, he just hides them better. I try to catch him at it, but I haven't managed yet.'

As I walked into the garden, I nodded at my brother. A difficult childhood is like an invisible enemy, I thought. You never know when it will strike.

Part Two

I recover remarkably quickly from my motorcycle accident. Soon I'm able to read, watch television and make phone calls again. I'm also given the full diagnosis: bruised spleen, right tibia and fibula broken, broken collarbone, severe concussion. The doctors say I was lucky.

Lucky. A word that means little to me right now.

There's a knock at the door. Marty has brought my children with him; Elena has come too, and even Toni, who's flown to Munich specially to see me.

My children run over to the bed and hug me. Vincent has painted me a picture; it shows a grinning man on crutches. Luise puts a soft toy animal on my bedside table to keep me company. They're seven years old now, yet still it seems like a miracle that they actually belong to me. That I'll always be their father, even if I were to emigrate one day, or something should happen to me, or they never want to see me again.

Luise points at the plaster on my leg, and the neck brace. As on her last visit, she asks me if I'm going to die, and I shake my head. She nods, relieved. Vincent doesn't seem all that happy with my answer. He wrings his fingers, and I see fear in his eyes.

I decide to pull myself together. I play the optimistic, cheerful clown I've always been for my children, telling them about daily life in hospital and asking them questions.

'How is it with Uncle Marty and Aunt Elena?'

My son is silent.

Luise answers for him. 'Nice.'

'What did you do yesterday?'

'We went to the zoo. We saw a lion, really close.'

She's happy, I think. After all that's happened, she's happy because of some poor caged lion. I take my daughter in my arms and give her a kiss.

'What about you?' I ask Vincent. 'Which animals did you like best?'

He lifts his head, but only manages to look me in the eye for a few seconds. 'The snakes,' he says quietly.

I shoot an anxious look at Marty, fervently hoping that, later on, my son won't dissect defenceless creatures and examine their blood under a microscope.

Then we all sit together drawing animals: an elephant, then mice, giraffes and a tiger. Toni's efforts are pitiful ('These poor animals wouldn't survive a single day the way you've drawn them,' says my brother), but Vincent draws with incredible precision. His giraffe turns out particularly well. When I praise him for it, my son smiles for the first time. The smile comes suddenly, and it's so disarming and beautiful that for a few seconds I'm not worried about him at all.

Once my visitors have left, evening falls. Pale clouds drift past outside, and suddenly it's as if the darkness is watching me through the window. I yearn for my wife, but she's away abroad on a trip that's very important for her. I told her I wouldn't disturb her, I'd manage on my own at home and she shouldn't even take her German mobile. She's in Russia, Yekaterinburg to be precise, and it could be days before she can get a flight. Until then I'm on my own.

In the night I sleep badly. My dreams replay the film of me coming off the road on the motorbike and crashing.

This is it, I thought at the last moment; or perhaps *This is going to be tough*, I don't remember which.

Then I wake up.

I switch on the light. At my request my brother brought me a photo album and two novels: *Time, Flying* by A. N. Romanov and *Tender Is the Night* by F. Scott Fitzgerald. I've read both books several times; again and again I find myself dwelling on familiar scenes and descriptions. Eventually I doze off. No dreams this time, just emptiness.

In the morning I'm lost in thought when she calls. She's still stuck in Yekaterinburg; there's a trade fair, all the flights are booked out.

'I can hardly bear it here,' I say. 'When are you coming?'

'I'll be with you soon.'

'I almost came to you; it seems easier.'

'Don't be so sarcastic. They won't let you through at the airport, anyway, with all your titanium screws and plates.'

She asks after the children. As my brother and Elena have always been good with them, she's reassured. I tell her I love her, and we hang up.

This time Marty visits me on his own. He stands at the window, gazing out into the light. His shirt looks tailored, the creases in his trousers razor-sharp, but his hair's been falling out for a while now. I look at my brother, who's never sentimental or nostalgic about the past but has fashioned every coincidence in his life into something original and special. Suddenly, in my mind's eye, I see us standing shoulder to shoulder at the age of seventy. I didn't choose Marty, and in fact we're completely different, but one thing sets him apart from all other people: he's always there. For forty-one years, at my side.

'Why did you do it?' he asks.

It's the question I've been waiting for.

'So you don't think it was an accident, either?'

'Why *either*?'

I think of the conversation with the young hospital psychologist, who was also of the opinion that it hadn't been an accident; they hadn't found any skid marks.

'So, what, a suicide attempt or something?' I answered, to provoke her.

She let the sentence stand.

'It's important that you face reality,' she said finally. 'I know you're taking refuge in your dream world again. But you have to accept what's happened. Your family needs someone who's living in the here and now.'

I didn't reply.

I fix my eyes on my brother and give him a long look. 'Why would I have killed myself? I have two children, I would never have abandoned them. It was an accident; I just lost control of the bike.'

Marty doesn't seem to believe me. 'The thing's a total write-off, by the way,' is all he says. 'I don't understand why you've suddenly become a motorbike addict. Far too dangerous.'

When he's gone I try to indulge in my daydreams again, but this time I don't succeed. I stare out of the window. A couple of swallows glide through the air. I remember how before, when things were bad, I used to imagine I could fly.

I leaf through the photo album for a while. Apart from the pictures of my wife, the photos I like looking at best are the ones with my brother and sister. Some show Liz at a party, cocktail glass in hand; her gaze is feisty, not a trace of doubt. That was fifteen years ago, and it's hard to put into words how much I miss her here.

A nurse knocks on the door. Supporting myself on crutches, I go with him for a first, careful walk in the hospital garden. My broken leg hardly hurts any more, the fractured collarbone is healing well, too, my headaches have almost disappeared. The unaccustomed daylight blinds me; I breathe in deeply and sit down on a bench. I am surrounded by birdsong; the sun shines down on the garden out of a cloudless sky.

She's dead, I think.

For a moment I have difficulty holding myself together. Distraction, distraction . . . The thoughts whirl about my head, and suddenly I'm picturing my years in Berlin. I remember how in moments of solitude I used to dance around my apartment, overcome by the silliness of desperation. I think about the cellar in Switzerland and the pack of rifle cartridges. Of how I found my way back to writing. A speeded-up montage of disconnected images – and then suddenly I see it all again: what happened before my motorbike accident. The abyss is staring me in the face.

And I stare back.

The Way Back

(2000–2003)

About two years after the holiday in France with my brother and sister, I gave up photography. I'd been rejected by a curator I was friends with, and in a fury I put all my cameras out on the street in a box. I went back to get it an hour later, but it was gone. Things really went downhill after that. I started sleeping into the afternoon, smoked too much dope, wrote a couple of short stories that I didn't show anyone, and quarrelled over everything. My then-girlfriend broke up with me. I was too uncommunicative, too *inauthentic*, and she couldn't stand that look of mine any more: like I was off in my own, inaccessible little world. It barely affected me. As in my previous relationships, I hadn't been in love, and deep down I felt that this wasn't my real life, anyway. That I was still going to swap it with the one in which my parents were still alive. This thought kept coming back to me; it was like a curse woven into my soul.

When Liz told me about the job at Yellow Records, I gave notice on my Hamburg apartment and moved to Berlin, near her. The music label was in a rear courtyard on the Kottbusser Damm and specialised in singer-songwriters and indie rock. And so it was that suddenly I was working as a legal adviser and, later, as a scout; but I might just as easily have gone off to live abroad or gone back to university. I couldn't have expressed it clearly at the time, but in my heart I sensed I'd lost my way. The problem was that I didn't know when and where. I didn't even know which way it was I'd lost.

*

Shortly after my thirtieth birthday, in January 2003, I was riding my Vespa through the city when a red Fiat stopped alongside. Why couldn't I take my eyes off it? Oh yes: Alva. She'd had the same car. Suddenly I found myself thinking about how it had all ended. I'd asked her to go to Munich with me. And she'd responded by sleeping with that man, and forcing me to watch. That was what had happened.

Well – not quite.

On our last weekend at school, Alva had come up to me unexpectedly. She'd beamed at me as if nothing had happened, and told me she might be going to New Zealand for a year of voluntary social service. We'd talked about how in future we'd hardly see each other any more, and how strange it was that you saw people every day for years and then never again. I was still hurt, but there'd been something vulnerable in her eyes that had touched me. Then she'd put her hand on my arm and asked whether perhaps we might do something together at the weekend. Some things had become clear to her; she'd really like to talk to me about them.

I was so surprised that at first I couldn't answer. I promised I would definitely call her, and Alva said she'd really look forward to it.

But I didn't.

All weekend I prowled about the telephone in the corridor of the boarding house. But I couldn't call her. Alva had deliberately hurt me, and despite all her protestations I obviously didn't mean that much to her, because it looked as if she would soon be leaving me forever. So how could I forgive her? At the same time I desperately wanted to see her. I hoped that maybe she would call me, but she didn't.

When I arrived at school on Monday, she didn't speak to me. She looked away the whole time, almost pointedly. I went up to her during break.

'Sorry,' I said, one hand propped against the wall, demonstratively casual. 'I was going to call you, but there was just too much going on at the weekend!'

I may even have told her about a party I'd been to; that I'd met
this girl there, someone Alva knew was keen on me. There was
certainly a delicious sense of satisfaction in being able to take
some small revenge for what Alva had done to me. I was counting
on her nodding regretfully, or that she would at least be surprised
by my cool behaviour. But she just looked at me enquiringly.

'Oh, right,' she said. 'Yes – I'd completely forgotten. Ah well,
never mind.'

That was the last time I'd spoken to Alva.

A few days after seeing the red Fiat, I picked Liz up from work.
It was now almost five years since our summer together in
Berdillac. She'd gone back to night school to take her school-
leaving certificate, and had done a teaching degree: her teacher
training in music, art and German was going well. I watched her
come out of the building with a few of the younger teachers.
From a distance Liz looked even taller, an imposing figure. She'd
slung a bag over one shoulder and was laughing. Clearly the
ringleader: the others were gazing up at her admiringly. Anyone
who didn't know she was well over thirty would have put her in
her mid-twenties; her face was just slightly fuller.

We cooked at Liz's apartment, which was crammed full of
paintings and knick-knacks and almost a little slovenly ('we
cooked' meant she cooked, I watched), and of course we talked
about our brother's move as well. Marty had recently sold his
company for an exorbitant sum and was now teaching at the
Technical University of Munich. He and Elena had bought a
house near the Englischer Garten.

'Just think!' I sat in Liz's kitchen, tilting my chair. 'He's living
just a few blocks from our former home.'

'I knew we'd go back there someday.' She was chopping basil.
'But I thought it would take longer.'

'I'm never going back to Munich. Why would I?'

'Because back then none of us chose to leave.'

Liz lit some joss sticks. There was Mexican folk music on her stereo, and she hummed along. I thought of her giving music lessons, playing her pupils something on the guitar, praising the younger ones by drawing little figures or animals in their exercise books, wanting to do theatre with them in the summer. Our sister may have lost her way for years, but it seemed to me that her life now finally approximated to the one in which our parents hadn't died. She'd made it back, and my brother also seemed to have found his place again. I, on the other hand, had noticed a group of people at a neighbouring table in a café a few days earlier, where a man my age was the centre of attention. He was making his friends laugh and dominating the conversation with almost infuriating nonchalance. I looked away, irritated, but there was something about his behaviour that stuck in my mind; and it suddenly occurred to me that, if a few things had gone differently, that man could have been me.

Shouts drifted up from outside. A horde of children was running across the concrete interior courtyard.

'How old would it be now?' I asked, still half lost in my thoughts.

The question was too sudden and inappropriate. My sister's eyes clouded. 'Five,' she said.

'Do you still think about it a lot?'

'Not as much as I used to. But sometimes I'm afraid that that was my chance, and that I won't have any children. The first time, at school, I was too young. But with Robert I was the right age. Who knows if it'll work out again.'

She still left her boyfriends so that they couldn't leave her; her last relationship, with a Dutch actor, had also failed. 'A man of enchanting stupidity,' Liz had once said.

Marty didn't have any children yet either, but for some years now he'd had a dog that, with a refreshing lack of creativity, he just called Dog. Recently he had announced that everything was doomed to destruction anyway, so why have children?

Liz could get worked up about this. 'That's Marty's nihilistic nonsense,' she said. 'But you know it's not true. All these nihilists and cynics are really just cowards. They act as if everything's meaningless because that means ultimately there's nothing to lose. Their attitude seems unassailable and superior, but inside it's worthless.'

She lit a cigarette, shaking her head. 'The alternative to the concept of life and death is the void' – stalk waggling between her lips – 'would it really be better if this world didn't exist at all? Instead, we live, make art, love, observe, suffer, laugh and are happy. We all exist in a million different ways so that there is no void, and the price we pay for that is death.'

I suddenly thought of Alva again, and the red Fiat. The night before, I'd dreamed I was walking through a war zone. Helicopters were falling out of the sky, bombs were dropping, people collapsing around me. The city was doomed to destruction but I kept on running, into the midst of the fighting, because I'd heard that Alva was imprisoned in a house in the centre. I roamed the city until I was exhausted; several times I almost died, but I never reached my destination. Then I woke up.

After that night it had all come back. Dreams always have their own sense of time, or rather there is no time, and so it seemed to me that it was just now that I'd run laps around the sports ground while Alva lay reading on the grass. Sometimes, back then, I used to lie down beside her and try to turn her pages by blowing on them. That had always coaxed a smile from her; but one afternoon Alva had reacted irritably. She was clutching her book with both hands; a beloved character was obviously dying between her fingers. It was only then that I noticed she was crying. I hadn't meant to disturb her, yet I couldn't alter the fact that I was sharing this intimate moment with her. I glanced at her reddened face, and realised how much Alva loved literature, so much more than all the other people I knew. And the fact that she was sitting beside me and had been so moved by a story also moved me. I would have liked to have taken her in my arms and protected her, from herself above all, and from all the things she never told me; and yet after that everything had happened quite differently, and now eleven years had passed.

That evening I found Alva's e-mail address and wrote to her. I wasn't anticipating a reply; I was following my instincts. At first it was a letter several pages long, but by the end only two lines remained:

I'm thirty and I don't have children yet.
How about you?

She didn't write back. For a few days, even weeks, I was still secretly waiting for a reply; then I gave up. I'd called out to the past, but it had returned no echo.

In the spring I took some time off and went to visit Marty, who had driven down to Berdillac with Elena for a few days. I parked my rental car outside the house at the end of the Rue Le Goff. The dog, a husky, immediately leaped towards me. Marty and Elena had got him as a puppy; now he was fully grown and strong, a majestic animal with white-black fur and clever blue eyes.

Elena's sister was also visiting with her three children. When I greeted Elena, I had the impression that she was oddly sad. There was, however, something eternally youthful about my brother. I teased him, saying that he looked increasingly like our father and I'd soon have to give him a pipe and a pale-brown leather jacket.

The seven of us went on an outing. The children played with the dog; Marty and I hung back a little. I sensed that his mind was elsewhere. Eventually he gestured towards Elena, who was just hoisting one of her nephews onto her shoulders. With her little relatives around her, she blossomed.

'She loves children,' said Marty.

'I know.'

'And she'll never be able to have any.'

I stopped. 'How long have you known?'

'Obviously we'd been thinking lately that it might be the case. We haven't been using contraception for two or three years; we've been actively trying for months. Then, when nothing happened, Elena got herself checked out . . .'

Marty looked me in the eye. 'You know, I'm not even sure that I necessarily want to have children. I like the idea of sitting building a remote-controlled car with my kid, but it's not a must, though; she *loves* children; she's always wanted to have her own. Our house has so many rooms . . . She's been crying a lot these past few weeks.'

We were strolling up the path that led to the familiar wood.

'I'm going to marry her,' said Marty, with the stoic calm that seemed to run through him like a watermark. 'We never actually wanted to, but now I think it's the right thing to do. What do you reckon?'

'I think that sounds good.'

Marty looked at me, embarrassed. 'And I'd like you to be my best man.'

'Best man? Don't people usually ask someone they like?'

'I thought I'd make an exception for you.'

The air in the wood was fragrant and fresh, and I could sense the approach of night. We came to the stony river with the old tree-trunk lying across it.

'Unbelievable that I simply walked across that as a child.' I tapped the wood with my foot. 'It's more than two metres above the river; if you fell off you'd be sure to break something.'

'You were never afraid as a child.'

I climbed onto the tree-trunk. It was as if I were entering an enchanted place, a door to the past. After just two steps I felt dizzy. The water rushed past beneath me; rocks rose up out of the river, though they weren't as sharp as I remembered. The trunk wobbled; with every step it felt as if I were about to slip and fall. I started sweating, and heard my father's warning voice in my ear, telling me that this was much too dangerous. All his fears, which now occupied my head like an unwanted tenant.

'Turn around,' Marty was saying too. 'That really doesn't look good!'

'I ran across very quickly when I was a kid, that's the only reason it worked.'

By now I'd managed a quarter of the distance, but the salvation of the other bank seemed infinitely far away. *Go back,* I thought. *Become the person you used to be.* Then I slipped. Only reflexes and luck kept me on my feet. My pulse throbbed in my throat. It was pointless. I carefully turned around and went back to Marty. Like a boxer staggering back to his corner, beaten by his younger self.

After they sold the company, Toni went to live in Los Angeles for two years, to study at the famous Chavez School of Magic and spend his free time riding his motorbike across the States or all the way down to Tierra del Fuego. Now he had unexpectedly moved to Berlin, and until he found an apartment he was sleeping on the sofa at mine.

One evening I was sitting with him in a bar when my sister happened to come in. She looked neither to her left nor her right and didn't notice us, but went to sit with a group of women at a corner table where she lit a cigarette and instantly monopolised the conversation. There was something glamorous about Liz, sitting there with the wine glass in her hand, and she talked as someone would drink if they were dying of thirst: greedy for every single word.

Toni wanted to go over to her, but I held him back. I could hear my sister speaking in her deep, theatrical voice; she seemed to be talking about chat-up lines. 'The best was at a Goth party on the Lower East Side,' she said loudly, 'when I was approached by a man dressed all in leather, with a beard and two stuck-on horns.'

'What did he say?' asked one of her friends.

Liz savoured the moment. 'He came right up close to me and asked, in this deep voice, "Are you ready to sleep with a demon?"' Her laugh echoed throughout the bar, rather dirty; the other women laughed as well.

Toni kept glancing across at her. 'Has she finally answered my letter yet?'

Later, we all went to the Club der Visionäre together. My sister and Toni sat beside each other on the jetty, dangling their feet in the Spree. Toni was flirting with her non-stop, which had piqued Liz's interest. She was seeing him no longer as just her brother's friend but as a man, and was leaning back casually, appraising him. One of the straps on her black dress had slipped, her blonde hair was loose, her bare legs crossed. She was lying in wait, wanting to know whether Toni was just joking when he teased her, and was in fact a nice guy, or whether he really did have that unfathomable, manly side. My sister was giving him her mocking, superior look again; there was something destructive in it and Toni needed to confront it. One second, two seconds . . . He avoided her eyes. Repeatedly. I could see exactly what was going on. He didn't stand a chance.

For my part, I tried to strike up a conversation with a couple of Liz's acquaintances, but it was rather stilted, and when the whole group decided to go on to another club I said goodbye. At home, silence awaited me, a sound I'd been familiar with for years. How I had come to loathe this hermit-like existence, this inability to participate in life. Always just dreaming, never truly awake. Look at you, I thought: why do you so often long for solitude in company when you can scarcely bear to be alone any more?

I flipped open the laptop. Two new e-mails. Marty wrote that his wedding was firmly in Elena's family's hands and he was excluded from the planning. The second message was from a former fellow student from my law course who'd sent out a round robin. Annoyed, I deleted it. I watched TV for a while, zapping through channels at random. Just as I was about to go to bed, another mail arrived. Written at 02:46. I rubbed my eyes and opened it.

I've thought about you from time to time these last few years.
Hope you're well. Would be nice to see each other again.
Alva

I spent the following weeks in a state of joyful suspense. Even Marty's wedding, with all its festivities and all his Croatian in-laws, could only tear me out of it briefly. It was as if a single message had brought my past back to life.

Alva was living in Switzerland. After much to-ing and fro-ing – she often took days to reply – we decided to meet halfway, in Munich. A little while later I travelled to my hometown and spent the morning visiting my brother. He and Elena had just got back from their honeymoon in Spain.

'Nervous?' asked Marty. We waded through the stacks of wedding presents, some of which were still unopened; the whole living room was crammed with them.

'I can't believe I'm about to see her again.'

'Has she got a boyfriend?' asked my brother, taking aim at a bright-green parcel. Elena's nephews had left their Softair pistols behind, and we were using them to shoot the wedding presents.

'I've heard she's married now,' I said, aiming at a long object wrapped in red paper. It rattled: clearly a box of cutlery.

'Uh-huh, so that's what you've heard.' My brother fired three shots in a row at a white parcel perched on a chest of drawers in the living room. It fell off, burst open, and a cheap kitchen clock with a Simpsons cartoon fell out.

Marty held it up in disgust. 'This is all tat.' He put the clock back on the chest of drawers. 'What sort of people give presents like this?'

'That's because you don't have any real friends.'

'You don't have any friends either.'

'I know. If I ever get married there'll be three people on my side: you, Liz, and possibly Toni.'

'Sorry, there'll only be two,' said my brother. 'I won't have the time.'

'You've really changed since you got married. For the worse.' I took aim at Homer Simpson, shooting him between his bulging eyes until he fell off the chest again and broke.

'Where exactly does Alva live?' Marty fired a whole volley at a blue parcel.

'In Lucerne; she's been there a few years. Maybe she speaks Swiss German by now.'

Suddenly Marty pointed his gun at me. 'What if she really is married?'

'I assume she is.' I aimed at him. 'She deserves to be.'

'But you're not really assuming it, are you?' Marty grinned. 'I can tell. You're hoping.'

'No comment.'

'Hope is for idiots.'

'So is pessimism.'

He jerked his chin at something to his left. The master present. A massive vase wrapped in shiny, candy-coloured paper, standing on the living-room table.

'On the count of three?'

'On the count of three!'

'One, two . . . three!'

Simultaneously we emptied our magazines. The vase teetered for a moment before falling to the floor with a crash. We laughed at each other, then looked around. The living room was now completely trashed. 'Let's tidy up,' said Marty, blowing down the barrel of his Softair. 'Elena will be back soon.'

The bar where I wanted to meet Alva was in the Glockenbach district, right next to my aunt's former apartment.

I was as nervous as a teenager, and got there a quarter of an hour early. I was about to leave again (don't be the first to arrive) when I noticed the red-haired woman at the table by the entrance. Her legs were crossed and she was talking to the waitress.

For several seconds I stared at Alva's narrow nose, the black-framed glasses, the beautifully curved mouth with the full lips, the delicate collarbone. Her pale, still-flawless skin and her slim figure. At first she seemed like a stranger to me: so grown-up. Her eyes had changed the most. They were still large and luminously green, but all the coolness in them had vanished. I was just wondering how that had happened when she spotted me.

'Hey,' she said.

How could I have forgotten the sound of her voice! A brief hug, and I was smiling so much my cheeks hurt, but I couldn't stop. She sat on the upholstered bench while I sat on a chair, a small round table between us.

'Since when are you on time?'

'Never, actually,' she said. 'But I was determined to get here before you and see you come in the door . . . And now I've missed it.'

Alva was wearing black jeans and a scoop-necked grey pullover; she came across as confident, mysterious, but also rather weary.

'I've got something for you,' I said, handing her my present.

'May I open it?'

Alva didn't tear the wrapping paper but opened the present carefully, almost lovingly. She pulled out the Nick Drake album. '*Pink Moon.*'

'Do you remember?' I asked. 'We listened to it the first time you came up to my room. I remembered that you liked it.'

I think she was pleased; at any rate, she kept looking at the album and stroking its worn edges with her fingers.

In my excitement, I initially talked too fast. Alva listened as I sketched a few details about my life; then she told me about her literature degree in Moscow, where she had dropped out after just one semester. A brief sounding out of each other's lives.

'And what are you working as?' I asked eventually.

'To be honest, I'm not working.'

'Why not?'

Alva shrugged. She acted as if it made no difference, but even after all these years I could tell when she was nervous. She was leaving key chapters out of her story, giving her years in Russia a wide berth, drawing a veil over what she was doing now, and only talking about events from long ago.

She ran her hands across the table, reaching for mine. 'It's so great to see you here. I was afraid you wouldn't come.'

'Why?'

Alva pulled her hands away. 'You look good' – she studied me – 'and you have a lovely smile, Jules. I wanted to tell you that back then, at school. When you smile you're like a different person, less reserved. You really should smile much more often.' She was elated now. 'Yes, just like that.' Suddenly assertive: 'But tell me, what are *you* doing these days?'

'I work for a music label.' I ordered a drink, she a cappuccino. 'I was actually going to move to Italy, then my sister told me about the position. Anyway, it's not a bad job. A lot of legal stuff, but I'm also spending more and more time looking after bands.'

My work usually went down really well, but Alva didn't seem too enthusiastic.

'Music suits you, of course. But I always thought you'd do something of your own – writing, for example. I thought your short stories were wonderful. Or why not photography? You always loved taking photos.'

I was touched by how much she believed in me. The only person who really liked my stories and pictures.

'I did try being a photographer, but it never really took off. Then at some point I gave up.'

'Why?'

'Too many rejections. Too much frustration.'

Alva considered. A quick look: 'Was that really the only reason you gave up?'

As ever, she saw through me.

'No. I just realised that I . . .' I shook my glass, and the two ice cubes bathing in the amber-coloured liquid slipped back and forth. 'Forget it – not that important. Another time.'

We sat in silence. The initial excitement of seeing each other again had evaporated; it was all so formal, so forced. For a moment I felt as if our real selves were far away, and we'd sent two negotiators to the bar who weren't authorised to talk about the really important things.

'What music are you listening to at the moment?' Alva asked eventually.

At her request I got out my mp3 player and sat beside her on the bench. We shared my headphones and went through a few bands. With each song she thawed a little more.

'This one's nice,' she said, when I played her 'Between The Bars' by Elliott Smith. She beamed. 'I really like this one.'

And for a moment, as we sat there beside each other listening to music, it felt as intimate as when we were at school.

'Are you happy?' I asked her.

She took off the headphones, confused. 'What?'

'I asked if you were happy?'

At first Alva seemed to want to avoid the question, and I worried that it was too direct, but then she just shrugged. 'You?'

I shrugged as well.

'Then we're on the same page,' she cried merrily.

I pointed to her cappuccino. 'I somehow thought we'd get drunk when we saw each other again.'

'We still can.'

'How about gin?'

'Preferably not. The last time we drank gin it was kind of weird, do you remember? You danced in front of me, and I was completely off my face. It wouldn't have taken much and I'd have thrown myself at you.'

She said this, casually, and turned to the cocktail menu.

Two drinks later we were sitting even closer together. I don't know whether it was the alcohol or listening to music, but our last meeting suddenly felt like yesterday again, except that yesterday was many years ago. I'd already missed one train, and I decided to miss the next one, too. By now I was slurring my words a bit, but at least I was finally saying what I wanted to say.

Alva was perking up, too.

'How's the women situation?' she asked.

'Oh, you know how it is. They fling themselves at me; there were two just now on the way to the bar. I can barely cope.'

She slapped my arm for that, and the evening turned into one long 'Do you remember?' and 'Unbelievable how we . . .', and we swapped lots of little stories: in her quiet voice she told me that she still listened to cassettes to get to sleep, or talked about her years in Russia and how the Moscow metro traders went from one compartment to the next, palming off sex toys or pirated DVDs and books on the commuters ('There are always a few key pages missing, but the books cost almost nothing'); in return I told her about Marty's wedding and how my brother had danced with the bride like an ill-calibrated robot, but on the other hand had given half his after-dinner speech in accent-free Croatian, and it had long since got dark outside while we talked about the loneliness that afflicted us now and then (me: 'This constantly being alone is killing me.' Alva: 'Yes, but the antidote to loneliness isn't just being around random people indiscriminately, the antidote to loneliness is emotional security.' Me, beckoning to a waiter: 'We'll drink to that!'), and all this time I couldn't stop staring at Alva's beautiful *film noir* face, looking into those big, luminous, pale-green eyes; and another drink, and we sank into blessed drunkenness, and to my astonishment I said, 'What I'd really like to do is leave my job, move away from Berlin and just *write*,' and suddenly it was as if I'd found my inner voice again, and I finally admitted that I had missed Alva; yes, that in all those years I couldn't help thinking about her again and again, and she said, her lips close to my ear, 'I thought about you, too,' and the back of my neck tingled, I was enjoying this velvety tension between us, and I realised that our legs were touching, and I kept wondering whether she'd noticed, whether it had occurred to her that as she spoke she kept coming so close to me that her hair tickled my face and I could smell her perfume, whether she was even doing it *deliberately*, and at that point I almost wanted to tell her that I'd understood too late, back then, that I loved her; but she was in the middle of talking about her internship in New Zealand, and I missed the next-to-last train, too, and watched Alva's hands, gesticulating as she spoke, or her teeth when she laughed, which she did a lot that evening, and she'd accepted her slightly crooked front tooth and didn't hold up her hand in front of her mouth any more.

'Why is eating pizza a way for you to overcome trauma?' she asked.

'Well, because of school,' I replied. 'Back then we often didn't get enough dinner, and if we did it was usually inedible. We didn't really have enough pocket money to order a pizza afterwards as well, but occasionally someone would. Then half an hour later the white pizza van would drive up in front of the boarding house. While the person who'd ordered it was paying and taking delivery of this delicious-smelling pizza, he was being watched from the windows by countless pairs of eyes. And he would scarcely have stepped back inside the boarding house before we all stormed him. *Please, just one slice, I've always given you one.* Or: *You'll get some next time, when I order one – a quarter of the pizza, I promise. Just one slice.* You had to give the other kids some, usually half the pizza, because next time you'd be dependent on *their* generosity. And so you never ate your fill. There's a hunger in me that has never been satisfied. Nine years of ravenous hunger, and no matter how many pizzas I eat these days, it's never enough.'

Alva sipped her drink. 'I'm just thinking about your mail.' An amused glance. 'Do you really still want to have children?'

I nodded. 'Yes, I'd like to be better at it than my father.' Even in this relaxed mood my voice started trembling. 'No, I'd like to be better at it than both of them. I'd just like to survive and *always* be there. When the children start school, when they reach puberty, when they fall in love, when they grow up. I'd like to see them do all of that. I'd like to know how it is for them not to go through that alone.'

Alva was suddenly serious. 'What was it actually like for you, coming to boarding school with your brother and sister? I often wondered that. All your old friends gone, your home, everything, in one fell swoop. That first drive to school must have been particularly awful.'

I considered. 'To be honest, I don't remember anything about it any more.'

'But you hardly ever forget things as a rule.' She pointed to the Nick Drake album. 'I can't believe you still knew that . . . You must remember, surely.'

'It doesn't interest me any more. We were at boarding school. How we got there . . . no idea.'

Alva was disappointed. 'I only started there a few months before you. We'd just moved house back then. Anyway: on my first day I almost threw up. I still remember every second of that day.'

This was news to me; I'd thought she'd always been at our school. How little we'd told each other back then of what was really important.

I racked my brains again, but my memory refused to provide any pictures of my first drive to the school; fragments, at best, that immediately dissolved again. Vanished places in the landscape of a past I had toured so thoroughly.

We looked at each other, feeling that we had said everything now, except the things we were determined not to reveal.

'Why don't you work?' I asked again.

Alva hesitated. She pushed back her hair, and it was only then that I saw the two delicate scars on her neck, right below her left ear. Two long lines. I wanted to run my finger down them, and only just managed to control myself.

'How did you get those?'

She looked at me, shocked, and immediately let her hair fall back over her ear. Uneasy now, she finished the rest of her drink, and for the first time that evening there was something dark, almost vacant, in her eyes again.

'I don't want to talk about it,' she said quietly. And from the way she put her glass down on the table, that soft clink, I realised that the evening's magic spell was broken; that time was no longer running backwards for us, but forwards.

Alva looked at the clock. 'When's your train again?'

I had to be at a meeting the next morning. She went with me to the station; in the taxi we didn't say a word. It had all gone so fast, and now I hadn't even asked her whether she wanted children, too. And why she suddenly seemed so tense.

We were already standing on the platform. 'Wouldn't you like to come and visit me in Berlin sometime?'

At first Alva seemed happy, then her expression became somehow distant.

'I don't know whether you've heard, but I'm married.'

For a moment I couldn't breathe; I stared at my hands and everything seemed to slow down. It was only now that I realised I'd never intended to take this last night train, that I didn't want to go back at all, ever.

When I looked at Alva again, she was fishing something out of her bag.

'I have a present for you too, by the way. I just didn't know when I should give it to you. It's from me and my husband.'

A book-shaped parcel. I took it, but didn't open it. And then I simply hugged her. Alva's hands closed around my back, and all of a sudden I realised just how starved I'd been all these years. She didn't let go of me, or I didn't let go of her. I believe we stood for a whole minute without moving, hugging each other tightly on the platform, and it dawned on me that after this evening we wouldn't see each other again. Because my time with her was unquestionably in the past, and because I couldn't bear that.

As I boarded the train I was trying hard not to let her see my face. I threw my coat and her present onto a seat, pulled myself together a bit and looked at other passengers, who were chatting or spreading their newspapers and laptops out in front of them.

Just before the guard blew the final whistle, I went back to her. I felt her hand on my arm.

'Take care, Jules.'

I nodded. 'You too.'

The doors closed. I saw her wave to me through the scratched window. The train was already starting to move, and as I walked back to my seat the station slid away.

I thought of my meeting the next day and the contract I was supposed to draw up with a musician; and then I thought of Alva again, standing on the platform. A sudden pain shot through me. I closed my eyes. It was night, and I was running through billowing fields of wheat, out into the darkness. As I ran I grew lighter and lighter, until all of a sudden I took off. I felt the wind, spread out my arms, moved faster still. Below me the forest, above me the void. I tumbled through the air and flew away, further and further, as if I were flying home.

The Flight of Time

(2005–2006)

I didn't unwrap Alva's present. After our meeting the silent hope I'd carried with me all those years was extinguished. From then on I met my fate with indifference, and what followed was a meaningless period, disposable as crumpled paper.

It wasn't until two years later that I heard from her again. By then I'd been with Norah, a former work colleague, for quite a while. She was from Bristol and, like me, a hypochondriac; both of us would immediately change the channel whenever a report came on about horrible diseases. She wasn't really surprised that I'd spent my youth in a home. 'The first time I saw you eating, bolting it like mad, I thought: prison or boarding school.' Norah had just returned to England for a three-month internship. Before leaving, she had dropped a few hints that she had fallen in love with me. I didn't love her back to the same degree, but that didn't seem as important to me any more.

At the label I'd risen to become head of the A&R department; I travelled all over Europe to see bands whose demos were promising. This job was a privilege, and there were younger colleagues who complained about my promotion. Why does Jules get to do all that, they asked, claiming that I was too anachronistic and too unimpassioned. But my boss backed me up, and the bands I signed were actually successful. I never looked for artists who were merely very talented, because there were an astonishing number of those. I looked for bands and singers who *wanted it*. More than I'd wanted it back then, as a photographer. I was convinced that you could *force* yourself to be creative, that you could work on your imagination, but not on your will. The real talent was the will. I'm sure now that this was the thought that bothered my younger colleagues most.

Meanwhile, Liz and Toni had become good friends; my sister often went with him to the flea market, she saw his magic shows, or she'd let him take her out with him on his motorbike. There was just one topic that was never discussed.

'Is there something going on between the two of you now?' I'd asked her once.

'Don't be ridiculous. Toni's far too short.'

'But he's only a couple of centimetres shorter than you. Is that really too small, full stop? Are you that superficial?'

My sister gave me a look that said I didn't have a clue. 'There's nothing going on, anyway; he just looks after me.'

I knew that at some point there'd been a night when Liz had taken something that hadn't agreed with her. 'A little episode,' she called it. She hadn't been able to reach me, and in her desperation she'd called Toni, who'd come over straight away. He'd sat on a chair beside her bed all night.

'And at some point I told her that I loved her, always had,' Toni told me later. 'And your sister said she already knew. Then I said I didn't expect anything, I just wanted to get things out in the open.' He laughed. 'I said it'd be enough for me just to look after her a bit in future. And you know what?' Toni looked at me. 'It really is enough. I'd like it to be more, of course, but it's fine like this as well.'

'May I quote you in a few months' time, when she has a new boyfriend?'

'Preferably not.'

Liz now had a permanent position as a teacher in a secondary school. Over dinner she told me about a pupil who secretly wrote her love letters. 'He's one of the worst in the class,' she said. 'He always misspells the word "feelings", without the "g". Cute, huh?' My sister smiled, like a bashful child.

And this smile reminded me of something I'd long forgotten.

I found myself thinking about Alva and the meeting with her in Munich. At first I thought it was just a sentimental relapse; then I realised it wasn't Alva herself who'd come to mind, but the answer to the question she'd asked me back then: what it had been like for me and my siblings driving to the home for the first time after our parents' death.

The image slowly emerged from white nothingness like a developing Polaroid.

More than twenty years earlier, in the tunnel of the past, I was sitting on the back seat of the car, my brother beside me. In front, at the wheel, our Aunt Helene, Liz alongside. All through the journey I'd been depressed at the thought of living in a home. I kept thinking about our parents' funeral. About the two tiny holes into which their urns had been lowered.

Barren winter landscapes rolled past outside; the last of the daylight disappeared. And in the midst of this sombre mood my sister started raving about our new home.

'I bet they have school uniform there,' she said. 'Shirt and skirt for the girls and suit and tie for the boys.'

'I don't like suits,' Marty replied. 'Or ties.'

'And the dining room must be huge,' Liz went on. 'I'm sure they've got a swimming pool, too. And sports grounds where you can play tennis, or even cricket.'

'I don't like cricket,' said Marty, whose every other sentence had started with 'I don't like . . .' for weeks now. 'Anyway, what makes you say cricket?' he asked. 'They only play that in England or India.'

But Liz had already moved on to descriptions of palatial dormitories and well-appointed communal kitchens. At the time I was surprised; now, decades later, I understood that she was just scared. She wrote her name on a napkin one last time. *Liz, Liz, Liz.*

The first signposts appeared, directing us to the school. I imagined how the pupils there would welcome me over the next few days, and my stomach clenched.

'It's going to be brilliant,' my sister said again. 'Don't you think?'

'No!' Marty polished his glasses and gave me a worried look.

Our aunt, who had picked out this home for us, also tried to be encouraging. 'When I was a child I always wanted to go to boarding school, but I was never allowed. I'm sure it's going to be great.'

'Exactly – it'll be *great*,' said Liz, in a silly voice. 'We're nearly there. I can hardly wait.'

When we arrived in the dark and saw the shabby, run-down boarding house with only a few windows still lit up, she too fell silent.

I watched from inside the car as the director of the home spoke with our aunt and my brother and sister heaved their luggage out of the boot and stood around uncertainly in the car park. I got out as well, and was about to join them with my suitcase when the headmistress said that Year Six and Seven pupils, of whom I was one, lived in special accommodation. Before I'd fully grasped that this meant I was to be separated from my siblings, I saw Marty and Liz shoulder their bags and, after a quick goodbye, disappear into the larger of the two buildings. At the door my sister turned and looked at me one last time, a look that already presaged all that would follow. She just managed to muster a smile, like a bashful child; then she was gone, and it would be years before she came back again.

In the late autumn of 2005 I paid my brother a visit after a gig in Bavaria. We went to the fair with Elena and her nephews and nieces. The afternoon sun shed its golden light on the carousels and snack stands; loud music and babbling voices surged at us from all sides, and we were enveloped in the smell of burnt almonds. Marty told me that soon people would only read books electronically.

'This is so crap,' I said. 'Stuff like that is hollowing out reality. Books and records and films are being thrown away and digitised into a world you can never physically enter. The children of the future will just sit around in empty white rooms.'

'White Wall Kids,' my brother interjected. 'Good name for a band.'

I frowned. 'You used to have to wait for a film to be developed. But it wasn't just the photos we loved, it was the anticipation of finally holding them in your hands.'

'Yes, Grandfather.' Marty gave the hint of a smirk. 'No one can turn back the clock.'

I waved my hand dismissively. But in retrospect something about our conversation bothered me, like a small cut on your finger that you only notice after a while. It was the sentence 'No one can turn back the clock' that preoccupied me for a long time.

'Everything okay?' Marty nudged me. 'You look a bit down.'

'Everything's fine.'

'I dunno,' he said. 'You'll be thirty-three soon, and I sometimes worry that time's running out for you. You told me recently that you hated your work.'

'I said I wasn't going to do it forever. So what? It's all okay. Please stop worrying all the time.'

I may have raised my voice a bit.

'Damn it, Jules, I don't want to fight with you. I just don't want you to suddenly wake up and you're nearly fifty and you've missed all your chances. You're still dreaming yourself into another life.'

Marty grabbed my shoulder. 'You have to finally forget the past. Do you know how many people had it worse than we did? Your childhood, our parents' death, are not your fault. What *is* your fault is what these things are doing to you. You alone are responsible for yourself and your life. And if you just do what you've always done, you'll just get what you've always got.'

I said nothing. For the remainder of our time at the fair I kept to myself. Then I caught sight of the high striker, and something came over me. Without stopping to think, I paid, grabbed the hammer and brought it whizzing down onto the mark with every ounce of my strength. The metal ball sprang upwards, but only reached eighty per cent.

I summoned all I had, all the pent-up anger and frustration, and hit it again. This time the ball only reached sixty-five per cent.

A tinny clown's voice mocked me from inside the device. 'Is that all you've got?'

I hit it again. Seventy per cent.

'That's it?' asked the shrill mechanical voice, and laughed hoarsely.

And I hit the little black mark again and again, but all I'd got wasn't enough, it just wasn't enough, and the ball never struck the top.

That evening I opened Alva's present.

It was a white paperback. *The Altered Thought and Other Stories* by A. N. Romanov. A nostalgic present, like my Nick Drake album; Romanov had been one of our favourite authors at school.

I read Alva's dedication first, which was fairly brief. Then it seemed her husband had written something as well.

Dear Jules,
My wife has only very good things to say about you.
I hope you enjoy reading this.
  Best wishes,
  Alexander Nikolai

I read these lines over and over again. Was it really possible? I remembered how Alva had raved about Romanov's short stories at school. Her reverential tone of voice whenever she read a section out to me. Why hadn't she told me when we met that she was married to him? Had she wanted to spare me humiliation because I could never hope to match him?

I took my Vespa and rode out into the countryside. Towards evening, at the blue hour, the landscape gained something mysterious, enticing. A light that seemed to come from another world. Only the dull grinding of the city was still audible in the distance, and out here on my own I realised, with a sense of physical pain, that I had not used my time. Had fought for minutes when trying to catch a bus; wasted years because I hadn't done what I wanted to do.

That same night, I wrote an e-mail to Alva and her husband, in a humorous tone, saying that I'd finally read the book with a delay of only a few years, and had been very pleased with both the present and the rather surprising dedication. Unlike last time, Alva answered immediately. She concluded with the following words:

My husband and I would be very happy if you were to visit us sometime. We now live in a chalet near Lucerne; you are always welcome.
  I hope to see you again soon.
  Alva

Her prompt reply and the invitation, repeatedly expressed, churned me up inside. I was hoping again, just as I'd hoped at fifteen. As I'd hoped at thirty. At the same time, I sensed that I needed to finally put this story behind me if I wasn't to spend my whole life chasing after a ghost. Norah rang shortly afterwards, as if on cue, and said she was looking forward to seeing me when she got back; she had a surprise for me. 'Something exciting,' was all she said. 'You'll like it.' After the call, I thought of how Norah loved to go dancing with me, of how she always brought my beloved scones for me from England, and of her lovely face with the tiny beauty spot above her lip that she'd jokingly named 'Simon'. I realised once more that I liked her, that I'd missed her these past few months, that she was real. A person to whom I meant something.

I made my decision after a conversation with Toni. His apartment was near Oranienburger Strasse. A huge billiards table in the living room, Rothko prints and photos by Will Steacy in the hall, the office full of toolkits, light generators, grinders, soldering irons and other things he needed for his magic tricks. Toni's latest number consisted of bending or knotting a green laser beam on stage, running his hand through it, then inexplicably hanging a coat-hanger on it that seemed to float in mid-air, held up only by green light.

We played billiards, as we usually did when I visited. We were already doing it back in boarding-school days, when we used to spend almost every weekend in the Jackpot with my brother. Marty had been one of the best billiard players in school, like a character out of a B-movie with his cue, long greasy hair, goatee beard and black leather coat. We were never in his league.

'She's got a boyfriend,' said Toni, while we were playing. 'Quite a nice one.'

'So what now?'

He stared at the billiard balls, at a loss, then took aim at the yellow. 'I don't know. I reckon that I love your sister, and that I'm in love with her. The part that loves her is pleased for her that she has a boyfriend. The part that's in love with her wants to rip him to shreds.'

He missed the shot. 'I know you've been asking yourself for ages why I don't finally give up on your sister,' he said. 'Why I don't just limit contact with her, find some other girl, have a fairly nice life with her. One where I sometimes sit and think to myself: shame it didn't work out with Liz, but this is pretty good, too; there just wasn't any more to be had from it.' He shook his head. 'I can't help myself.'

'I know.'

'It'll never work out, and perhaps in six months' time I'll say something different and start deceiving myself, but at least now I've been honest for once.' He put down the cue. 'I mean, if you spend all your life running in the wrong direction, could it be the right one after all?'

A January day: grey, sooty evening light slanted into the compartment, the edges of the clouds had a metallic sheen. The train decelerated, rolled to a halt. In Lucerne, Alva was waiting for me on the platform. She kissed me on the cheek, three times, then led me to her car where her husband was waiting for me.

'I can't believe you've actually come,' she said as we walked, summarising what I was thinking, too.

A. N. Romanov was already sixty-seven, but looked at least ten years younger.

'Alexander,' he said, and held out his hand. 'Very pleased to meet you.'

His accent was barely noticeable. Romanov was a tall, slim, distinguished figure with wavy grey hair, still elegant that evening in a suit and shirt with the top buttons left undone. His angular face looked chiselled, there was an impish set to his mouth, and he also exuded an old-fashioned manliness; you couldn't imagine him dodging a fight in his younger years, or not knowing how to repair a leaky drainpipe.

Alva called her husband not Alexander but Sasha, the Russian diminutive. As she drove us up to the chalet, Romanov told me about the area. I was overwhelmed to be listening to this man's sonorous voice after reading so many of his intimate thoughts on paper. Romanov had had his breakthrough in his early twenties: an intellectual dandy whose novels and novellas had been translated into thirty languages. Now, though, his fame had waned and was only to be found online, where, alongside articles about his first marriage, I'd also found lots of black-and-white photos, some taken with famous artists of the day, some of him smoking alone outside a club in Camden.

He and Alva no longer lived in Lucerne; for the past two years they'd been in a small mountain village called Eigenthal, at the foot of Mount Pilatus. It was a very rural area; hardly anyone lived up here apart from a few farmers and locals, and most of the holiday homes appeared to be unoccupied. In the distance, the melodious honking of the yellow postal van.

We reached an extensive property enclosed by a rotten wooden fence. The chalet itself was a massive building with a stone base; the uppermost floor with the shingle roof was made of wood. Behind it lay a garden and a meadow, both coated in a thin layer of ice. An isolated place that seemed never to have made the connection with the modern world. I stowed my things in the guest room, and wondered for a moment what I was actually doing here.

For dinner there was raclette, potatoes and white wine. The record player on the chest of drawers was playing jazz.

'*Time Further Out*,' I said. 'You listen to something like this during dinner?'

Romanov was pleased. 'Sometimes. Do you like it?'

'My mother liked Brubeck a lot.'

'I saw Dave in San Francisco once. Very sociable guy; we ended up in the same bar after a show, chatted for hours.'

Alva glanced at me briefly. 'What you have to know is that Sasha stalked him all through the Sixties. He followed him around from one concert to another. At some point Brubeck talked to him for five minutes out of pity.'

Romanov put his hand on hers. 'I hardly know how to impress her these days. I offer her Dave Brubeck, but still she wants more.'

Alva stroked the back of his hand in amusement. It pained me to see them exchanging intimate looks. To see how his manner pleased her, his enigmatic smile, as if he were the only person who'd noticed something amusing but was keeping it to himself. I pictured the happy years she must have spent with him. How at first perhaps she had still been distant, before thawing at his side. She often used to lend me Romanov's books. Certain passages had been underlined; they'd been about the death of his father, or his corrosive fear that he was incapable of being happy. And she still admired him even now, I could see it clearly.

'I reread "An Indomitable Heart" on the way here,' I said. 'Along with Hemingway's "The Snows of Kilimanjaro" it's the best short story I've read.'

'Thank you, but it's a little overrated.' Romanov sprinkled pepper on his cheese. 'You have to realise I was twenty when I wrote it. That's more than . . . It's a long time ago. The story is imprecise, kitsch, and full of mistakes.'

'I found it moving.'

Romanov looked at Alva. 'How much have you paid him to say that?'

'Our accounts are now empty.'

He held out his hand to me, as before, at the station. 'Jules, thank you for your words.'

After dinner we went and sat in the living room. We all drank a bit too much wine; Romanov's cheeks were flushed. He told us, cheerfully, that he had a precise idea of what his soul looked like. 'It's about twenty-five centimetres in diameter and it hovers at chest height,' he said. 'It's a shimmery greyish-silver, and when you touch it it's like stroking your hand over the finest velvet before passing straight through it, as if through air.'

Later he talked about his friendship with Nabokov, and a trip to China. 'I was your age, and I spent every evening with friends in an illegal casino in Macao.' Romanov put down his wine glass so he could gesticulate with both hands. 'It had this marvellously criminal atmosphere, people making the most unequivocal offers; you'd flirt and chat with crooks and dodgy businessmen. The first evening, my friends want to play the slot machines while I want to play roulette, so we agree to meet at the cashier to exchange our chips at the stroke of midnight. Over the next few hours, with a bit of beginner's luck, I win two thousand dollars – an inconceivable sum for me at the time. Then at midnight on the dot I'm waiting at our rendezvous, but my friends aren't there yet.' Romanov took a sip of wine. 'While I'm waiting, it occurs to me that on one table red has already come up an incredible twenty-three times in a row. This is the ideal moment, I think, so I go over there and put a hundred dollars on black. No risk. Red comes up again. I put another hundred dollars on black, but red comes up for the twenty-fifth time. To get my money back, I put two hundred dollars on black. Red again. Now I have to bet four hundred dollars. Again, nothing. Eight hundred dollars. Red. Just at that moment my friends come along. I borrow money and put two thousand on black. Two thousand! But it comes up red for the twenty-ninth time. And as I'm leaving the casino a broken man, I hear the croupier behind me call out, "Black."'

As an anecdote it wasn't outstanding, but Romanov told it with such masterful timing that you had to laugh at the punchline.

He fished a cigarette out of a silver case. 'My goodnight cigarette. Would you like one, too?'

I thanked him but declined, admiring the relish with which he puffed the smoke towards the ceiling, how much he was able to enjoy this simple moment. 'Alva says you've known each other since you were young?'

'That's right.'

'Why did you lose touch?'

'Because . . .' A glance at Alva, but her head was bowed. A scene I'd suppressed for years came into my mind: a bleak, austerely furnished house. Me running up the stairs, and how it had secretly aroused me to see Alva naked while at that very moment our friendship was falling apart. And, as so often, I wondered: did her mother send me upstairs on purpose?

Romanov studied me, then looked at Alva, and suddenly there was a touch of melancholy in his eyes.

He stood and walked towards me. We were the same height. 'You're young, Jules. Remember that. You have time.' I was fascinated by the pointed way in which he said the word 'time'. He took one last drag, then stubbed out his cigarette in the ashtray. 'It's nice to have you as our guest. Stay as long as you want. We sleep superbly up here, as you'll see.' He kissed Alva, then went upstairs with slow, deliberate steps.

When he'd gone, I dropped onto the sofa and poured myself another glass of Fendant. 'Are you his groupie?' I asked, only half joking. 'His muse?'

'Both, probably,' she said. 'Incidentally, Sasha hasn't talked that much in ages. I think he wanted to impress you. He even walked without a stick; he never does normally.'

'I like him. How did you meet him?'

Alva sat on a chest of drawers and drew up her legs. 'It was ten years ago, at a symposium in St Petersburg where I was working as a student translator. He was in his mid-fifties then and looked like an actor, but there was a bit of George Gershwin about him, too. I noticed him mainly because he spoke excellent German and the women were really hurling themselves at him, I'd never seen anything like it. He was coming out with his spiel, and as he did he kept looking over at me. I don't know, there was something so laid-back about him . . . It fascinated me.'

'How did your parents react? Do they visit you here?'

'My father comes a few times a year. I'm not in contact with my mother any more. We haven't spoken since I left school.'

Outside, all was quiet: the nearest people lived a long way off, hidden behind a bank of inky stormclouds. I looked at Alva, who had aged hardly at all in the intervening years. She was wearing her glasses and had put her red hair up. On her neck the two ivory-coloured scars.

She tilted her head back. 'You know, I want to be honest. I love Sasha' – suddenly dejected – 'but you mustn't let this evening deceive you. He hasn't left the chalet for months, and recently he's become rather . . . *forgetful.*'

We heard the gushing of the tap upstairs, then footsteps again.

'We used to spend a lot of time travelling. Trips, readings, symposiums – he has so many friends all over the world. But above all he was so lively, so curious. Before I got to know him I'd always thought he was melancholy, because he'd written all those sad things. Instead, he radiated this childish optimism, and it was just infectious. That was what I loved best about him.'

Alva poured us more wine. 'Sasha was seriously ill two years ago. For the time being he's recovered, but it's changed him. It's as if his magic's disappeared, as if he's suddenly become an ordinary old man, with the usual fears and eccentricities. He spends all his time upstairs these days, writing; he's determined to finish his book. He told me recently that he could sense the end. *The end is here in this room*, he said, *can you sense it too?* I hugged him, and the crazy thing was that I could sense his end as well.'

She grimaced, and paused for a moment. Then she composed herself and turned to me. 'He knows you write too, by the way.'

'But I don't write, Alva, how many times. That's all years ago.'

'Maybe you're not writing on paper, but you're doing it in your head,' she said, in her quiet voice, and touched my arm. 'You always have. You're a rememberer and a preserver, you just can't help it.'

In the distance, the Pilatus massif in the red light of dawn. The rushing of a stream. Inhale deeply: the clear air. I went for a run along the river in the early morning, passing farms and patches of forest. I arrived back at the chalet an hour later, sweating and panting. To my surprise Romanov was waiting for me on the steps outside the front door.

'Aha, a sportsman,' he said. 'My wife loves sportsmen, but I presume you knew that.'

'Your wife loves writers above all.'

He put his hand on my sleeve. 'Jules, come with me a moment.'

Romanov led me upstairs to his study. It smelled of dry, warm dust. A big desk with an Olivetti, a little table in the corner, a piano, some manuscript pages lying around, and a wooden crucifix. That was it.

'My mind needs space,' said Romanov. 'I used to have two bookshelves here as well, but then I'd read instead of writing, and so they had to go again. I have to work. Time's flying.'

'Time's flying' seemed to be his motto; he repeated it constantly. Once, he said that as a child he'd written a poem, 'Time, Flying', but it had got lost in a house move. He'd taken the title from an opera by Schubert, only slightly altered. The first lines of his childhood poem had been:

> *Time, flying away,*
> *take me with you.*

I pointed to the piano. 'Do you play?'

'A little.'

Romanov struck up one of Shostakovich's *Fantastic Dances*. His fingers seemed to know what to do of their own accord, effortlessly finding the right keys. 'I was rejected by the conservatoire,' he said, 'but at least I still had my Olivetti. So you could say I've spent my whole life bashing the keys, with varying degrees of elegance.'

When he'd finished the piece he closed the lid. He seemed to have something on his mind. Finally he pointed to the table in the corner. 'If you want, you could work or write up here.'

'Thank you, but I don't want to disturb you.'

'You won't be disturbing me; on the contrary. I used to like writing in libraries; it spurred me on to see other people working. In the beginning Alva would often sit with me, but she's too curious, it made me nervous.' He looked at me. 'So, what do you say? I'd be happy to have some company.'

It sounded quite offhand, but I could tell that it was a request, so straight after lunch I went and sat with him in the study. His desk was in front of the window, mine by the wall. Romanov looked out at the Swiss mountain landscape, I at wooden beams. He had a leather chair on castors, I a plastic folding stool. Clearly a two-tier society.

To begin with I went on editing a report for my label, but I found it difficult. Eventually I closed the document and just started writing. Absurd though it had seemed, to be sitting here next to an author I had once revered, it also motivated me. My imagination was an abandoned mine, and as I headed down into it in the wagon I was amazed at all that was down there, waiting to be brought to light. I immediately came up with several ideas and outlines that must have been lying dormant in me for years.

Romanov was watching me.

'What is it?' I asked.

'You write so fast. You're really pounding at the keyboard. *Clack, clack, clack.*'

A glance at his Olivetti. The white page rolled onto his typewriter had only a few lines on it. He was wearing his glasses and pursing his lips with effort.

'So what are you writing about?'

'Remembering. A novel, consisting of five stories. They're all connected, and essentially it's about how memories define and direct us. It's . . .' Romanov thought for a moment, then snorted. 'It's all *dreadful*.' He stood up. 'So dreadful that what I'd really like to do is take the typewriter and throw it out of the window. My last publication was six years ago; I've postponed this book over and over again.'

Romanov paced about the room, leaning on one of the walking sticks that stood in a basket in the corner, which he'd relied on since a hiking accident some years earlier. He tapped his forehead. 'There's simply nothing left in there. Like a pantry that's been eaten empty. It's all in published books, crumpled pages, spoken words. I can't . . .'

He seemed to have forgotten mid-sentence what it was he was saying. Abruptly he turned away. Only now did I hear the ticking of the clock that hung on the wall in the corner.

'When I was your age, Jules, I would write that much as well. *Clack, clack, clack*,' he said again. 'I was so carefree. I thought it would go on like that forever. But gradually there was less and less. I ought to come to terms with it. But I can't. Not so long as people think "An Indomitable Heart" is my best story. I wrote it when I was twenty, more or less in passing.'

He paused. And then came the chilling moment when he simply changed the subject and told me the story about the illegal casino, word for word, all over again.

The first days with Alva felt like coming home after a long journey. All those moments from our youth meant so much more to me than everything that had come afterwards; every conversation with her, every look, even every disappointment from that time stood out in my memory like a monolith. And now I was back at the source. When we sat in the kitchen drinking wine and being silly, when we walked through the forest and didn't say a word, when she played me something clumsily on the piano and I told her stories about my brother and sister, or when we sat on the living-room sofa at night listening to music and

Alva leaned against me: in all these moments I could virtually see our past delicately reconnecting with our present and future.

On the third day of my visit, Alva and her husband drove to the city in the early morning. After they'd gone, I went up to the second floor. Discovered that the two of them slept in separate bedrooms. This part of the house was suffused with the sharp tang of herbs, salves and medicine. Alva had told me that Romanov had been on strong medication since his prostate operation. His room had the air of an antique-shop storeroom; on the night table, beside an Asian wicker lamp, a globe and some notebooks, sat a greying toy rabbit. Alva's room, on the other hand, looked provisional: a round bed with a tower of books beside it, hip-high; the dracaenas and yuccas by the window were as tall as the ceiling.

This time, when I went out jogging, I picked a path that led through wet mountain countryside surrounded by firs. The trail led me up and up, all the way to the Chräigütsch. An icy wind whistled over the fields below.

When I arrived back at the chalet, it wasn't Romanov who was waiting for me by the front door but Alva. 'I was watching you from the window,' she said. 'Who'd have thought I'd see you run again?'

After a late breakfast the two of us went for a walk. The chalet backed onto a piece of forest; in places the trees grew so close together that you could no longer see the sky, and the forest seemed to me like a shadowy, magical underworld. Alva walked close beside me, her face red from the cold.

'I often thought about your sister over the years,' I said, after a while. 'About them finding her jacket. I wish you'd told me earlier; I would have understood you much better.'

Alva was silent. She picked up a stone from the ground and stared at it as if it were something precious.

'It was too much for me to tell you about it all.' She threw the stone away. 'When my sister disappeared, my father almost went mad. For him, the worst thing was that they didn't find the slightest clue on her jacket. He gave up his job, joined every single search party, went around speaking to witnesses on his own initiative. He was hardly sleeping any more, and when he couldn't go on any longer he had himself admitted to hospital. My mother cried non-stop for a few weeks, then she never talked about it again. As if Phine had never existed. She just never mentioned her.'

Alva's voice grew quieter. 'All my parents did after that was fight. When they got divorced, my mother and I moved to another village quite a long way from home. We never told anyone about it. I had depression back then, and suicidal thoughts. But I kept thinking: what if Phine comes back one day and I'm not there any more?'

I tried to give her a hug, but she moved away. We were passing a frozen meadow. For a moment I was tempted to touch the electric fence.

She put her hand on my shoulder. 'The others in our class had no idea what I'd been through. They just talked about the holidays and their parents, and they all seemed so happy. Only you . . .' – a shiver ran down my spine – 'only you didn't seem happy. That's why I sat next to you back then.'

We were heading for an Alpine inn with the peculiar name Unterlauelen.

'So you know that feeling,' I said calmly, 'when life has been poisoned by something, right from the start. Like black liquid poured into a basin of clean water.'

'I thought travelling would help. After school I went to New Zealand for six months, then Russia. Later, with Sasha, I went everywhere. But it doesn't help.'

'And literature, does that help?'

'Sometimes.'

'And A. N. Romanov?'

She smiled. 'Sometimes he does, too. Actually, the reason I was always reading was simply to escape, to let myself be comforted by a few sentences or a story. When I was younger I wanted more than anything to be a character in a novel. To be immortal and live forever in a book, then everyone can read me and watch me from the outside. Daft, I know.' Looking sheepish: 'Although, if I'm honest, the thing I'd still like best is to be a character in a novel.'

And that was when I realised why she had lured me to Switzerland. She felt betrayed. She must have married Romanov in part because he manufactured two of her favourite drugs: confidence and beautiful words. Now, though, the supplier was almost seventy and had become unreliable. I imagined how Alva had spent the last couple of years in the mountains: a lonely satellite, circling the study in the chalet where her husband toiled ever more fruitlessly at his typewriter and scarcely spoke to her any more.

We sat down at a table in the inn. She told me about her father: how he had given her the red Fiat for her eighteenth birthday, and how nowadays he was a keen mountaineer. 'He was very amused, incidentally, when he realised that his son-in-law was ten years older than him.'

'How is he?'

'Pretty well, I think. He's working again now, as an internist in a group practice. He always loved talking to his patients. I often used to visit him at work when I was a child.'

'You never talked to me about him before.'

She stared at her plate. 'When my mother got custody, my father moved to Augsburg. To begin with I still visited him every other weekend, I had my own room, he gave me books and took me hiking. Then all of a sudden there was no contact, for years. I thought it was my fault, that perhaps I reminded him too much of my sister; but when I was eighteen he contacted me and we talked things through. I was so happy that I had him again! It was only then that I found out my mother had never given me his letters. She'd told him I didn't want to see him any more.'

'Why did she do that?'

'I don't know. She always loved Phine a bit more, and she never got over losing her. We used to fight a lot. We said terrible things. She was so cold towards me; I was glad when I was finally able to get away. I thought that was it, but a few years ago she sent my father a letter to give to me. No return address. She's living abroad now, but she didn't write much about that. It was a nice letter, anyway: a sort of farewell.'

Alva shook her head. 'I just wish she'd said all those things to me when I was younger. I hated life so much back then. I had the feeling that if my sister disappears and my mother still doesn't love me, it must mean I'm not worth anything. I wanted to become the person who deserved all this.'

Tears shimmered in her eyes. I leaned over and hugged her. 'Will you stay a bit longer?' she asked, in my ear.

I saw her beseeching expression and realised, perhaps even before she did, the full extent of what she was asking.

It took me two attempts to hand in my notice. In the first call I pretended to have pneumonia, but as I'd never been a good liar I called again and told my boss, much to his surprise, that I wouldn't be coming back to work. Contrary to my usual way of doing things, I didn't think for one moment about the potential consequences. And I replied to a very affectionate mail from Norah by saying that for the time being it wouldn't be possible for me to go on seeing her, and I would explain everything at a later date. She wrote to me several times after that, called and left messages, but I didn't respond.

In the space of just a few days I had drawn a line under my old life. Yet I wasn't even sure what kind of future I might have with Alva. I just knew that I couldn't let her go again. That I didn't want to spend my whole life paying for the mistakes I'd made as a teenager.

'I don't like to say this to you again, but you can't bring back the past, or change it,' said my brother, on the phone.

'Yes,' I said, 'you can.'

I'd been surfing the net in the living room for a few hours before I realised Alva wasn't in the house. At first I'd thought she was keeping Romanov company upstairs, but then I noticed I hadn't heard either her footsteps or the gushing of the tap, which in the poorly soundproofed chalet were always audible at the same times of day. I waited downstairs in the living room for a while before going up to bed. It was the end of February, and it was snowing heavily outside. At six in the morning I was woken by the sound of the front door closing. Later, when I asked Alva where she'd been all that time, she just shrugged and looked at me as if she didn't know what I was talking about.

Her passion for gardening was also new to me. When spring came, she spent hours tending vegetables or repotting and watering her plants, and when she came in from the garden she had dirty fingernails and was happy. Romanov's realm, on the other hand, was the chalet, and if I had to use a sound to describe it, it would be the slow, indefatigable clacking of his typewriter.

One day he suddenly took up his walking stick and challenged me to a duel. I grabbed another of his walking sticks and we fenced for a moment. When I asked him what this was about, Romanov replied laconically, 'The best to be said of him, if you can, is: he was a child, and he was a man!'

The fencing had clearly exhausted him; he sat down on a chair and wiped the sweat from his forehead. 'What do your parents do, Jules?'

'They died in an accident when I was ten.'

'I'm sorry.'

I gestured dismissively. 'What about your parents? What were they like?'

He told me about his mother, a poet, who came from an old Petersburg family. 'She loved German literature and the German language, so we always had a nanny from Germany. My father, on the other hand, had a much simpler upbringing, near Yekaterinburg. A *muzhik* dreamer who always had some great business idea in his head but never successfully realised a single one. He too fled with his family when he was still a child, before the October Revolution. He met my mother in America, and later we lived in the Netherlands. That's where my father killed himself.'

I looked at him inquiringly.

'Lack of success,' he said. 'He'd ruined yet another company; we were at our wits' end and literally out on the street. It was his fault. So he put an end to it. Some of our acquaintances thought it was cowardly. I thought it was logical.' He looked me in the eye. 'A son always has an instinctive, good relationship with his mother. His father, on the other hand . . . He watches him, he mistrusts and reveres him, he measures himself against him. I've thought about him all my life.'

'I hardly knew my father,' I said. 'I often wonder what our relationship would be like if he were still alive. Would we have much to do with each other? Or perhaps we'd even be friends? I'd like to sit in a bar and chat with him, the two of us, as adults. I missed out on everything. Conversations, little moments, father–son stuff. It wasn't until I was twenty that I realised I was shaving wrong. I was standing in the bathroom with my flatmate. *Always upwards under the chin*, he said. I didn't know.'

I sat down on a chair next to Romanov. He patted my shoulder. 'You're a good man, Jules. I'm sure your father would like you.'

Embarrassed, I asked, 'How did you end up in Switzerland?'

'How I ended up here? My first wife was from here, and I immediately liked the country. Also, Alva wanted to go abroad again, after so many years. So did I, to be honest. I moved to Russia after *perestroika*, but I never felt at home there the way I'd hoped.'

'By the way, I've started reading your correspondence with Nabokov. Is it true you went to visit him when you were a little boy?'

Romanov laughed and stroked his hair off his forehead. For a moment he was ageless. 'I wasn't actually that little any more. I think I was sixteen or seventeen, and I'd just read *Lolita*. It was the first book that really inspired me, although I'm sure I only understood half of it. But that playful wit, that linguistic brilliance – I had to meet him. We were still living in Oregon then, and one night I ran away and took a Greyhound bus to New York to visit him at Cornell University. But that day, of all days, he wasn't lecturing. I laid the Russian accent on thick, said I was a nephew of his, and they gave me his private address. A few hours later I rang his door-bell. He stared at me in astonishment when he heard that I'd run away on his account. We called my parents, then we drank tea and talked about authors and tennis players we both admired. Naturally I sent him all of my stories; to Switzerland, too, later on. He always read them, even though he was forty years older.'

Short silence. 'What does Alva do when she goes out at night?' I asked. 'She's disappeared several times now. What does she get up to?'

'I don't know. She doesn't tell me, but she's been doing it as long as we've known each other. I always had the feeling I shouldn't ask her about it. I don't think she'd like it, and she needs these nocturnal walks.'

I nodded. 'Alexander, may I ask you something else? Why did you marry Alva?'

'Why did I marry her?' These days Romanov often repeated the questions I asked him. All in all, the moments when he forgot things, lost concentration or went looking for his glasses were becoming alarmingly frequent. 'I'm sure Alva's already told you about the symposium and how she came and spoke to me. But I was already very aware of this young woman who was always explaining things to the others and who was so assiduous in all that she did. Assiduous, yes, but mysterious, too. You sensed that she'd been through a lot.' Proudly: 'And of course she was stunning. Sometimes you see people better from a distance, and she seemed to be someone who could be sad, warm-hearted and cheerful all at once. And she read. My God, how this woman read! On steps, on chairs, on the floor – every spare minute she had a book in her lap.'

'And then?' I asked quietly.

He thought for a moment. 'Alva was very reserved. We went out to eat a few times, but she was almost shy; she hardly said anything to begin with. At moments like that I usually feel duty-bound to keep the conversation going, maybe even perform a bit. But when I was with her I found myself, for the first time, enjoying the silence within me. She was like a cold hand on a hot brow.'

Later, I was standing alone in front of the panoramic window in the living room, watching it get dark outside. I found nights in the chalet a bit uncanny at first. The laughing African masks on the walls seemed eerily to come alive; the stags' heads and other hunting trophies stared down at the observer, and often, looking out of the window, you'd see nothing but an underworldly twilight over the valley, followed by black nothingness. Sometimes we didn't see anyone else for days, and it felt as if we were the only ones still up here. The sounds of civilisation were what brought us back to reality: the gurgle of the heating, or the whistle of the kettle on the stove. It was a monotonous, almost bizarre daily existence, and it soon dawned on me that we were stranded here, and that all of us were waiting for something. It came as a shock when I realised what it was.

It was on one of these evenings that the curious scene I'd been suppressing since childhood came back to me again. We'd been to see a Billy Wilder film at an art-house cinema in town, and had gone for something to eat afterwards. Romanov, who didn't usually like to be around other people, had come with us for once. On the way back to the chalet he told us about how the sociologist Max Weber had quarrelled with his father, who had died shortly afterwards. There had therefore been no reconciliation, and after his father's death Weber became a nervous wreck.

'He had to give up teaching,' said Romanov. 'It even caused him to lose the power of speech.'

'Just because of this one quarrel?' I asked.

'I'm sure there were many reasons, but he simply couldn't cope with the fact that he hadn't reconciled with his father. It ate him up inside. Weber's wife called it an evil thing from the unconscious underground of life that stretched out its claws towards her husband.'

Back in the chalet, when Romanov had gone upstairs, Alva put on the Nick Drake album. 'I listened to it a lot after our last meeting in Munich,' she said. 'I was sure then that we wouldn't see each other again.' She was sitting on a sideboard, and snapped her book shut. Alva loved to sit in the most ridiculous places in the house.

'Sometimes I hear you upstairs talking with Sasha, and I can't believe you're really here. Being with you, talking with you or listening to music, was once such an important part of my life, but in recent years I often thought it was just a dream. As if it had never happened. And now, suddenly, it's as if it were yesterday.'

'That's because right now we're listening to the same music as we did then. Time isn't linear; nor is memory. You always remember more clearly things you're emotionally close to at any given moment. At Christmas, you always think last Christmas has only just been and gone, even though it's twelve months ago. On the other hand, the summer just gone, which is actually six months closer, feels much further away. Memories of things that are emotionally similar to the present take a kind of short cut. Here . . .' I scribbled it down on a piece of paper and showed it to her:

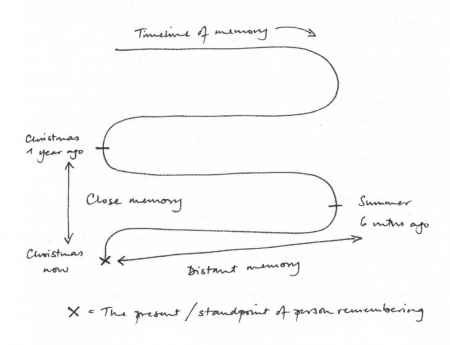

'Uh-huh. So this is the sort of thing you think about,' she said.

I grabbed Romanov's walking stick and took a few steps with it across the room. Alva just came over and took it away.

'Are you walking around with this as well now?' She ran her finger over the polished mahogany.

'Give me back the stick. I need it.'

She laughed. 'No.'

A quiet rumble of thunder. A storm was gathering in the mountains; from time to time bolts of lightning flashed above the peaks, lighting up the night. It felt especially cosy to be sheltered inside as the wind whistled over the trees and tugged at the branches.

Alva moved closer. 'Why did you really stop taking photos?'

'I always felt that when I was taking photos I was close to my father. But then I realised it wasn't true.' My face grew hot. 'But mainly I started because I just . . .'

She took another step towards me. 'Just what?'

A scene I thought I'd forgotten surfaced before my eyes: a taxi driving away from me at night under lamplight and turning a corner. I wanted to shout something after it, something important, but I couldn't . . .

Dazed, I looked at Alva. Should I tell her what I only surmised and could barely admit to myself? That it was an unconscious sense of guilt that had made me waste the best years of my life, stumble into the wrong university course and pick up the camera again? That all these years I'd denied myself the chance to write, even though I loved it?

'I'll tell you another time.'

'*Another time, another time*,' said Alva, rather adorably, and without thinking my hand landed on her elbow. The hand developed a life of its own, crawled tentatively up her arm and reached her cheek. Another half-step towards her; my chin almost touched her forehead. I looked down at her, she up at me, momentarily uncertain. She reached for my hand. But at the same instant she stepped back, poked me in the stomach with the stick, and said goodnight.

I still didn't imagine that Romanov's condition would deteriorate so fast, not even when he let the bath overflow twice within a fairly short space of time because he'd forgotten he intended to bathe. He was an expert at hiding his true condition. A house with the façade still intact while everything inside was collapsing.

I accompanied him down to the cellar of the chalet, where you could regulate the heating and do the laundry. I was assailed by a strong odour of cleaning fluid, old newspapers and damp masonry. A wine rack and a gun cabinet stood apart in an insulated area. Romanov took the various guns out one by one and explained them to me. There were small- and large-calibre rifles, Zimmerstutzens, muzzle-loaders, and an over-and-under shotgun.

'I used to hunt a lot,' he said. 'But I haven't for years now. My father taught me. I was a little boy then; nine, maybe. He was an excellent huntsman.'

Romanov saw my expression and nodded. 'He did it with that one. A Browning: his favourite gun. My father was a man who was able to *let go*. His death was terrible for us, but I always admired him for this act of courage – now perhaps more than ever.'

He touched the barrel of the rifle with his fingertips. 'Listen, Jules,' he said, suddenly switching to the familiar *Du* form of address. 'Two years ago I had cancer, and I said hello to Death. He said I only had a little time left. Since then, I've had to write. I know that my wife is suffering as a result. She's cut off from the outside world up here; I keep telling her she should get herself a flat in town, but she wants to stay with me. I'm sorry I'm no longer the man she fell in love with. But I can't help it. I hoped that in you she'd have a companion she could talk to and spend time with. It means a lot to me that Alva isn't so isolated and alone. You're our friend, and I value that.'

He put his hand on my shoulder and looked me in the eye.
Then he abruptly turned away.

'But don't you dare screw her.'

It was a few seconds before this registered. I instinctively took
half a step back. 'I didn't want—'

'I'm not a fool.' Romanov still didn't look at me. 'The future
is something I'll leave to you youngsters. But as long as I'm still
alive I don't want her cheating on me. A few years ago I'd have
made sure of it myself. I know how to keep a woman. But now
. . . Promise me you won't touch her.'

I said nothing. I contemplated first the guns, then him.

'Promise me, Jules!'

Romanov was looking at me again. For a moment there was
something furtive in his expression, and his otherwise friendly
eyes were staring at me implacably.

In June I'd been in the mountains for five months. I had sublet
my apartment in Berlin through Liz so as not to use up all my
savings. How far away that all is, though, I thought, as I drove
with Alva to the little ice-cold mountain lake. Shivering, we
climbed out of the water and lay down on our towels to dry off
in the sun. It smelled of grass; the sky was cloudless blue. For
a while we watched a paraglider drift down into the valley in
the distance. I lay on my back, Alva on her stomach. She kept
bending her legs, deliberately poking my left shin with her toes
each time.

'Is that fun?' I asked.

'Kind of . . . Have you actually read *The Heart is a Lonely
Hunter* yet?'

'Yes, I read it ages ago, at school. I found it really moving. I
even wrote you a letter back then.'

'Funny,' she said, 'I never got a letter from you.'

'I thought it was too kitsch and didn't give it to you after all.'

'Have you still got it?'

'No.'

'You're lying, Jules, I bet you've still got that letter.'

A brimstone butterfly flew across the grass and landed right in front of me.

'I'd like to read something of yours,' said Alva.

'I'm not ready yet.'

'What do you two actually do all the time? I hear you talking constantly.'

'Mostly we talk about you.'

Her toes tapped my shin again; this time it was a gentle warning.

'How's Sasha getting on?'

'Hard to say.' I considered how to put it. 'Have you noticed how absent-minded he's been lately? I have the feeling he's worse than just a few weeks ago.'

'I know,' said Alva tonelessly, as if from very far away.

'And what does that mean?'

She was silent. It was the question none of us could answer.

While I was making good headway and working on two novellas, for Romanov progress was slow. From time to time he would read out a few sentences to me, or even ask for my opinion. Sometimes, though, he would just watch me writing. '*Clack, clack, clack,*' he'd say then, again, sometimes amused, sometimes depressed. It made no difference that he was the better writer: he would never again be able to sit there enthusiastically pouring forth as I did.

'Shall we go and see a film afterwards?' asked Alva.

'Only if you don't cry.'

'I'm sure I won't cry.'

She said that every time. And then she would cry after all. Melodramatic scenes were guaranteed to bring tears to her eyes; she found even the most clichéd turns of events tremendously moving: when a couple got together after all, for example, or an old, injured footballer triumphantly turned the match around at the very last minute. She was ashamed of this, and I loved to wind her up about it.

'Watch out, they're going to kiss in a second,' I'd say. 'Would you rather look away?'

What I appreciated most about Alva these days, though, was her *gentleness*. It was as if the word had been invented for her. She was gentle in the way she repotted plants, formulated a thought, or tenderly stroked the nape of her husband's neck; the way she wrote a letter, or laid the table, always placing cutlery, plates and glasses with precision. As if she didn't want to leave anything else to chance.

In the early evening I took my notes up to Romanov's study. From a distance I could already hear music. The door was ajar, and I peeped in. Romanov was sitting at the piano, Alva on a chair beside him. He whispered something to her that made her laugh. They kissed, not very passionately, then Romanov played again. His fingers danced elegantly across the keys, but suddenly he played a wrong note. He kept trying to pick up the melody again, in vain. He simply couldn't remember the notes. Finally he closed the lid of the piano. Alva said something in Russian, then she leaned her head against his chest and Romanov stroked her hair. His eyes were lowered, and the look on his face engraved itself on my mind.

That night Alva disappeared again for several hours and only came back to the chalet in the early morning.

I wasn't sure how my brother and sister would get on with Alva, but as soon as they arrived at the station they greeted her with a hug. Liz and Marty had come to stay for the weekend, and we all drove up to the mountain village together. Alva negotiated the hairpin bends with almost excessive caution, and I couldn't help thinking of how she used to drive as a teenager.

'It's like the Shire here, but without the hobbits.' Marty stared, fascinated, at the gold-veined clouds in the evening sky. He'd had back problems for a while now, and was sitting rather stiffly in the passenger seat.

'We even get our milk straight from the farmers,' said Alva.

'We have a two-litre churn, and we carry the foaming milk back ourselves.'

'You mean, *I* carry the milk,' I interjected.

'And I've been cooking for you here for months.'

'I think it's such a shame Jules doesn't cook any more,' said my brother. 'When he was little he was always in the kitchen. Sometimes he'd even throw our parents out because they kept butting in.'

'I didn't know that,' said Alva. 'I asked him the other day if he wanted to cook sometime, and he told me he couldn't.'

Instead of answering I looked at my siblings. 'Alva's husband is really pleased you're coming.'

'I googled him,' said Marty. 'America, the Netherlands, Russia, Switzerland – he's had a colourful life. How old is he now?'

'Sixty-seven.'

Marty's gaze wandered from me to Alva. She sat at the wheel knowing that everyone in the car was thinking the same thing, but it didn't bother her.

'I think that's great,' said my sister. 'When I was a teenager I always wanted a much older man.'

'God, I know,' said Marty. 'You had a thirty-six-year-old boyfriend for a couple of months back then. Your weird fiancé was almost twenty years older, too. And he never talked to us.'

'My brother doesn't know what he's talking about,' said Liz to Alva. 'He's been with the same woman for a hundred years. The only one who would ever have him.'

Marty kissed his wedding ring and made a superior face.

The car stopped on the gravel drive with a satisfying crunch. Romanov watched us from the balcony like a hunter watching game from a raised hide. He greeted my siblings and was remarkably friendly, but then disappeared up to the second floor and wasn't seen again until dinner.

'He's just not used to visitors any more.' Alva stood in the kitchen, chopping an onion. 'Why did you never say you liked cooking? It'd be nice if you cooked a meal for me sometime.'

'If a few things had worked out differently, I would have cooked for you once.'

'Aha. When?'

'When we were still in school. I asked you if you wanted to share an apartment with me in Munich; we were going to discuss it that evening over dinner. I'd already gone and bought everything; I thought if you ate my *farfalle* with ragout you'd forget about your plans to emigrate.'

She smiled. 'Ah, yes, I remember. So why didn't we have dinner in the end?'

I stared at her, speechless, and suddenly her smile vanished and the kitchen fell quiet. The furrow in her brow reappeared. She stirred the saucepan of risotto, silent and clearly tense. Eventually she put down the wooden spoon. 'I'm sorry.'

'Never mind.'

'Will you still cook for me one day?'

I looked at her closely for a moment. Then I nodded.

During dinner Romanov sat on his chair at the head of the table as if turned to stone, not knowing how to interact with the unaccustomed visitors. He was wearing a black shirt and a grey jacket, still outwardly immaculate. But unlike the day I met him, he was mostly silent.

Marty talked about his postdoctoral qualification, and how Elena was going to open a psychotherapy practice in Munich. Liz, on the other hand, hardly talked about her work or everyday life any more. She seemed restless, as if she were waiting to break free. The wild animal in my sister, which had dozed contentedly these last few years, was stirring again, licking its paws and starting to pace about its cage.

Later, as we sat in the living room, Romanov gradually came to life. I don't remember what he spoke of to begin with, only that he talked about his first wife, the daughter of a fabulously rich Zurich industrialist. Romanov had been at the Kronenhalle restaurant, celebrating the publication of his novel *The Perpetual Virginity of the Soul*, and had met her there at the bar.

'She died far too young, sadly,' he said. 'I always thought it was the great misfortune of my life. I went to Russia, prepared to retreat from the world. Then the good Lord blessed me all over again.'

Romanov raised his glass to Alva. I knew that he was serious about the good Lord; he often held forth to me about how only fools were unbelievers.

He poured himself some more wine and started telling stories, jumping from anecdote to anecdote, thinking that he was entertaining us, but that evening I realised that he didn't have the stories under control; rather, the stories were controlling him. His brain seemed to be working overtime, wrenching open all kinds of drawers. I could see that it pained Alva, although she tried not to let it show.

Then Romanov stopped in the middle of a sentence and scrutinized my siblings. His eyes betrayed uncertainty; for a moment he no longer seemed to know who he actually had in front of him. An unnatural pause. Eventually he smiled and, with startling self-assurance, asked Liz and Marty whether this was their first time in the region and how they liked it here. General questions he could have put to any stranger, which I'd come to recognise as part of his disguise. Shortly afterwards Alva took him upstairs.

In the living room an awkward silence fell. Marty frowned, but said nothing at first.

Liz lit a cigarette. 'He's got something about him.' She considered. 'He must have been incredibly good-looking once.'

'He seems a bit . . .' Marty hesitated, '. . . *confused*. Not the whole evening, but you keep seeing flashes of it. How's Alva coping?'

'It exhausts her. But she doesn't want to talk to me about it; she hasn't even told me what exactly's wrong with him. I assume it's Alzheimer's, but I'm not sure.'

'And how are *you* coping?' Liz looked at me. 'We're starting to worry about what exactly you're doing here. I mean, how are things with Alva, are you . . .?'

I shook my head.

Liz rolled her eyes. 'My dear Jules, you really are at heart one of the most romantic people I know. And I'm sure it isn't easy with her husband' – she tapped a column of ash off her cigarette – 'but, bloody hell, how long have you been here now? A few *months*?'

A creak on the stairs. Alva returned; she picked up a glass of wine and nodded at us. 'It's nice that you have siblings,' she said to me.

'It's nice that my little brother has a woman,' said Liz.

I shot her a dirty look, and was immediately cross with myself because it meant I'd missed seeing Alva's expression.

It was one of the first mild summer nights; we went and sat outside on the veranda. Marty lay on the ground because of his bad back. The valley before us was shrouded in darkness, and on the other side of it someone had lit a big campfire on the mountain.

'Shame Toni couldn't come,' I said, looking at my sister. 'Have you already broken his heart with your new boyfriend, or is that still to come?'

'I think we're currently in the process.' Liz gestured apologetically.

My brother turned to look at Alva. 'You know, we're the loneliest siblings in the world,' he said, still lying on his back. 'All three of us share one and the same best friend. *Best-friend-sharing*, I sometimes call it. We could almost start an agency, hiring Toni out to people like us. He could be friends with you, too, for a monthly fee.'

'At least you've always had someone,' said Alva. 'I lost my best friend for almost fifteen years.'

She left my look unanswered.

I was glad my brother and sister got on so well with Alva and seemed to like her. When Liz asked whether Alva also had siblings, she fell silent for a moment; but then, after a little hesitation, she told them about Phine, who might be alive somewhere or was long since dead, and to my relief it seemed to be a release for her to talk about it.

The soft grey of dawn grew paler. I couldn't recall many occasions when I'd shared the sunrise with someone. A few times at school, and with Liz and Marty in Montpellier. It was as if in the half-light of morning people's true nature was revealed, as if there were no more pretending. And so the four of us sat there, talking and watching the first rays of sun hit the tops of the mountains.

After Marty and Liz had gone, the chalet suddenly felt empty and too big. If at first we hadn't known how to deal with the noise my siblings brought with them, now it was the silence they left behind. Romanov could still converse lucidly, but sometimes he was no longer able to speak in the abstract or connect general ideas, obsessing over details for minutes on end instead. He also misplaced things more and more often. Sometimes I'd find a few books in the bathroom cupboard, or a teacup in the shoe compartment underneath our coats.

One evening I was sitting with Alva in the living room; we were playing Scrabble. The room was lit only by a small lamp and a smoking candle. It was raining quietly outside, accompanied by the ringing of cowbells. Alva was sitting cross-legged on the armchair. She was just about to place a word when we heard Romanov's footsteps upstairs.

Suddenly she slammed the letters she was holding onto the board.

'I CAN'T STAND THIS ANY MORE!' she screamed. 'I can't go on like this. He's going mad, Jules.' She stood up. 'He's nothing like the man I met any more. Sometimes I feel as if I'm living with a stranger.'

Her mouth twitched. 'Every day he loses a bit more of himself. Every day he forgets more of me. Then from time to time he seems completely normal again, but I know he's disappearing inside.'

'Can't you talk to him about it? Help him?'

'Sasha doesn't want to. And anyway, there is no help.' She let these words sink in.

Then she sighed. 'I need something to drink.'

She took a bottle of Scotch from the pantry. We knocked back a few glasses without really getting drunk and sat, stupefied, on the kitchen worktop beside the fridge.

'How did you actually get that?' I pointed to the delicate scars under Alva's ear.

'It was during my first years in Russia, long before I met Sasha.' She spoke quietly, and not in my direction. 'I was still living in Moscow back then, and my life was a bit like a nightmare. I was a complete stranger there, and I met the wrong people. I just went along with everything, and I did things you shouldn't do.'

'What sort of things?'

'I'd rather not get specific.' She brushed it away. 'Anyway, it's a long time ago. Eventually I put a stop to it. My father sent me some money, and I went to St Petersburg.'

Alva seldom talked about her years in Moscow, and at times it seemed to me that something in her had got broken back then, or she had left a piece of herself behind in that darkness. I wished I'd been there and could have prevented it.

'What do you do when you go out walking at night?'

'Nothing. I just walk. I like to be alone at that time and confront all the things I never want to think about otherwise.' She looked at me; then she said: 'I started doing it because I was sure that one night I'd go for a walk and wouldn't come back. That I'd simply disappear. It was a feeling of limitless freedom every time.'

'Did you want to *kill yourself*?'

'I didn't say that. And besides, I always have come back, so far.' A little more conciliatory: 'Sometimes I think I just do it now out of sheer habit. It is a bit strange, I know.'

She emptied her glass in a single gulp. Then she looked at me, and her expression seemed somehow lost. 'Jules, I want you to go. Tomorrow, preferably.'

I couldn't believe what I'd just heard.

It was only now that the alcohol hit me. I felt paralysed, tired. Incapable of reacting appropriately or meeting her eyes.

'I don't want to carry on like this with you,' I heard her say. 'I know what's in store for Sasha, there's no denying it any more, and I don't want to drag you into it as well. It's better if you leave us now. It's my husband who's dying here; this is *my* responsibility.'

I sat there, stunned. Pictured myself leaving the chalet with my suitcase in the morning. Leaving Alva and her husband behind, and, as so often in my life, heading off into a pointless freedom.

It's my husband who's dying here.

Suddenly, in all that she had said, I heard the constant refrain of her youth: a quiet 'I'm not good enough'.

In my mind's eye I saw eleven-year-old Alva once more, shyly visiting me in my room at the boarding house and inspecting my things. Then the unattainable nineteen-year-old who hated herself so much there'd been no place for me. The twenty-five-year-old I'd never met, newly in love and, presumably, happy. The gentle, married thirty-year-old who accompanied me to the train in Munich. And now, years later, here she was, sitting beside me with her wounds and fears and unable to make the right decision.

The fridge hummed away; rain pattered down outside. My breathing quickened as I put my hand on Alva's cheek and turned her face towards me. She jumped; her whole body tensed.

She seemed to be about to say something; I heard the delicate sound of her tongue releasing itself from her palate. In that moment I kissed her on the mouth. I could feel her surprise; her hesitation, too. Then she returned the kiss.

The next morning I woke in my room just after six. I put on my running shoes and stepped outside. Raindrops were falling from the leaves of the trees; wisps of fog drifted across the landscape, and a milky haze was thickening in the valley. A picture straight out of legend. Now, though, the sun was slowly coming out. For a moment I felt twenty again; then I set off.

At first Romanov didn't notice anything of the change that

was taking place right under his nose. He was too preoccupied with himself and his scattering mind. Alva continued to sleep in her own bed, and we avoided any expression of tenderness in his presence.

However, one day he said, from his desk, 'Jules, you seem happy. You've been typing away quietly and cheerfully all week. What are you working on at the moment?'

'The two novellas, still. The first is about a married man who loses control of his dreams. He doesn't dream something different every night, but always the same thing. About a different life, different people, a different job and a different wife, whom he also loves. Soon both realities are equally strong. When the wife in his dream dies, it has big repercussions in reality, too.'

I'd titled the novella 'A Different Life'; it was set during World War One. At the end the protagonist was called up, while in his dreams he was living peacefully in the countryside.

Romanov reached for his stick and walked over to my desk, his glasses on his nose. He read a few lines. When he'd finished he rested his hand on my shoulder, which felt to me like a compliment or encouragement. I outlined the second novella to him, too. It was a little like Fitzgerald's 'The Curious Case of Benjamin Button', in which a man aged backwards: mine was about a man for whom time moved faster. If you talked to him for a few minutes, half an hour had actually gone by. If a woman went out with him and for her the date had lasted precisely three hours, seven would have passed, or sometimes twelve. The man remained lonely all his life. People avoided him as soon as they found out about his secret, and he was looking for a person who was willing nonetheless to grow old by his side because a few years and the memories with him were worth more than a whole life without him.

That day I was filled with optimism. I fetched the milk, washed up, and decided to do the laundry. Early in the evening I opened the cellar door, whistling, and got a shock. Romanov was standing alone in the middle of the room, talking anxiously to himself. When he noticed me he fell silent and gave me a narrow look.

'What time is it?' he asked.

'Quarter to seven.'

This information seemed to confuse rather than calm him.

'Quarter to seven in the *evening*,' I added.

'And what am I doing here?'

My eyes fell on the gun cabinet. 'You were turning up the heating. It's too cold in the house.'

Romanov seemed to consider this. Then he nodded. 'Yes, that was it.' He gave me a friendly look and went over to the thermostat.

I spent a couple more days working on the two texts, then I gave them to Alva to read. They were pretty long for novellas, and not quite finished. But it wasn't the stories that were important; it was the insight into my inner self. There were things I couldn't say; I could only write them. Because when I spoke, I thought; and when I wrote, I felt.

We lay on my bed. Alva bit into an apple and skimmed the lines. I watched her eagerly. Once, as she read, she laughed aloud, and I felt as if I were on a street at night and all the streetlamps had gone on all at once. At some point I fell asleep. I woke, briefly, in the middle of the night, and Alva was still reading beside me; she seemed upset, and said she found the story very moving. I saw her reach for her bottle of water and drink, then I closed my eyes.

Hours later I woke again. It was already light outside, but it could only be early morning.

'Finally!' Alva sat on my lap in her underwear and circled my belly button with her fingers. Her red hair was tied in a plait; she wasn't wearing her glasses. I must have given her a questioning look, because she pointed at the two stories lying in an untidy stack on my bedside table, somewhat the worse for wear. Then, just before she threw herself at me, she said five magic words, and I can still hear them today.

'Jules, this is really good.'

*

That afternoon I was sitting in the study. Romanov wasn't even trying to write any more; he was just staring at me the whole time instead.

'Is everything all right?' I asked him.

He nodded absently and stood up. Then, all of a sudden, he clutched his chest. 'It hurts,' he said, his voice cracking.

I ran over to him, prepared for the worst. A firm grip: suddenly, before I knew what was happening, my head was clamped under Romanov's arm. He rammed my skull against the desk and slammed it down a second time on the keyboard of the Olivetti. I finally managed to free myself from his clutches, and he slapped my face. Then he sat down on the chair, panting.

I was so shocked by the attack that I sat down as well. My head was hammering. The metallic taste of blood in my mouth.

'Do you think I don't notice when someone is fucking my wife?' I heard him say. 'I'm old, but I'm not blind. Who do you think you are? Casanova, a master seducer? Old people sleep badly. I'm awake at five o'clock every morning, and ever since I've been living here with Alva I've visited her at that hour and watched her lying asleep in her bed. Not last night. And she wasn't on one of her walks, either. She was with you.'

I probed my lip with my tongue, checking for injuries, and said nothing.

'I asked you not to touch her before my death. It was a request.'

'It was a threat.'

Romanov's jaw was working. 'You stole from a dying beggar. You couldn't even wait till he was dead . . .'

He started talking to himself in Russian; the words sounded bitter. I could imagine what he was saying. It was like an hourglass turned on its head: with every second, more grains of sand fell from his chamber into mine, and there was nothing he could do about it.

Slowly I approached him. 'Alva has been the most important person in my life since I was eleven years old. I couldn't . . .' Instinctively, I decided not to tell him that Alva had tried to send me away. 'I'm sorry, Alexander,' was all I said. 'I'm so sorry. But it's not just about you and me: it's about Alva, too. What *she* wants.'

Romanov didn't answer; his gaze slid past me. Eventually he pointed to my desk. 'I would like to read both your stories.'

'You've never read anything of mine. Maybe you won't like my style; maybe you won't think they're any good.'

'You're sleeping with a woman you love,' he said dully. 'Everything you write now is either terrible or very good.'

Romanov and Alva had a long argument; I heard Alva's voice becoming increasingly emphatic. All in all she barely seemed able to cope any more with his gradual deterioration. She slept badly and dragged herself about the house with shadows under her eyes. I wished I could do something for her, anything. It was as if every day she grew more afraid of a clear decision and longed for it at the same time.

Low-hanging fog in the treetops, sky grey over the mountains. The first snow fell early, at the end of October, which meant we were even more housebound. I still went for my run every morning, but the icy air cut my face and the cold twisted in my bones.

Romanov had let me know that he liked the two stories, but he never mentioned them again. Instead he went on tapping slowly but indefatigably on his typewriter. It felt to me as if he were constantly reminding us of his presence with his interminable tapping.

Once we were making love in my room when we heard the plaintive admonitions of the typewriter. We tried to ignore them, but the clacking didn't stop, and eventually Alva pushed me away. Close to tears, she silently got dressed and went to him.

I can't say whether Romanov was still angry with me. However, one morning he got lost on the road further down the hill and fell over, and when I helped him up he hugged me, which he'd never done before.

These days he always carried around a book by Nabokov. Wherever he was he had it with him; only once he left it on the kitchen table. I was about to take it up to him when I discovered the piece of notepaper stuck between the pages. My name immediately jumped out at me. Beside it, in an almost illegible scrawl, was a brief description of my appearance and the word 'Friend'. Underneath: 'Alva, red hair, glasses, young. My wife', and further descriptions, of his study or bedroom, for example, his date of birth, and a big 'Switzerland, 2006'. But what really made me shudder were the two words he had scribbled along the right-hand edge:

1. Write
2. Cellar

I took the book – *Speak, Memory* – with the note in up to him on the first floor. Romanov took them both without a word. I'd feared I would be speaking to a person of confused mind, but he understood immediately. It was to be the last lucid conversation I ever had with him.

'As I'm sure you've noticed, I am ill,' he said, sitting on the chair in front of his desk. 'My wife thought at first that the prostate operation had changed my life, but it was the general examination beforehand. Alzheimer's, still in the early stages then. I tried to keep it from her to begin with, but she soon realised.'

He lowered his chin. 'I'm not right in the head any more, I can feel it myself. I wanted to come out here, to the countryside, because the city felt as if it was too much for me. Friends and acquaintances came to visit in the beginning, but I want my peace and quiet. Up here there are only a few things I need to remember. Myself, my wife, you, this room, my book. But my mind is disintegrating more and more quickly.'

'Why won't you let us help you? We could have a nurse come in.'

'I talked about it with Alva. I don't want all of that: constant check-ups at the doctor's, the pills and memory exercises. Writing is my therapy.' He turned away. 'And I don't want Alva to have to look after me. I want my wife to be able to be free.'

'So you'd rather go to a clinic?'

'You don't understand.' Romanov paused after every sentence, weighing his words. 'My mother developed dementia very early on; she died in a care home. By the end she was a slobbering creature that was happy if it got to watch a puppet show. My mother was a poet, a sharp-minded intellectual. But she wasn't able to let go, to react in time. I still have a few weeks left of being in command of my own life. I know I'm not that far now from the moment when my brain finally disintegrates and I'm not my own master any more. When that happens I'll no longer be capable of bringing things to a proper end. I'll end up vegetating in a home instead.'

He opened a drawer. 'But there are a few things I need to settle before then. This' – he took out a large envelope – 'is for you. Read it after my death. Not before.'

I took it, hesitantly. 'Why are you telling me all this? Why would you still trust me?'

'Because you owe it to me, Jules.' Romanov took a deep breath, in and out. His hand reached out towards me. 'Lately I've been seeing my childhood again, very clearly. Cold winters, an evening meal in America, conversations with my parents that I'd long forgotten. All these moments are surfacing again; they're haunting me.' He massaged the back of his neck. 'I have to let go; do you understand what that means? To know that your own life will soon be over? That you have to bid farewell to your mind because it's leaving you, never to return?'

He shook his head. 'I can still remember being the same age as you with everything before me; how I was able to defy death. And now here I am, sitting in a burning library, and I can't save a thing.'

His mouth began to tremble.

'Just let me put my affairs in order,' said Romanov quietly. 'I can't let go yet. But I will manage to in time.'

Over the following weeks, whenever Alva wanted to talk about her husband's future, I played down the problem. I wanted to buy him time; I did his laundry, ran errands, and supported the two of them as best I could. Romanov had always been proud of his ability to do pretty much everything himself, but now he even found getting dressed difficult, and often had to let Alva help him.

Every now and then he would make plans that were mired in the past. One evening he talked about visiting his long-dead brother in America. When he saw us glancing at each other, and realised his mistake, he grimaced. 'Unbelievable,' he murmured to himself.

Also new, and alarming, were his fits of rage.

'I don't need you!' he screamed at Alva once, in front of me, and before I could intervene he shook her violently. 'I can do it by myself!'

Alva didn't defend herself. I stepped between them and grabbed hold of him. Romanov tugged at my arms and yelled something in Russian that I didn't understand. It took us a long time to calm him down, but a little while later he seemed not to remember the incident, and reached tenderly for Alva's hand.

Later, as we were all eating lunch together, she announced that she couldn't go on like this. In the conversation that followed she made a few tactful omissions in order to spare me certain details of his disintegration.

'Someone could come and look after you,' she said.

Romanov didn't answer. He hardly spoke any more these days for fear of getting something wrong, and had even stopped reading the newspaper in the mornings. Only when eating was he completely himself, and I watched as he cut off a piece of meat, inhaled its aroma, put it in his mouth and closed his eyes appreciatively as he chewed.

'They can make life easier for you,' Alva began again. 'And for us, too.'

Romanov stared at his plate. 'No nurses,' he said. 'I don't want anyone coming here.'

He took her hand and kissed it, then just stood up and shuffled to his study. In the dining room we could hear him upstairs, hammering slowly and defiantly on his typewriter. These were the blossoms of fear. I'd rifled through the wastepaper basket; it seemed that he was unable to write a single proper sentence any more. They were more a list of names or cryptic notes:

> *Montagsregen . . .*
> *Evenings a player. Leaves if he stays.*
> *Not important in the end*
> *what one wanted*
> *But the question remains*

And with the same stubborn pride that made him keep on sitting at the typewriter, he continued to refuse to let Alva nurse him. Every day was full of rows and accusations, and after he got lost outside yet again and ended up with hypothermia, Alva said the best thing would be if, after Christmas, he were entrusted to the care of the Christian Foundation in Zurich, a private nursing home. She had explained the situation to the director there, who had immediately assured her of a place.

Romanov had shown no emotion after this announcement, but these days I often saw him staring into space, brooding.

And then came the seventeenth of December, the day that would have been my Aunt Helene's birthday. 'Exactly one week before Christmas,' she'd always say, whenever we children had forgotten it again. 'Very easy to remember.'

I'd had a peculiar sense of unease all morning. There was something different about today, but what? Alva was in town. I called my brother and sister. Two months ago I'd invited them to spend the Christmas holidays with us; now I had to cancel.

Liz said she and Toni would celebrate in Munich with our brother. I replied that I'd join them there for a day, if it somehow could be arranged.

'Get out of there,' said my sister, before hanging up.

I went over to the window. Garden and meadow had vanished; before me lay the valley, covered in snow. The chalet was absolutely quiet. And then I knew what was missing. The sound of Romanov's typewriter upstairs.

I ran into the study – empty. When I pushed the cellar door open seconds later, Romanov was standing in front of me with a laundry bag in his hand. Cheeks waxen and pale, chin studded with grey stubble. It seemed to take him a few moments to recognise me. To my relief he called me by my name.

'Jules, you have to help me,' he said amicably, suddenly using the informal *Du* form of address again. He took a folded slip of paper out of his pocket. On it was written just one word: *Cellar.*

'What did I want to do here?'

I thought of Alva, who was doing the shopping in town, after which she had an appointment with the director of the Christian Foundation to discuss the next steps. Meanwhile I was standing here with her husband who wanted to know whether he was planning to do the laundry or kill himself. I remembered his piece of paper where, next to a description of my appearance, he had written the word 'Friend'. My temples throbbed as I went over to his father's favourite weapon and touched the heavy metal barrel.

I put the gun in Romanov's hand.

Years later I would still see this scene before me with the utmost clarity. I sometimes dream about it to this day.

'The Browning,' he said at once.

'Do you remember your father?'

'Of course.'

'Do you remember how he died?'

'He shot himself. Believe it or not, this was the gun. I used to hunt with it a lot. My father was a keen huntsman, too.'

Romanov stared at the gun, lost in thought. Then his expression changed. I saw fear and panic rise up in him. His mouth convulsed and his hands began to shake.

'Oh my God, I know why I'm here,' he whispered.

The realisation shocked him. He stared at me, wide-eyed, and I was aware that this could be the last moment in which he still had control over his actions. After this, all that lay ahead of him was the expanse of madness.

'Am I doing the right thing?' he asked, the gun still in his hand. 'Tell me, Jules? Is it the right thing?'

'Your wife is in town.' My mouth was dry. 'She's meeting the director of a nursing home. She . . .'

Romanov gave me a questioning look.

'You don't want to go into a clinic,' I said. 'Not like your mother. Do you understand?'

I could practically see him desperately searching for these memories.

'No, I don't want that,' he said at last.

I walked up to him. 'Can you let go? Alexander, can you let go?'

Romanov didn't seem to hear me. 'My mother was all wrong at the end,' he said, his voice almost childish. 'She was like an animal. She didn't know anything any more, not who her son was nor who she used to be.' He went over to the cabinet and took out a pack of ammunition. Then he loaded the gun. A cartridge fell to the floor; laboriously he picked it up.

'Should I tell your wife anything? I'll tell her that you love her.'

Romanov didn't answer. He stroked the gun with trembling hands. I could see he was very scared.

'As a little boy I always used to watch the migrating birds,' he said. 'Where are they flying to, I used to think. Where on earth are they flying?'

A voice in my head ordered me to snatch the gun from him and call the emergency services. But I hugged Romanov and left the cellar without a word.

Hastily I went up to my room, fetched my jacket and ran down the slope towards the valley. At one point I slipped and fell in the snow. I scrambled to my feet and ran on. The whole time I was waiting for a shot, but it didn't come. I imagined Romanov standing in the cellar with the gun, alone with the decision: whether to lose his mind or his life. A few more last moments, taking leave of everything a few more times, then using that one second of courage, staying strong and letting go.

I had already reached the road when I heard the report. Several agitated birds fluttered up above the trees, then silence settled over the valley once again.

The Genesis of Fear

(2007–2008)

We'd rented a car for the drive to Italy. Just before we set off we went to take another look at our new living room. Freshly painted walls, floorboards sanded and varnished; we'd finished only a few hours earlier. Alva talked about how we would furnish the apartment when we got back, and I don't know whether it was because I had a home again or because she was six months pregnant, but my eyes suddenly filled with tears of happiness. Embarrassed, I turned away.

We left Munich in the early evening and took it in turns to drive. 'You know what?' Alva drummed her fingers on the steering wheel. 'I think I'm going to go back and study again after all. I've missed university and learning. I'll just be the oldest one there; so what?'

'What will you study? Literature?'

A vehement shake of the head. 'I've spent so much time around authors; I need something of my own now, just for me. I want to do something for my brain.'

Her eyes sparkled behind the lenses of her glasses, and as I gazed at her face – her white, delicate skin, her fine black lashes, the rich red of her hair – I was momentarily overwhelmed by her beauty.

We talked about the trips we'd taken together as youngsters, to far-off lakes and festivals. In my exuberance I said something like, 'Isn't it crazy that we didn't see each other for so many years?'

Alva shrugged. 'When we were at school I thought the two of us as a couple would be complicated. It was only later that I realised I loved you' – she was in the middle of changing lanes and didn't look at me – 'but by then I was already in Russia. I used to think of you a lot back then, but there came a point when I just wanted to forget you.'

'So you missed me?'

'Yes, sometimes,' said Alva. 'On the whole, though, I was glad to be rid of you.'

She smiled. I put my hand on her belly. We still didn't have names for the twins. At first she'd wanted to name our daughter after her sister, but then she'd decided against it – 'What if Phine's still alive?' While looking for names I'd discovered that 'Alva' meant 'forest sprite' in Scandinavia. I liked that. Alva was watching over the forest I hadn't left since childhood.

Ahead of us dozens of lorries, the smell of petrol, the light of innumerable headlamps. We passed the Italian border, looking forward to the hotel on the Amalfi coast where we planned to stay for two weeks. I was paying for the trip out of my savings, although that wasn't strictly necessary. After Romanov's death, Alva had inherited what was to me a shockingly large sum; added to that, the sale of the chalet and the surrounding land had fetched almost another million Swiss francs. Whether I liked it or not, money was no longer an issue.

'Did you manage to speak to the publisher again?'

'Yes,' I said. 'They're putting his book in the spring programme after all.'

'Can you do that?'

'I've almost finished.'

Romanov's last work – *Time, Flying* – would consist of five novellas. Three of them he had already deposited with a notary in Lucerne months before his death to protect them from himself. The first story was about a travelling salesman in Poland in the late 1940s. He'd lost his family in the war and was travelling in winter through a cold, barren country that held nothing but his memories. The next novella, 'Against the Light', was set in America; it was about a married couple in Oregon who were splitting up. The woman was just realising that her husband had been cheating on her for years, and now all her happy memories of him were cracked. The third story was about himself: it told of the forgotten author Aleksandr Nikolai Romanov. It described how he lost his mind and ended up in a home, where he was constantly taking his life apart and reconstituting it wrongly. Its resolute consistency made this my favourite of all his stories, even more than 'An Indomitable Heart'.

The last two novellas were by me.

The envelope Romanov had given me a few weeks before his death had contained thirty pages with scenes, notes, memories and ideas. There was also a letter.

We are both thieves, Jules . . .

it said.

So I'd like to offer you an exchange. A book for a wife. You owe me that.

He wanted to have the two stories I had written in Switzerland, reworked according to his guidelines.

'I still don't understand why you're doing this for Sasha,' said Alva. 'It was just a request, and he wasn't himself any more.'

'He was pretty serious about this request.'

'Even so . . . You're throwing away your future as a writer. Why are you doing that?'

I just shook my head. I couldn't tell her.

Sometimes it had been surprisingly easy, but sometimes also practically impossible to let Romanov's ideas flow into my novellas. Incorporating someone else's scenes into a manuscript was like performing a transplant. Often I'd had to invent whole new plotlines to accommodate the ideas he wanted. After a while, though, I could no longer separate his scenes from my own. His last book would be full of tragedy, too, but Romanov had once said he had never dramatised life, never added anything. It was just that he had never looked away.

Alva sighed. 'And what will you do when you've finished his book?'

'I'll look for a job.'

She waved dismissively. 'You'll look after the children while I'm at university.'

'And what am I supposed to *do*?'

'You're supposed to write your *own* things again. I'll happily spend my money supporting a promising writer. Call it a grant.'

'Very funny.' I pulled in at a petrol station.

Alva moved closer. 'That's always been my dream, Jules. My very own court poet, wholly dependent on me.' She gave me a kiss. 'My *household slave*.'

'You're getting very cheeky nowadays, Crooky Tooth.' I kissed her back, but bit her bottom lip at the same time. 'Be careful all that money doesn't corrupt you.'

'It already has.'

We stocked up on coffee and *tramezzini*, then drove on. The sky was pitch black, the dashboard illuminated, and it was very cosy, sitting here in the car with her. We talked all night, listened to Italian songs on the radio and messed about, and Alva said yet again that I had very small ears, the smallest she had ever seen, and I claimed it was a sign of great intelligence.

'When we get there, the first thing we'll do is have breakfast by the sea.' She burrowed down in her seat, pleasantly tired. A seam of sunlight appeared on the horizon, and we watched silently as the country road gradually materialised in front of us out of the darkness. Alva's fingertips brushed my forearm, up and down, up and down, and perhaps this was the moment when I no longer wanted to exchange my life for another, not even the one in which my parents were still alive.

When Romanov's Swiss publisher brought out his book nine months later, there were several reviews in the feature supplements, some of which also looked at his life's work; sales, however, were disappointing. The name A. N. Romanov was burnished one last time, then it was over.

'At least he isn't here to see it.' Alva gazed bitterly at the little white book in her hand. 'In five years no one will read it any more. It's too dark.'

'I'll read it.'

'When?'

'When things are bad. It'll comfort me.'

Alva went over to the cot. 'Why would things be bad for us?' She gazed at the babies. 'There's a calculation I like to make, even though it's a bit macabre. Life is a zero-sum game. On the debit side I've already got my sister's disappearance, my child-hood, my mother, Sasha's death, and the manner of it above all. So a lot of good things have to happen to us now so that things balance out again.'

'Life is not a zero-sum game. There are people who just have bad luck, who lose everything they love, little by little.'

'And of course you believe you're one of them? My darling Job.' Alva ran her hand through my hair. *Gentle*, I thought.

'Trust me.' She gave me a kiss. 'The next few years are ours.'

I lifted our daughter out of bed. Still an overwhelming feeling to hold one of the babies in my arms. As if the brightest part of me shone not in me any more, but in them. 'Did you hear that?' I whispered in Luise's ear. 'The next few years are ours.'

I was thirty-five now, almost the same age as my parents when they died. About to cross a threshold they were denied. It pained me that the time I'd spent with them was receding further and further into the past, that it was now just part of the long-ago first third of my life. Seeing Alva as a young mother, I often thought of my own mother and regretted knowing so little about her. My memory of her was more a feeling: her warmth, her irrepressible cheerfulness. As a person, though, she remained a stranger to me, and it was only now that I understood why. I had never seen a moment of weakness in her. Never experienced a time when she was down or depressed. She had glided through my childhood like an actress hiding her true self behind the mask of radiant mother, and so all I had were the few stories I knew about her, always the same ones.

'Your father wasn't actually my type at all,' she had told us once. 'But there was just no getting around him. He was the leader of a little clique of students, and every day they'd wait for me outside the university and he'd ask me if I'd go out with him. And every time I said no. *Until tomorrow, then*, he'd say, and he'd grin and bow. I liked it that he was so persistent. And he always pronounced my name wrong.'

With these words she would look across at my father who, as if on cue, would say, 'Magdalena Seitz' with an exaggerated accent.

When I think of her portrayal of him as a dashing young man, I can hardly believe how different my father apparently was compared to his anxious later years. Back then he presumably had the borrowed confidence of almost all people in their early twenties. Or else it was the opposite: the only authentic period in his life, before the events of his youth dragged him into their net.

To shed some light on his past, I trawled through the attic. This was where all the boxes of mementoes from Berdillac, Munich, Hamburg and Berlin were stored. In one of them I found, along with some old family photos, the red notebook of short stories I'd written as a child, as well as the broken Leica and the letter in French.

Dear Stéphane, this camera is for you. It's to remind you of who you are, and of what life must never be allowed to destroy. Please try to understand me.

I put the letter away. What did I actually know about my father? As a young man he had been a keen footballer and had wanted to become a photographer, but had lacked both courage and support. It seemed certain, too, that he and his elder brother, Eric, were beaten by their father, usually when he'd been drinking.

Our Aunt Helene had intimated as much. Everything else I had to piece together from what we had *not* been told. Why had my Uncle Eric died so young? His death was a tragic secret that was never talked about in our family. Now it was too late to ask. My father had deliberately effaced his past, and I could no longer bring it into focus.

I was just putting everything away when one of the old family photos caught my eye. It showed my parents with the Lehners, a couple with whom they used to be very good friends. Hanno Lehner, a good-looking diplomat, who would often talk to us children about his travels in Sudan or Iran. And Elli Lehner, a teacher, like my mother. They seemed to have fallen out at some point, though, because in the years prior to my parents' death they had suddenly stopped coming to visit. In the photo, the four of them were sitting at the dining table in our apartment. My father was watching Elli Lehner gesticulating as she talked. Hanno Lehner was also watching his wife in fascination. My mother was the only one not watching her. And she wasn't looking at my father or into the camera, either. She was looking at *him*. I knew that look all too well. It was the same adoring, hungry gaze my sister turned on men she wanted. And whom she then obtained. But could that be right? Was the photo telling me this story, or was I telling it to myself?

I made myself a coffee and sat down to work on my novel. I was making hardly any progress these days. The almost manic energy I'd experienced during my time at the chalet had vanished, and Romanov's death was still affecting me. Alva had never found out that I had put the gun into her husband's hand, and although I knew that wasn't why I'd done it, I sometimes accused myself of having found an elegant way of eliminating my rival.

I tapped away for a while, and then suddenly my thoughts turned to my father again. To my last encounter with him. Although I'd had a different recollection of it for years, I now trusted the impressions that had come to me during the acid trip.

It was a truth I'd long suppressed that had been stuck inside me like a poisonous thorn, defining me from the darkness of my subconscious.

It's correct that on that last evening I spoke with my father about the camera he'd given me for Christmas, which I hadn't used. It's also correct that we settled this little argument and he offered to show me how to use the Mamiya. He said he'd be very happy if I were to get into photography; he'd often noticed I had a good eye for subject matter.

But that had not been the end of our conversation.

Our relationship at the time was tense, not only because of the camera. My mother was always self-assured and even-tempered; I would never have disobeyed her. But if my father told me to go to bed I would shrug my shoulders, and if he feigned authority and reprimanded me, I just laughed. Because his fear and insecurity showed, and I couldn't stand it.

The weekend my parents drove to France, I was determined to go to a party being thrown by an older boy. He already smoked and drank, and to me it felt like a great honour that he'd invited me. However, my father told me I couldn't stay the night.

'But everyone's going, Papa. I promised I'd be there, too.'

'We've already talked about this boy; he's not the sort of person you should be hanging around with. I'm certainly not letting you stay there unsupervised.'

'But if I don't go they'll think I'm a coward.'

'Well, then that's what they'll think. In any case, you're not going.'

As far as he was concerned the discussion was over. He zipped up his suitcase and started to fill his pipe.

'Yeah, right,' I said. 'I didn't think that would matter to you. *You're* a coward, after all.'

I immediately sensed I'd made a mistake. My father turned to look at me, as shocked as I was, the pipe still in his hand.

'What did you say, Jules?'

'That you're a coward,' I heard myself stammer. I was turning

hot and cold; this was going way too far, and yet I couldn't stop.
'You never dare do anything. You won't let us do anything because
you're afraid of everything. You're a coward and you want us to
be like you.'

The slap hit my left cheek.

Tears sprang to my eyes. 'Piss off,' I yelled. 'You and your
bloody camera.' I glared at him furiously. 'I *hate* you!'

Sudden silence.

I took a step back. I felt as if I was really seeing my father for
the first time. He looked deeply wounded, and his expression
was the same as after the telephone call when he had lost his job.
Part of me instantly felt sorry for him. Then I ran to my room.

Half an hour later my mother came to see me. She was wearing
her beige coat, and she hugged me goodbye. I smelled the lilac
scent of her perfume. 'Don't be like this,' she said. 'Papa didn't
mean it like that.'

'He hit me.'

'I know. And he's so, so sorry. He can't believe he did such a
thing.' She paused. 'At the moment he's got some . . . Things
aren't going too well for him.'

'Is that why you're going away?'

'That's one of the reasons.' She stroked my hair. 'Wouldn't
you like to say goodbye to Papa? He'd so like to say bye-bye to
you; the taxi'll be here any minute.'

'No,' I barked.

My mother kissed me on the cheek, then I heard her saying
goodbye to Liz and Marty in the corridor as well. My father asked
after me.

'You know what he's like,' she said. 'He's stubborn.'

'Damn it . . .' he murmured; he still sounded dejected. Then
he came to my room himself and tried to talk to me, but I silently
rebuffed him. Shortly afterwards the taxi arrived, and I heard the
apartment door close.

I was never able to add anything to the 'I hate you', so it
remained the last thing I said to my father before his death.

Back then, I watched them from the living-room window as they got into the taxi. Stéphane, my father, held the door open for Magdalena, my mother, and then they drove away, and to this day I can see the taxi in my mind's eye, turning the corner in the lamplight and disappearing from view.

That Which Cannot Be Changed

(2012–2014)

April 2012, more than two and a half years before my motorbike accident: Easter in Munich with the family. The copper-coloured roofs on our street glowed in the afternoon sun, and the smell of freshly baked cake hung in the air. Marty kept making faces all through the meal to try and make my son laugh, but it was a hopeless undertaking. At four and a half, Vincent was already a reserved sort of child, and my brother wasn't exactly a born children's entertainer.

After dessert the twins hunted the Easter eggs Elena had hidden around the house. Whenever she was with my children she blossomed, so I liked bringing the two of them to see her and did so frequently. From time to time, though, I would visit her alone, at her practice. I'd started going when I discovered I was going to be a father and wasn't sure I was up to the role. Elena didn't say much during our sessions; instead, she listened as I talked about my silent fear of losing everything all over again. And she saw through me, usually without a word. A single look, sometimes friendly, sometimes admonishing, was enough: I knew what she meant. It became increasingly clear to me what Marty had looked for and found in her. Elena was a corrector: she sensed when you were losing your way, and led you back again with gentle insistence.

Toni hadn't come to Munich. I decided not to ask Liz about him. Back then, whenever Toni picked up a woman after a performance he would tell her everything in minute detail and they'd laugh about it together. Liz would lean against him, take his hand and call him affectionate nicknames. But it never went further than that. Then, when she had a boyfriend again, my sister would tell him nothing about it and withdrew from him almost completely. 'The sadist and the masochist,' my brother once said, jokingly, but of course it wasn't a joke.

Luise came running to her aunt and sat on her lap. As she did every time she came from Berlin to visit us, Liz solemnly announced that she wanted to have children as well. She was now forty-two, and I was no longer counting on her becoming a mother. 'I'd like to have one exactly like this,' she said. 'This one's perfect.' She kissed the top of my daughter's head, and they both grinned.

But even though my sister acted as if she enjoyed family life, she could only ever bear to spend a few days at a time in Munich. I remember how even before, when we used to celebrate Christmas with our aunt, she would always head off to a party just when everything seemed too harmonious and happy, and I thought of the Jack Kerouac quotation she had on the wall above her bed as a teenager:

The only people for me are the mad ones, the ones who are mad to live, mad to talk, mad to be saved, desirous of everything at the same time, the ones who never yawn or say a commonplace thing, but burn, burn, burn like fabulous yellow roman candles exploding like spiders across the stars.

Laughter from the living room. Alva and the children cuddled up together on the couch. She had read aloud to them, and now they were messing about. I could never get enough of seeing Alva as a mother. She always found the right tone; unlike me, she knew exactly when to be strict and when playful, and seemed to want to give them everything she had been denied. The children worshipped her.

I went over to the record player. 'Listen up,' I said, and for a moment I had the same sense of anticipation as when I was a boy and wanted to show something to my siblings. I put on an album. Noisy guitars, vocal harmonies. All eyes on me.

'Papa, what's this?'

'This is the Beatles,' I said. '"Paperback Writer".'

Luise seemed to find the music funny. Vincent, on the other hand, was tapping his foot in absolute astonishment, eyebrows raised, and when the song finished he immediately said, 'Again.'

That night our children stayed over with Marty and Elena so we could go out, just the two of us again for once.

'We're watching a film, then I'll send them to bed,' Elena said on the phone that evening. And, for the third time, 'We're taking good care of them.'

'Yes, yes, I know you are,' I said, almost laughing.

When I'd hung up I sensed Alva's eyes on me. 'What is it?'

'You look so contented. You're really grinning.'

'I don't grin.'

'Yes you do, you're still doing it now.'

I took her hand and pulled her flamboyantly towards me. 'Alone with you again at last' – my arms on her shoulders – 'how about we leave the children with my brother and run away together?'

'And I thought you'd never ask.'

Later, in the restaurant, Alva talked about a lecture Marty had recommended to her. They'd become good friends over the past few years; I'd often come home and find them in the middle of an intense conversation. Sometimes I would join them, but I actually liked it that the two of them got on so well, independently of me. 'Have you noticed how similar she and Liz are in many ways?' Marty asked me once, after one such meeting. At first I just laughed incredulously, but later on I often thought about this remark.

Alva had finished her philosophy degree some time ago; now she was working on her PhD and making improvements to our shabby inner courtyard at the same time. At her suggestion, the property management had laid a new lawn; now it was putting up a swing and a treehouse for the children (and also, a bit, for me).

But something still vibrated darkly inside her. From time to time the past seemed to clutch at her; scenes from her youth and from her years in Moscow, which I could not conceive of, would overtake her. Then she would sometimes have nightmares, and was nervous and restless in her sleep before cuddling up to me and growing calmer. I'd had to learn early on that there were two Alvas, and I couldn't have one without the other. Since the birth of the twins she'd stopped going for walks at night, but part of me was still worried that she might disappear again one day and would not be able to come back to me.

'By the way, I had a look at the children's book by that Swedish author.' Her head popped up from behind the menu. 'Magnus whatsit. Liked it a lot.'

I'd long since got used to her sneaking a look at the manuscripts I was editing. Nonetheless, I pretended to be outraged.

'What?' was all she said. 'As long as I'm not getting anything of yours to read, I'll read that instead.'

I'd got the editing job through Romanov's publishing house. They liked the work I did on his manuscript, and recommended me, at my request, to a publisher in Munich. Work on my own novel, however, was sporadic. I'd probably have abandoned it long ago if Alva hadn't kept asking me about it.

That evening we drank a bit too much, and Alva talked about the time before we met, and how as a child she'd loved going skating with her father on a frozen pond behind their house. As she spoke of it, it was as if she were suffused with an inner light. I leaned over the table and kissed her, then I poured us some more wine, and she asked if I were trying to get her drunk, and I said that had always been my intention.

She really was swaying a bit on the way home. I was going to support her until I realised that I wasn't steady on my feet any more, either. We started giggling and, leaning on each other, we trudged towards the underground.

In the night I was woken by a sound. I'd been having a very intense dream, and it took a while for me to return to my body. Alva was crying beside me. Shocked, I turned on the light.

'Why aren't I happy?'

She was speaking indistinctly and too fast. 'I love you, I love Vincent and Luise. I love all that we have. But sometimes it's as if it's not enough, as if nothing will ever be enough. Then all I want to do is go away and never come back, and I don't know why.'

Her remarks sank into me like a stone dropped in a lake.

I put my arms around her. 'It's okay,' I kept saying. Gently, I kissed her head. 'I love you the way you are.'

'I never wanted to be this way,' she said quietly. 'I can't do anything about it.'

'I know.'

I held her tightly for several minutes, talking to her, trying to comfort her. As Alva couldn't get back to sleep, we watched films until the room grew pale with the bluish light of dawn. And of course all this had nothing to do with what happened later, but after that night I came to appreciate the light-hearted moments just a little more than before.

A few hours before the flight, I was playing with the children in the courtyard. Luise insisted on being Peter Pan; Vincent took on various supporting roles. The recently completed treehouse was the pirates' bay, defended by me, a cunning Captain Hook. Romanov's mahogany walking stick served as my sabre; my children, meanwhile, attacked with branches, and naturally vanquished me in a bitter battle at the end of which I died an agonising death.

'He's dead, he's dead.' They ran around me, laughing and poking their sticks in my belly.

My brother appeared in the courtyard with a bag over his shoulder. He saw me rolling around on the ground and grinned. 'We have to go.'

A short trip to Berlin; we wanted to surprise Toni for his birthday. He was celebrating in a pub, and seemed really happy that we'd come to visit, but I was shocked by the state he was in.

Nothing of his former, attractive aura remained; he had aged, and seemed unhappy. That evening, as ever, his attention was focussed on Liz, who chatted affectionately with him to begin with, then later on was sitting at the bar with some man I didn't know. I could see Toni constantly glancing over at her, and even his artificial cheerfulness gradually dimmed, until he was just standing silently in the corner. Marty and I went to join him but we couldn't cheer him up, and he went home alone shortly afterwards.

That night we sat up for a long time in our sister's kitchen. She seemed to sense what we were thinking.

'I've had enough of this,' Liz said finally. 'It's not as if I enjoy seeing him so depressed.'

'That's not the point,' said Marty. 'It's that you've been torturing him for years. Toni could have had a family of his own by now; he could have been happy, but you don't want to let him go. You never quite close the door, you always leave it open just a tiny crack so you can be sure he'll keep on running after you. Because basically you couldn't stand it if he were suddenly gone.'

'And what am I supposed to do? Go out with him just because it'd be the *right thing?*'

'Why not? I don't think that's such a bad idea.'

'You're mad.' Liz stared at him in disbelief, then looked at me. 'What about you? Is that how you see it, too?'

'Well, you're certainly part of the reason why he's not in a relationship now, or married, and lives alone instead.' Liz was about to reply, but I held up my hand. 'Even if he were, though, he wouldn't be happy. Just as it seems you simply can't feel anything for him, he can't help loving you. It's his decision; he doesn't want anything else, which is why there's nothing to regret.'

Liz chewed her fingernails. 'I can't choose what I feel,' she said quietly. 'Even if he were Mr Right, I don't love him.'

'But love is just a word,' said Marty. 'What matters is being content.'

Liz laughed. 'That's such feeble nonsense, Marty. Sorry, but fuck contentment. I want excitement, tension, a challenge. Toni's great, and – honestly – I can even imagine that he's the man I'll grow old with. But just as a friend. He's someone you can love, but not someone I could fall in love with. I want someone who pushes me away sometimes, someone who treats me badly, whom I can fight for.'

'But why? Who can want something like that?'

She shrugged. 'There are women for whom it's not enough just to have comfort and security.'

Marty walked right up to her. 'Oh, like my wife, for example. I get it – of course, that's a perfect example. She sees me, thinks to herself, hmm, he's got potential, and then latches on to me for twenty years. Because maybe I'm a bit boring and not the greatest catch in the world, but I'm nice and I'm well-off. And maybe she hoped for something else when she was a teenager, but it'll do for marriage. And how nice that her husband thinks the same and everyone's settled for good old mediocrity. Something like that?'

There was an embarrassed pause, because that was indeed what we'd sometimes thought about his relationship.

My brother seemed to realise this. He quickly packed his bag and headed for the door. 'The way you always think about things, I don't see them turning out well for you,' he said to our sister. 'Because at this rate you're going to spend your whole life being unhappy.'

He disappeared down the stairs.

'At least it'll be my own life, then,' said Liz, but he was already out of earshot.

Alva usually went to the city library to write her dissertation, but one evening in late autumn she was working from home. A light was on low in the study: I stood in the doorway and watched her. Suddenly that line appeared between her eyebrows; she stared blankly into the distance and chewed her finger, lost in thought. I loved it when she had that air of industrious concentration. For a long time now I'd been able to tell from the set of her shoulders if she was tense; but the way she'd left the door ajar indicated that she wanted company. There was a familiarity between us that seemed infinite, like two mirrors reflecting one another.

I cut a banana into two halves, took my laptop and sat down at the desk opposite her. We ate the banana and typed without speaking; from time to time we exchanged brief glances. At moments like these, with Luise and Vincent asleep next door, I felt more secure than at any time since my childhood.

I remembered the fearless, confident boy I used to be back then. However, when my parents died he hadn't been strong enough, and had given way to another side of my personality. I didn't miss him. I only, sometimes, missed the high spirits that often used to seize me when I was ten. Would there ever be an event in my life that would catapult me back into that ecstatic, silly light-heartedness, even if only for a moment?

'I keep thinking about something.'

'Fire away.'

I snapped the laptop shut. 'I was wondering what would have happened if I'd gone to France and lived there. If I'd had an accident. If we'd never seen each other. There've been so many other paths in my life, so many possibilities of being someone else.' A glance at Alva. 'I mean, have you never wondered what would have become of you if your sister hadn't disappeared? I'm sure you'd be different now.'

She considered. 'Yes, for sure.'

'The question is, what *wouldn't* be different? What would be the immutable part of you? The bit that would stay the same in every life, no matter what course it took. Are there elements in us that survive everything?'

'And?'

I thought of Liz, who had always been skittish and solitary, even when our parents were still alive. Her fascination with boys seemed to be an integral part of her, too, as was her susceptibility to addiction, and the fact that she liked to sing and draw little stories. It made no difference that she'd stopped doing that and had lost her way for years. The catalyst was irrelevant: finding an inspirational children's book in a shop one day or dropping acid with her siblings, there would always have been a moment in her life that would have reawakened her desire to draw or make music. And Marty may not have become a doctor or researcher, but the immutable element in him seemed to be that rare fuel that allowed him to achieve every goal. He would probably have become a professor in other scientific fields, like biology or physics.

'I don't know . . .' I looked at Alva. 'What about you? What do you think?'

'Hmm . . . Kierkegaard says *the self must be broken in order to become itself.*'

'Which means?'

She frowned. 'Well, we come into the world and we're influenced by our environment, our parents, strokes of fate, education and random experiences. Then at some point we say, "I am such-and-such", as if it's something that can be taken for granted, but we just mean the surface, the primary self.' She sat down on my desk. 'To find your true self you need to question everything you encountered at birth. And lose some of it, too, because often it's only in pain that we discover what really belongs to us . . . It's in the breaches that we recognize ourselves.'

Her feet dangled in mid-air. 'On the other hand, I've no idea what would have happened if my life had been different, or easier. I'm not sure we'd have got together, for example. I'd probably have looked for a carefree, go-getting sort of man instead, someone less reflective. But as things were, you were the right person. You and only you.'

'That's honest, but it does hurt a little.'

She gave me a tender kiss on the temple.

'And why was I the right person?' I asked.

'Because you understand everything.'

Brief consideration. 'What else? My good looks, my not inconsiderable intelligence . . . my modesty?'

'Perhaps your modesty as well.' She examined my mop of hair. 'Still not a single grey one. How do you do it?'

Instead of answering, I stretched out my hand and touched her cheek. She closed her eyes.

I thought about our wedding a few years earlier. The little party in my brother's garden, decorated with Chinese lanterns, and the speech her father had given. He and Alva had their own particular way of dealing with each other. Although they had a very affectionate and close relationship, they saw each other only rarely. They wrote often, though, and back then her father had also insisted on paying for the wedding.

'Do you still think a lot about Phine?'

She nodded. 'I don't think that'll ever stop.'

Alva took off her glasses with a sigh and polished the lenses. She was pale. For a few weeks now she'd seemed tired, and had often had a fever.

I prescribed her a break and fetched a bottle of wine from the kitchen. She put on George Gershwin. I couldn't get into his music, but Alva loved *her* Gershwin – she always called him 'my George'. Old age used to scare me, but now there was something reassuring in the thought of still living with her in forty years' time. We'd sit together, read, talk or play chess; sometimes we'd tease each other, then we'd look back again on the treasury of memories we'd amassed together. I wondered what her face would look like with wrinkles, and how she would dress in her late seventies. In that moment I realised that none of this would matter to me, and the thought of growing old no longer held any fear.

Later, I went into our children's room. They were both asleep, and I stood listening to their quiet breathing. I sat on Luise's bed first. A lively, cheerful girl, almost too confident. She already knew her own worth, knew that we all thought she was sweet and so forgave her a lot. She still liked to cuddle with me, but she saw through me now. Instinctively, she rebelled only with me but obeyed her mother. I gave her a kiss on the forehead and went over to Vincent's bed. He had kicked off the blanket in his sleep again. He was more of a daydreamer than Luise, and frightened of all that was unfamiliar. Often he would keep me company when I was editing in the study; he liked the peace and quiet, and would play on the floor with a lorry or repeat to me the stories Alva had read to him. Even as a baby he'd been this quiet; but why? When had that been decided?

I covered him with the blanket, then I fetched a beer from the kitchen and went out onto the balcony. A breath of cool wind brushed my skin; the smell of damp leaves drifted up from the courtyard. I took a few swigs, felt the tranquillity of the night flowing towards me, and was suddenly overwhelmed by a sense of wistful, almost pleasurable melancholy.

In January 2013 I flew to Berlin for a few days to work with one of our authors on his manuscript. I met Liz one evening for a meal as well, and to my surprise she brought Toni along with her. He was in a good mood, talking about a magic show in Edinburgh where he'd performed as a guest act, and generally made a much better impression than last time. He and Liz weren't together, but she seemed to be treating him more seriously and not torturing him any more with her affairs.

Darkness was falling as my plane flew in over Munich, the scenery fading into a twilight peopled with shadows. The sight triggered a vague sense of unease in me, but it dissipated as soon as we landed. On the train I checked my mobile. Alva had called several times without leaving a message. I called back, but she didn't answer.

Nearly home, I wrote. *What's up?*

On entering the flat I saw that the children were quarrelling. Luise had taken a soft-toy giraffe from Vincent and wanted to marry it to one of her toy animals, but he didn't approve. They were squabbling over the giraffe, and I had to intervene.

'Give it back to him,' I said, in my strict father disguise; but Luise just ran away, and when I shouted at her to come back she laughed so cheekily that I almost started laughing myself.

Finally Vincent got the toy back, by which time my daughter had lost interest. She took a hairbrush from the bathroom and started singing loudly to herself.

Vincent tapped his forehead. 'She's so stupid.'

I told them both to get ready as we were going to dinner soon with their uncle and aunt; the evening had been planned ages ago.

'But Mama cancelled dinner,' said Vincent.

'Why?'

He shrugged. It was only then that I noticed Alva wasn't home. I looked in the bedroom for a note, or some indication of where she'd gone, but didn't find anything. When I called her again I discovered she'd left her mobile on the bedside table.

'Mama wanted to pop out,' said Luise, behind me.

I wheeled round. 'When?'

'Just before you came.'

'Did she say where, or when she'd be back?'

Luise shook her head. 'No, she just said you'd be back soon and you should go ahead and make dinner.'

I started to get nervous. It wasn't like Alva to leave the children alone, even if only for a few minutes. I persuaded myself that I was worrying for no reason; she'd probably just gone to the library for a bit, or was copying something for her dissertation. I cooked for the children, played Snakes and Ladders with them and put them to bed. It was only when I was alone again in the living room and the silence in the apartment began to grow oppressive that the sense of unease returned. The library would be closed by now. I called Marty and Elena, but they didn't know anything. For a moment I considered calling the police, but I decided to wait.

I stared at the phone, drank two bottles of beer, stared at the phone, walked round the block, stared at the phone, sat for a long time in the icy cold on the little steps outside our front door, watching for Alva. Two o'clock, three o'clock, four o'clock came and went. I made a strong coffee and tried to distract myself. Zapped through the TV channels at random and started reading

Un amour de Swann, my mother's favourite book. But I was so
tired I couldn't keep my eyes open.

Just as I was about to lie down for a moment I heard the key
in the lock. Pure relief. I hurried to the door. Alva was back, but
her eyes were dark and stained with tears. She seemed altered,
like a creature of the night that had only just resumed its human
form.

'Where were you?'

She hung her jacket over the chair without speaking.

'For God's sake, tell me, where were you?'

'I needed to be alone for a while.'

I could have done with a decent apology. Or a logical explanation for her disappearance. Something to placate me – not this.

'Did you go for a walk? Are you going to start all that again?'
I was right up in her face; I realised I'd lost control. 'You have
children, for crying out loud. How can you just run off and
frighten us like that?'

She stared at me. Her eyes were still shimmering and dark, but
my angry words had intimidated her.

'I was suddenly scared witless that you were never coming
back.' I was shaking with emotion. 'You know you can talk to
me about anything. I mean, can you imagine what we—'

'I've got cancer.'

A second passed, then I reeled back as if struck by an invisible
hand. Those three simple words unleashed a force so archaic that
I was instantly struck dumb; it robbed me of all feeling, and for
a moment I didn't know what to say or do.

'I tried to reach you,' said Alva, in the silence. 'Several times.
At some point I just had to get out. Sorry. I shouldn't have done
that.'

A paralysing, tingling sensation was spreading throughout my
body, from my chest down my arms and legs; for a moment it
felt as if I were floating away.

'What kind of cancer?' I said eventually. It sounded as if
someone had turned my voice down to minimum volume.

'Leukaemia.'

'Is it definite? How do you know?'

'I went to the doctor last week, when you were in Berlin. I had a fever again, but I'd been feeling ill before that as well. They did a series of tests, but I didn't tell you because I didn't want to worry you. Then today I got the final results.'

I realised I'd sat down. When I felt Alva's hand on the back of my neck I unconsciously flinched, and she withdrew it again.

'Look at me,' she said.

Dumbly, I gazed up at her.

'I'm going to survive this, Jules. I know it.' She seemed surprisingly calm. 'I'm going to survive it.'

I looked her in the eyes and believed every word.

Alva's prognosis was not that good, but she'd been given a real chance of defeating the cancer in her blood. She immediately started chemotherapy and had to spend weeks in hospital for the initial treatment. The medication was given intravenously. *Cytostatics*: another word for hope. Another word for poison.

A new, hyper-real reality, scarcely endurable with a lucid mind. I was like someone in a fog, a mute ghost sitting beside her hospital bed, watching over her. But even when her hair fell out Alva didn't let it get her down. She endured the painful injections and the interminable nausea; sometimes she even made jokes about it. She told the children it was nothing too bad and she would soon be better. I tried to do the same. Optimism, optimism. Only once did I let slip that yet again Fate was against us, but Alva immediately interrupted me.

'I don't want to hear that sort of thing,' she said firmly. Then, more amiably, 'You can moan and groan when I'm well again.'

I nodded. We were standing in the bedroom at home; it was the first time she'd been allowed to leave the hospital for a few days. A song was playing on the radio. I must still have looked despondent, because she took my hand and did a few dance steps.

This came as a surprise: in all the time I'd known her I'd never seen her dance, apart from a few tentative steps at our wedding.

We moved to the music, closely entwined, and slowly, as Alva was still weak. She had closed her eyes. At that moment it seemed incomprehensible to me that the life of this person, so close and familiar, this person whose breath, warmth, trauma I could feel, was in danger.

'Where are you right now?' I asked.

'I'm here' – eyes still shut – 'I'm dancing with you and trying not to think of anything else.'

'Isn't it strange that we've never danced?'

'I'm not that keen on it, as you may have gathered.'

The walls of the bedroom receded and dissolved, our skin smoothed, we were back at boarding school. We were nineteen and had fled to my room to escape the rain; we were getting drunk on gin, and I . . .

'Do you remember me asking you to dance once?'

'You've never done that.'

'Yes I did; I even put on a song my mother said would help me win any woman, but you didn't want to dance with me. And so of course I thought you didn't want me.'

Alva grimaced. 'It was *her* thing, you understand? Not mine. She was the more talented one; she had ballet lessons almost every day, from when she was little, and when she disappeared I wanted nothing to do with dancing any more. It reminded me too much of her.'

I felt as if an icy wind had blown through me. 'If only I'd known,' I said, more to myself than to Alva.

For a while we moved to the music without speaking. I inhaled the familiar scent of her perfume: sandalwood and gardenia.

'Tell me something nice about your sister,' I said. 'Whenever I think about her, the only thing that comes to mind is that all they found was her jacket. Tell me something, so I get a different picture of her.'

Alva thought for a minute. 'Phine was very lively, almost

fidgety,' she said. 'And she loved opera. She was already listening to Mozart a lot as a child. Once we went to a performance of *The Magic Flute*, and she was so excited that she hyperventilated during the show and had to be taken out by the theatre doctor.' She laughed. 'We were often very boisterous when we played together. We had a set ritual before going to sleep. After our mother had said goodnight to us, Phine and I would always do two somersaults on our beds. One forwards and one back; it was only after that that our mother would turn off the light.' She shook her head, but I could see she liked this image salvaged from the ruins.

At the time I was doing what I could for Alva: I cared for her, tried to fulfil her every wish, hardly left her side, and still felt useless. It helped a little that my brother was with us almost every day; Elena also came straight from her practice to our apartment every evening. In her gentle way, she made sure that we all stayed calm.

The first, aggressive phase of treatment finished, and the months of consolidation therapy began. Alva could now come home for a few weeks at a time to recover between each cycle of chemo. Sometimes she was so tired she would sleep until evening; on good days she was often out in the courtyard, which had nearly transformed into a garden. I liked to watch her from the balcony, kneeling down there on the ground, turning over the earth or planting something. Best of all, though, I liked the moment when she finished her work and stopped to survey it. Usually she would wipe her forehead one more time, or rub her hands, but above all she seemed so *content*.

When summer came we still hadn't been given a clear prognosis. By now we were thinking only in blast and leukocyte counts, and to distract ourselves we went to Berdillac. Alva was really looking forward to the trip; the first thing she wanted to do was go to the seaside.

'Get yourselves ready,' she called out merrily to the children before going upstairs to fetch her things.

I got Vincent and Luise into the car and buckled them up, then went back into the house. As I passed the bathroom, I saw Alva's face in the mirror. I'd never seen this expression. Not even the first time she told me about her sister. Her mouth was contorted, tears pouring down her cheeks. What I was seeing in her face was pure terror.

When she noticed me she wiped her eyes. 'I just had this feeling that I'm not going to make it.' She took off her wig. 'What if soon I'm not here any more? I simply can't imagine it.'

She looked at her bald head in the mirror.

'That is not me, Jules. THAT IS SIMPLY NOT ME!' she shouted suddenly, and I flinched.

Then she sank down onto the tiled bathroom floor. 'They're only six,' she said quietly. 'They're far too young.'

The children started school in September. I felt as I did when Alva was about to enter puberty and I'd understood that from then on I had to share her with the world. She, on the other hand, just felt uncomfortable about taking the children. 'I look godawful in this wig,' she said. 'They're all going to stare at me.'

'Rubbish, you look great.'

She sighed. 'Jules, you were never a good liar, but you've just surpassed yourself.'

Nonetheless, she did come with us on the first day of school.

Luise was hugely looking forward to everything, but Vincent was sceptical. 'Can't I keep going to kindergarten for another year?' he asked me.

'Don't you want to learn things?'

'Yes. But it was so nice there.'

'School will be nice, too.'

Those big, incredulous eyes again.

'Well, I think it's great,' said Luise.

'Well, I think it's great,' Vincent mimicked her.

Although they were twins, they didn't have much in common.

Luise was still livelier, wilder, almost rebellious. With an enthusiasm that reminded me of the young Liz, she couldn't wait to show the other children in the class that she already knew how to read and write. Vincent could read a few words, too, but his confidence was very fragile. His mother's illness had made him even more mistrustful and solitary. These days he seldom told me what was on his mind, and he was becoming increasingly withdrawn. Football was the only thing that brought him out of himself. Sometimes I would play with him and Luise in the courtyard, and it made me think of my father and how he used to play in the Englischer Garten, a sweeper dribbling forwards with elegance and panache. I imagined what he would have been like playing with my children, presumably as a wrinkled seventy-year-old, and it was one of those moments when I really missed him.

In the mornings Alva and I had time to ourselves for the first time in years. At first we hardly knew what to do with it, but soon we were enjoying long breakfasts on the balcony discussing newspaper articles and listening to music. Afterwards I would grab a couple of manuscripts and edit them in the bedroom to keep her company. If she was feeling weak Alva would lie in bed, but sometimes she would take a book and sit on the chest of drawers with her back against the wall. Her favourite spot. She was still a strangely catlike creature who eschewed chairs and sofas and preferred to sit in alcoves or on worktops and tables.

If she was feeling better we'd go for long walks, too. 'I miss university,' she said once, in her quiet voice. She touched my arm. 'I think it's a shame I was never able to share that with you. That feeling of taking your mind seriously, of learning, it's so . . .'

She made a sweeping gesture, because she couldn't think of a suitable word. 'Jules, next year, when I'm feeling better, I'd like you to take a course with me. I know I'm blackmailing you a bit, but this illness has got to be good for something.'

Autumn had spread a carpet of leaves over the Englischer

Garten. A swan clambered out of the lake and waddled awkwardly towards us.

Alva nudged me. 'What would you wish for in the coming year? If you could do anything at all, what would it be?'

'Ride a motorbike,' I answered, without thinking.

'Really?'

'I've wanted to ever since I was a child. I always envied Toni whenever he went for a ride and said afterwards that it was a bit like flying. I'm sure it was a massive exaggeration, but I'd like to find out for myself.'

'Then why don't you?'

'Well . . . something could happen.'

'Millions of people ride motorbikes and nothing happens.'

'Luck.'

'Maybe,' she said. 'But why shouldn't you be lucky?'

Later, as we were standing in the kitchen preparing lunch, Alva's phone vibrated. After a brief hesitation, she answered it. We exchanged looks.

'The hospital,' she whispered.

My pulse immediately started racing. I put down the wooden spoon and paced nervously about the room, watching Alva's face, searching for possible signs of good or bad news. Why was it taking so long? She briefly narrowed her eyes, which instantly plunged me into deepest despair, but then she was listening intently again.

All of a sudden a hot, almost electrifying feeling shot through me. At first I didn't understand why. Then I realised that Alva was smiling. She kept nodding, with a huge grin on her face. 'Yes, of course,' she was saying. She grabbed my shirt hard and pulled me towards her, wanted me to listen in, but the call was already over. Then everything happened very fast: she put down the phone, we were in each other's arms, I heard myself yelling something I barely understood myself, then squeezed her to me again. I could feel her whole body shaking.

The consultant had told her that the cancer had completely disappeared. He advised her to dispense with the stresses and risks of a bone-marrow transplant and start maintenance therapy right away instead.

I wanted to hear this over and over again, in different words, and then again and again. I called Marty and Elena, then Liz; and Toni, who was on the subway and could barely understand anything, and that was best of all, because then I was able to bellow it: 'I said, Alva's beaten the cancer!'

The real pleasure, though, was not that initial, bubbling joy, but the dull, deep relief that followed. In the afternoon we went to the park with the children and played football. We kicked around there together until evening, sat on the swings in the playground dangling our legs in the air, ate chips from a snack van and chatted, all with that light in our eyes. None of us wanted to go home and end this magical moment too early.

Lying in bed that night, neither Alva nor I could sleep. Euphoria still burned in us, and we were wide awake. At her request I went and got her favourite ice cream from a nearby petrol station, vanilla with biscuit pieces. I started walking back normally, then speeded up before finally running the last few metres to our front door, bag in hand, laughing.

As we ate the ice cream, we made plans for the future. The past few months we'd never thought any further than the next call from the hospital; now the horizon was widening before us and we talked of secret wishes, possible trips, or what we wanted to do with Vincent and Luise when they were older.

'Admit it' – I stroked the two delicate scars on her neck – 'you knew all along that it would be all right in the end.'

'Of course. After all, it's a—'

'Zero-sum game, I know.'

'Besides, I couldn't have left you alone with the children. It wouldn't have been so bad for me, but the poor children.'

We talked about what would have happened if I'd had to bring up the twins on my own, and pictured the worst. Luise a strung-out punk with a Mohican, playing bass in a horrendous band and getting kicked out of school. And Vincent a lonely esoteric, joining a dubious sect and disappearing forever into the Canadian wilderness with his new friends.

'A sect? Would I really be that bad a father?'

'Well, maybe not quite that bad.'

'It's just that they never listen to me, only to you. How do you do it?'

She shrugged.

'Strong in the egg,' I said quietly.

When Alva fell asleep I stayed awake, looking at her. It was raining outside; the drops hammered against the window, but she looked peaceful: sleep seemed to have erased all the dark thoughts. She rolled towards me; her arm lay on my chest. I held it tight. Waves of tiredness overwhelmed me, but I kept gazing at her until I found myself in a dream in which I was roaming with my brother's dog through an endless forest.

By the time winter arrived Alva's hair had already grown back quite well. We spent Christmas at my brother's house, which had plenty of space for such occasions. A modern building, surrounded by thick hedges and standing alone on a big plot of land. The ideal home for a film baddie, with countless superfluous rooms, a huge garden, and technical gadgets like an Internet-connected fridge and a retractable video screen.

'Marty is the emperor of the futile,' my sister had once said.

Everyone had come; Alva's father, too – a small, wiry, rather eccentric man with a Roman nose and a melancholy set to his mouth that didn't quite go with his otherwise cheerful manner. His gaze was steady, his skin weather-beaten from his many climbing trips in the Alps. First he hugged Alva for a long time, then he picked up our children. He asked them lots of questions and neither of them left his side all night.

We all sang songs together. Liz played the guitar, but refused, as always, to sing 'Moon River'.

'I'm not singing that stupid song again until I have children of my own.'

'Huh, so never,' said Marty.

She gave him a reproachful look.

Afterwards the children were allowed to open their presents – books and Lego from us parents, clothes from Elena, video games from Toni and Marty and watercolours from Liz – while we sat at the big table in the living room and watched them. We had a difficult year behind us, so it was all the nicer to sit here now together and be able to look back on it as if on a bad dream.

My brother was standing with Toni in front of the stereo, arguing about who got to choose. He came back to the table, shaking his head. 'As of today it's definitively clear that Toni hasn't got a clue about music.'

'Don't believe a word he says,' called Toni. 'He listened to black metal for years at school; I'm scarred for life.'

As always when the two of them saw each other again, their initial excitement meant they kept making fun of each other, before sitting down in brotherly companionship and chatting for hours.

Liz, on the other hand, was very reserved all evening. The first wrinkles had incised themselves on her previously flawless face. It wasn't noticeable when she smiled, but when she didn't she looked pinched. She didn't take drugs any more, but I knew she still drank too much; a glass of red was as much a characteristic of hers as the blonde hair. My sister was now forty-four, and seemed to have nothing to set against the ageing process. She had always just enjoyed the moment, had relinquished everything in her life in order to be free, and now her hands were almost empty.

When I asked her about her work, she made a face. 'I keep getting older, and they always stay seventeen. They'll always have their whole lives in front of them, whereas mine is increasingly behind me.'

We were sitting on our own in the kitchen; it was already late. Liz was telling me that she had just split up with her boyfriend, a journalist. It hadn't worked out, again. She ran her fingers along the notched edge of the table, and suddenly all the confidence drained from her face. Her mouth twitched; she tried to disguise it, but the twitch returned. Eventually she came and stood behind me and wrapped her arms around me as she used to when she was a child. I held her tight, and thought of a boat that had been pushed away from the bank, very gently, a long time ago. In all those years there'd never been anything to check that first, tiny impetus, so the boat went on drifting out to sea, alone . . .

'I don't know,' I said. 'Perhaps once in your life you should hold on to something until the end, instead of always moving on.'

'I knew you'd say that.' She let go of me. 'But there's no point in living like that. Everything's over so quickly and you can't hold on to anything. All you can do is *be*.'

She gave me that look again, *her* look; and this time I withstood it, because now I knew what she meant.

In the new year I enrolled Vincent in a football team. He reacted with panic, while Luise thought it was unfair because she wanted to be on the team as well. But it was important to me that Vincent should have something that was his and his alone, where his universally talented sister couldn't outdo him. I also wanted my son to learn to play in a team and not end up, later, on the lonely hundred-metre track, vying against himself and against time.

Little by little the dark moments of the previous year seeped out of us. I saw Alva sitting at her laptop in the study again every day now, writing her PhD. She was still threatening to look for courses we could attend together the following term. 'Unless you *finally* give me some of your novel to read.'

'I'm not ready yet. But you will get to read it, I promise.'

'Sasha always said that, too, and in the end he didn't give me anything any more.'

Our children had now grown accustomed to school. During the day they had their own lives, which I heard about but never saw. Once, though, while we were eating, Vincent said a teacher had been talking to them about 'Muhma Dali'. When I asked him about this, he said he'd been a boxer.

'You mean Muhammad Ali,' I cried. 'He was the best boxer of all time.'

Vincent looked at me with an expression along the lines of 'If you say so . . .' My daughter also made no attempt to disguise her lack of interest.

'Ali was magnificent. He always had an incredibly big mouth. Watch this.' I rose from my chair and bellowed, wide-eyed: 'I am the greatest! I done tussled with a whale. Just last week I murdered a rock, injured a stone, hospitalised a brick. I'm so mean I make medicine sick. Float like a butterfly, sting like a bee.'

I bobbed and weaved around the dining room. The children watched their father's unexpected outburst with amazement.

'And Ali always insulted his opponents. Like this.' I walked provocatively up to Luise. 'You're so ugly that when you cry your tears turn around and go down the back of your head.' She laughed. I punched the air foolishly a couple of times and went up to Vincent. 'And I bet you scare yourself to death just staring in the mirror. You ugly bear!'

Then I tried out the Ali shuffle and bobbed quickly on the spot, but I wasn't so good at it any more. Soon I was panting, but I didn't stop. The children roared with laughter, and when Alva just shook her head in amazement I bobbed about in front of her until she, too, had to laugh.

At the end of February I picked Marty up from the university to go for lunch. As he came out of his institute he was discussing something with a group of students, some of whom were only half his age. What good taste my brother had now, quite unlike his youth! He was wearing an elegant grey suit with a blue shirt, light-brown Budapester shoes, and a peaked cap, probably to conceal his hair loss. He listened to music by Springsteen, Talking Heads and Van Zandt, wore almost invisible glasses, and looked like someone you could rely on absolutely.

'What were you discussing with the students?'

Marty pushed open the restaurant door. 'Oh, one of them asked at the end of class whether there was such a thing as free will.'

'And?'

'There has to be, of course. But the question is actually less important than the attitude towards it. Because even if brain research could prove that we never consciously have a choice, I wouldn't accept it.' He smiled. 'If free will were just an illusion, it would still be all I have.'

I was just about to answer when my phone rang. Alva.

'Come home quickly, please,' she said.

I felt a powerful tug in my chest. For some reason I immediately thought of Vincent. If something had happened, it must be to him.

'Is something wrong with the children?' I asked when I arrived at the apartment. 'Is Vincent hurt?'

'No.'

Relief. I walked up to her. 'So what is it?'

Alva smiled, but it wasn't a real smile. Her eyes shimmered, then she looked away, and I sank down silently beside her on the bed.

Life is not a zero-sum game. It owes us nothing, and things just happen the way they do. Sometimes they're fair and everything makes sense; sometimes they're so unfair we question everything. I pulled the mask off the face of Fate, and all I found beneath it was chance.

Since learning that Alva's disease had come back, I was just stumbling through the days. The cancer had spread; tumours had formed in her liver and spleen. The doctors prescribed chemo- and radiotherapy and upped the dose. Huge quantities of poison were pumped into her, and once again it was unclear whom it was killing, the cancer or her.

During this time Elena and my brother moved in with us, and the three of us took care of the children. Marty played with them; Elena read to them in the evening and drove them to school in the morning, when I was already on my way to the hospital. We all did our best to radiate optimism, but Vincent was the first to see through it.

'Is she going to die?' he asked.

I looked at him in dismay. 'No, of course not.'

'So why's she been gone so long?'

'So they can help her better. Your mother's invincible, don't you worry. She got well again last time, didn't she?'

This seemed to allay his fears. Luise gave the impression of being a bit more confident than her brother, but as often as she could she would visit Alva in hospital and slip into her bed. I can still see her now, lying there beside her mother, neither of them saying a word, one out of weakness, the other out of fear.

'We're doing everything that needs to be done,' Elena kept telling me. 'You don't need to worry about the children.'

'Thanks.'

'And if you want to talk—'

'I know.'

Up till now I'd always been able to rely on Alva not to give up hope, to keep going, but I could tell she hadn't expected to relapse so soon. I wanted to show her the way, and so I eventually called Toni.

One month later – by now it was May – I ran up the hospital steps and rushed into Alva's room. She was dozing, books for her PhD piled on her bed. The spring had been intoxicatingly beautiful so far, and this too was a glorious, sunny day; the little room was practically bursting with light.

'Can you get up?' I led Alva to the window and pointed at the motorcycle down below in the parking lot. She looked first at the bike, then at me.

'But you were always too scared.'

'That's over,' I said. 'No more fear.'

She gave me a long kiss and hugged me. I was still holding the helmet in my hand and I tossed it onto the bed. Then I realised Alva was crying. I held her tight without saying a word.

'But *I'm* afraid,' she whispered in my ear, as if telling me a secret. 'The chemo isn't working properly.'

'They'll increase the dose, or try a different drug.'

'I'm in here almost all the time now.'

It took her a while to calm down; then she let me tell her about my secret driving lessons, and how Toni had advised me when I bought the bike. It was always nice telling Alva about something. Her eyes would widen; she would lean forward, touch your elbow without realising, completely absorbed in her curiosity. She never fell asleep during films, either, not even if she was completely exhausted; she always wanted to know how the story ended.

'When you get out again, I'll take you for a spin on my motorcycle.'

She looked at me sceptically. 'Can you actually ride it properly?'

'Well, I made it here without having an accident.'

We lay down on her bed, which wasn't really wide enough for both of us.

Alva snuggled up to me. 'I like lying here with you.' Her fingers stroked my chin, my mouth, wandered over my eyebrows and temples. 'Did you know I like your little ears?'

'Somehow I guessed.'

'Your little ears are the best thing about you.'

She stared at me for a long while, as if she were really seeing me for the first time. Finally she touched my hair. 'So much grey,' she said, and then fell silent.

My sister came to visit a couple of times at the weekends; she looked after the children, or went for walks with me, and of course she also went to see Alva in hospital. But I sensed that she too was struggling. Her career bored her, and she was increasingly haunted by the thought that she might never have children. One evening we were watching a report about India on TV, and

Liz remarked that she'd never been there. It sounded casual, but I saw the lust for life flare in her eyes and knew that soon she was going to *do* something. When we switched off the TV, she gave me a consoling hug. Or I her – it wasn't quite clear.

I did most of my work at night now, as I could hardly sleep anyway. I told the doctors to be honest with me, but they reassured me. There was still no reason to give up hope, they said. That was enough to keep going. Every morning I ran through the park, often with my brother's dog at my side. Afterwards, I tried to use every second of the day to support Alva: I tidied up, ran errands, shuttled between hospital and home, looked after the children. I myself was completely subsumed by the desire to be there for the two of them. But Vincent and Luise fought more often now, and when I tried to mediate or put them to bed they ran away in tears, howling that they wanted their mother back.

Marty helped; he put on an optimistic front, but sometimes I'd see him staring into space looking gloomy and disheartened. I knew he liked Alva very much, and that his nihilistic world view contained little that might be constructive in this situation. People were born, lived, died, their bodies decomposed, then all was forgotten. I, on the other hand, said a few prayers for Alva to get well again. I didn't really have much time for religion, but I'd never been a complete unbeliever. I recalled a conversation I'd had with Romanov. We'd been standing in his study discussing theodicy.

'Jules, stop giving me all this,' he'd said. 'Sometimes there just isn't an answer: that's the way it is. We humans have been left completely to our own devices down here. What sort of a world would it be, anyway, if every prayer were heard and we knew for certain that we'd carry on after death? What use would we have for life any more? We'd all be in Paradise already. Do you know the saying, "Give a man a fish and you feed him for a day; teach him to catch fish, and you feed him for the whole of his life"? That's exactly how this works. God wants us to learn to look after ourselves. He doesn't give us the fish and hear all our prayers, but He listens to us and observes how we cope with everything down here – sickness, injustice, death and suffering. Life is there in order to learn how to fish.'

These words were a comfort to me now. I thought of Romanov's magnanimity in inviting me to his house back then, and of how much he must have loved Alva, and I promised myself I'd go and visit his grave in Lucerne one day.

July came, and although Alva was now too exhausted to work, she still sat in bed reading books for her dissertation: Spinoza, Locke and Hegel. It was as if she were trying to ignore the body that was betraying her.

I just said, 'All that difficult stuff.'

'I like it. I've always enjoyed engaging with other people's ideas.'

I couldn't say what I wanted to say, but she knew anyway.

'If I really have to die,' she said, 'it'll be with my head held high. The same way I've lived, for as long as possible. Reading and learning.'

Back then I was sure she missed her nocturnal walks. I often imagined Alva secretly roaming the hospital at night. I almost wished she would: that in a mortal sense she would never leave, but would mysteriously disappear into the darkness forever.

'How are the little ones?' she asked.

'Luise's doing okay, she's just been very quiet lately. She asked me if she could skip school and come with me. And Vincent had a fight with a teammate.'

'Look – he drew that.'

Alva pointed to a picture lying on the table. It showed her with a dog, clearly my brother's. Beside them, Vincent had drawn a black circle. He must have used all of the crayons to make that black. The black circle is death, I thought in alarm.

'I suppose we'll have to postpone taking that philosophy course together,' she said, with apparent amusement. 'You've got away with it again.'

I smiled briefly, then was assaulted by fear, violent and physical, like a fist slamming repeatedly into my stomach. A pain that tied up the world in one big knot.

Alva reached for my hand. A familiar, lovely feeling, holding her hand in mine; they fitted together perfectly. I'd noticed it even back then, all those years ago, in the red Fiat outside the village pub. I stayed with her until it started getting dark outside, then I got on the motorbike. But I didn't head home, to where Marty had already put the children to bed; instead, I rode out of the city. Once on the country road I opened the visor. The wind sliced at my face. I loved this feeling.

Sometimes I stared at the road so hard that everything disappeared. Then I'd see her sitting beside me at school. Red-haired, shy, with too-big horn-rimmed glasses, very pretty in spite of her slightly crooked front tooth. Alva, such a mystery to me.

I now knew all the things I hadn't known back then. That this girl had lost her sister, and that later she would go to Russia and get married. That she would meet me again and have children with me. I knew about her nocturnal walks, and also that one day she would be a brilliant mother; and I knew that eventually she would get sick and be lying in hospital. Back then, when Alva came to sit beside me in school, we could never have suspected any of this. She was just a country girl beside a city boy who had recently been orphaned. The beginning of a story. Our story.

And then I thought about death, and how in the past I'd often imagined it as an infinite expanse, like a snowy landscape over which you flew. And where you touched that whiteness the emptiness was filled with the memories, feelings and pictures you carried within yourself, and it acquired a face. Sometimes what was created was so beautiful and strange that the soul dived in to linger there awhile before finally continuing on its passage through the void.

Sometime in late July I found myself alone in the apartment. It was early afternoon, the silence felt strange, and I watched the wind whipping across the courtyard and burying itself in the bushes. It had been raining non-stop for several hours, but broad beams of sunlight were now stabbing through the slate-coloured clouds. I decided to look for the letter I wrote to Alva when I was nineteen, shortly before our friendship fell apart. I'd agonised over it at the time, and in the end I hadn't given it to her after all; I'd found it too childish and melodramatic. Instead I'd quoted my father, that nonsense about how she was just my one true friend. And so she'd never read these handwritten lines, dated 26th May 1992:

Dear Alva,

I hope you like the short stories I wrote. If not, please don't be too harsh. By the way, I finally finished The Heart is a Lonely Hunter *last weekend. Now I know why you like McCullers so much; I found the story moving, too. I quite understand now why you want to be like a character from the book and always go to cafés after midnight. But actually those people who come together there every night are all restless and a little bit broken. So I hope you won't be like that. Incidentally, what touched me far more was the way one character separates life into an outside and an inside world. I've thought about that a lot these past few days, because I've realised that I do something similar.*

The outside world is what other people call reality. A world where my parents have died, where I have no friends, where my brother and sister went away and left me without a backward glance. A world where I'm going to study some arbitrary thing in order to do some arbitrary job. Where I simply can't open up to people, where perhaps I seem cold and have lost part or even all of myself. Where death is waiting at the end, and where I sometimes feel as if I'm simply disappearing.

The inside world, though, is different. It's just in my head. But isn't everything just in our heads? You've often asked me what I'm thinking when I'm daydreaming or not paying attention in school. The truth is: I'm not thinking, I'm just being. Sometimes, in these moments, I imagine that I grew up in America, or that my mother and father are still alive. For example, in class today I drove through Italy. With my parents, my aunt, my brother and sister, all of us together in a cosy caravan. The feeling was so intense I can hardly put it into words. We were children again, driving along the Amalfi coast, and I could describe to you precisely what it smelled like there – lemons and seaweed – and the already autumnal colours of the leaves, and how the watermelon slices we ate glowed red in the sunlight. I could tell you what we talked about, my brother and sister and I, and our parents' expressions as they looked at us, and how we ate in this little Italian restaurant and my sister sipped a glass of wine for the first time and acted as if she liked the taste, but I know that really she thought it was disgusting.

Of course I realise that these fantasies are childish. And yet I'm sure there must be a place in this universe from which you can look at both worlds and they're both equally true. The real and the imagined. Because in a billion years, when everything's gone and forgotten, when time has erased everything and there's no proof any more of anything what-soever, what reality was will be irrelevant. Perhaps then the stories I invented in my head will have been just as real and unreal as what people have called reality.

I expect you're asking yourself why I'm writing all this to you. And I'm sure you'd like to know why I'm only asking if you'd like to share an apartment with me in Munich instead of telling you what I feel for you, even though it's probably obvious. I'm not doing it to offend you – on the contrary. The truth is I just can't yet. Because I don't know what you think of me, or feel for me. And I'm afraid of risking what we have, and, after my parents and siblings, losing you as well.

But after all these years this letter is my first big step back to the outside world. I've confided in you something I've never told anyone before. Because I know it's wrong to retreat so much into oneself. I want to be wherever you are, and that is – reality.

Your
Jules

A day in August, I no longer remember which. The ceiling light in the hospital corridor is flickering, which bothers me terribly. The smell of disinfectant irritates my nose; someone runs along the corridor, trainers squeaking on the floor. I watch the mechanical movements of the doctor's mouth; the words take a long time to reach me. The treatment isn't working any more; further metastases have formed; they're fighting a losing battle. The cancer is everywhere now in Alva's medicine-weakened body; it's gained the upper hand. The doctors recommend withdrawing treatment and providing only palliative care.

They give her only a few more weeks. I keep repeating it in my head. *Only a few more weeks.*

Even though we'd secretly been reckoning with this for a long time, right to the end we'd hoped against hope that there would be a miracle cure. Even after this inconceivable diagnosis I still couldn't believe it. It must be a hallucination, and in a minute we'd all be sitting round the table together, having dinner, playing board games afterwards. It simply couldn't be true. It wasn't possible.

I hardly felt anything any more. I trudged along the hospital corridor, my mind a blank, and opened the door to Alva's little room. I entered it as I had hundreds of times in recent weeks, but this time everything was different.

'It's happened, then,' said Alva, when she saw me. 'Game over.'

I'd expected to find her in floods of tears, not reading a book. She still wouldn't let go of her PhD, even though it was clear now that she would never finish it. I sat down beside her on the bed and tried to hug her, but she gently pushed me away.

'I can't bear to be close to anyone just now,' she said. 'This is something I have to go through alone. Give me a bit more time, okay?'

I stepped back. 'Of course.'

'I'm sure I'll feel better again tomorrow.'

She looked away. I gazed at her for a moment, then left the room.

It was too bright in town; the sun poured down over the streets and houses. I didn't call anyone; I let myself be borne along by the stream of people. The smell of pretzels from a bakery. Workmen mending the paving. An elderly couple strolling along the pavement hand in hand. *Only a few more weeks.*

At home Elena had cooked for the children; she seemed to have heard the news already because she gave me a wordless hug. The children sat silently at the table. I assumed no one had told them yet, but they seemed to sense that something had fundamentally changed.

I hugged my daughter, then my son, ate a few mouthfuls, went to the bedroom and lay down on my side of the bed. The other side would now stay empty forever. Immediately I was annoyed by my self-pity: don't be pathetic. Eventually I fell asleep.

In the evening I was woken by my brother. Without saying a word he lay down beside me on the bed where Alva had always lain. His face was pale.

'I called Liz,' he said. 'She didn't say much, but she seemed pretty down already. With all that's going on at the moment we're forgetting what a state she's in. She told me recently that she really wants to resign. I said she should come to us in the holidays.' He turned to me. 'And Toni said to tell you he's always there for you if you need him. He'll come straight away if you'd like.'

We looked at each other.

Marty shook his head. 'I just don't know what to say to you. I've been trying all day to think of something comforting, but there just isn't anything . . . At least your children will be able to say goodbye. That's not much, but it's more than we were able to do back then.'

'They're only seven,' I said. 'In thirty years' time they'll hardly be able to remember their mother.'

'Then it'll be up to you to tell them about her.'

We lay there like that for a few minutes; then Marty got up. He and Elena looked after the children that evening. I lay motionless in the bedroom, heard Luise and Vincent asking for me and the sound of clattering plates or a running tap. But I couldn't bring myself to get up. I went on lying there until the apartment gradually fell silent and everyone was asleep. Then I switched on the light and picked up Romanov's last book.

I don't want to describe what the disease did to Alva's body at the end. Or detail the moments when she lost her composure and despaired. I felt as if she were dangling over an abyss, clinging on to the cliff with just one hand as the disease loosened her fingers one by one.

But although her body was destroying itself, the spirit it housed was still strong. After a few days of utter dismay and helplessness, Alva had decided to face death bravely. I didn't know where she found this strength, as by this point she could hardly stand and spent more and more time dozing in morphine-induced sleep. But when she woke it would flare up, this strength.

Alva had been transferred to the palliative care ward. Not a drab, white room any longer; this one was almost comfortable, with a laminate floor, watercolours on the walls and a red imitation-leather armchair. I sat there beside her bed from morning till evening. I made use of every second she was conscious; I wanted to steal as many last memories as possible from whatever time we had left. Sometimes, during these conversations, I would be inundated by a sense of loss and would fall to pieces; but then she would smile, even though it wasn't her old smile any more, and tell me to pull myself together; whatever would Death think of me? She always behaved as if he were standing there with us in the room.

'You can speak openly, don't worry,' she would say. 'I have no secrets from him.'

The mornings were hardest for her; she would lie in bed stiff and silent, incapable of talking to me. 'When I'm dreaming, it's all gone,' she murmured. 'Then I wake up, and every day I have to find out all over again that I'm going to die soon. And then I forget again at night in my sleep.'

She was too weak and tired now to read, and her philosophy books stayed on the bedside table. Instead, I read aloud to her: excerpts from novels, and poems, too. Her favourite poem was by Rilke; I could recite it by heart now.

> *Before us great Death stands*
> *Our fate held close within his quiet hands.*
> *When with proud joy we lift Life's red wine up*
> *To drink deep of the mystic shining cup*
> *And ecstasy through all our being leaps –*
> *Death bows his head and weeps.*

She liked it best, though, when I read to her from my own stories, the two novellas in Romanov's book. About the man who led a second, different life in his dreams. And the one who remained alone until he died because he stole time from people, and never found anyone who would forgo a long life to spend just a few years with him.

'Unfortunately I won't get to read your novel in this life any more,' said Alva, during one of our last longer conversations. Later, when the doctors increased the dose, she was mostly too tired or confused from the morphine to be able to talk to me properly, but that afternoon she was awake.

'There are so many things I'd still have liked to have done. So many places I would have liked to have seen.' She looked at me. 'You were always going to cook for me.'

'I've often cooked for you.'

'But never the way you were going to back then, at school.'

I had to admit that was true.

'And the two little ones,' she said. 'I wanted to watch them getting older. I would so have liked to talk to Luise when she reaches puberty and has problems. Or when Vincent falls in love for the first time.' She reached for my hand. 'You're going to have to do that instead.'

In the previous weeks I'd convinced myself that I would somehow manage all of this, but suddenly I erupted in despair and anger. I got up and paced about the room. 'But I can't do all this,' I said loudly. 'I can't replace you. I'M JUST NOT READY YET.'

'You're a brilliant father.'

'Only because I've had you. You raised them, you did all the important stuff. I just played with them. I'm just not *ready* yet to look after them on my own. The children don't listen to me as it is, they don't buy me in this role.'

Alva shook her head wearily. 'You'll grow into it, I know you will. When they need you, you'll be ready.'

'I just don't want their lives to be like mine was, back then.' I sank into a chair; my foot jiggled nervously.

She stayed calm. 'I understand. But what I see in you as a father is not so much the cheery joker you are with the children as the serious man you've always been. And your brother and sister will support you.'

'Liz is in India,' I said, still incredulous.

'I didn't know that.'

'She handed in her notice three days ago and just ran away to Mumbai instead of helping me here. She's gone and buggered off, as always.'

For a moment Alva didn't know how to answer this.

'Even so,' she said eventually. 'I couldn't imagine a better father for the twins. You're just going to have to take my word over yours on this one.'

I sat down beside her on the bed. 'Okay,' I said quietly.

Her hand in mine again.

'Are you frightened?' I asked.

'Sometimes. When I still can't get my head around the idea that I'm going to die soon, I get frightened. But just as often now I can get my head around it, and then I feel good. It would have had to happen sometime anyway.'

I nodded. Our conversation was like a race; we both kept wanting to add something. 'It's only been eight years,' I said. 'Just eight years that we were together. We wasted so much time.'

'I've often thought about that as well.' With an effort, Alva sat up and gazed at me. 'Jules, do you remember the last time we talked to each other at school?'

'At the leavers' ball?'

'No, you didn't even look at me then. It was before that.'

'Right,' I said. 'You came to me all of a sudden and suggested we do something together on the last weekend of the school year; you absolutely had to talk to me. And I didn't call – I was too proud. Although of course I wanted to see you. But when I mentioned it to you later, you'd forgotten anyway. You couldn't care less.'

She pulled her hand away. 'No,' she said. 'It was the other way round. *I* asked *you* after the weekend why you hadn't called, but you . . .'

Her voice in my ears was suddenly muffled. A hairline crack appeared in reality once again, and now, in my mind's eye, I could clearly see myself standing in the classroom telling her that lie, with a complacent grin: that I'd forgotten about our date and had got off with another girl at a party.

Alva looked at me. 'All weekend I'd hoped you'd call. I'd finally . . . *understood* you, Jules. Every time someone called our house, I hoped it was you.'

'Is that true?'

'Yes. And when you didn't call I was sad, and annoyed, but mainly with myself. After that I just wanted to get away.'

For a while I struggled for words. But when I began to reproach myself, she interrupted me immediately.

'We just weren't ready.'

'But we would have had so much more time.'

'We had our time anyway,' I heard her say. 'Better eight years with you than fifty without.'

I rested my head on her bed. When I closed my eyes, I was able to go back to that summer of our youth and recognise her timid signals. The memento album she'd given me so casually back then, that contained only photos of the two of us for which she'd written little poems. Or how she'd once said, mockingly, that she wanted to go abroad and would have to fall in love if she were to stay. We'd kept missing each other back then, had needed each other as friends and realised too late what we felt for each other. I could correct our mistakes now; it was so infernally easy. Never mind where, in her Fiat, in my dormitory room or at the mountain cabin, all that was needed were fewer words, fewer deeds, and suddenly everything was different . . .

But then I had to open my eyes again and face what was to come. That which could not be changed.

Some neighbours and some of Alva's fellow students came to say goodbye, and her father visited regularly from Augsburg and brought her flowers. It was only right at the end that he couldn't bear it any more: knowing that, after the first, he was actually going to lose his second daughter, too. He asked me to give her a letter.

And eventually the day came when our children saw Alva for the last time. The doctor was in the room, so I waited with them on a bench in the corridor. Both were silent, and clearly out of their depth. They were only seven, and certainly weren't aware of the true finality of this goodbye; but on another, deeper level they understood all too well what lay ahead of them.

Two nurses passed our bench, chatting, then there was silence.

'Is there really a Nangiyala?' asked Luise.

'What's that?' I asked.

'It's from a story Elena read us.'

'From *The Brothers Lionheart*,' added Vincent quietly. 'Nangiyala is a country you go to when you die.'

'Is it nice there?' I asked.

'Yes,' they both said. They looked at me expectantly, as if it were entirely up to me what happened to Alva after her death.

'I'm sure she'll go there if she wants to. But maybe she'd like to go somewhere else. In any case, she'll be somewhere where she can see the two of you clearly.'

They both believed it straight away, and for a second I believed it, too. Then the doctor came out of the room and we could go in.

I was afraid Alva would be asleep, or woozy from the drugs. I was relieved to find her looking reasonably alert. When she saw the children, her expression changed. At first she seemed glad, but when she realised why I'd brought them her eyes were filled with such pain I could hardly bear it.

Wordlessly our children put their gifts on the bedside table. Vincent had painted her a goodbye picture of his favourite animals and another of him with her, and Luise had brought her a particularly beautiful stone she'd come across while playing in the park, which was supposed to bring her good luck.

They hugged Alva, then climbed into bed with her once more. When at last they wept I turned my head away and left the room. Eyes blurred with tears, I sat on the bench again, so powerless, so useless. An emptiness inside me the like of which I'd never felt, not even when my parents died.

After a few minutes Luise and Vincent came to me in the corridor. I don't remember what we did or said after that.

My brother and Elena were now looking after the children almost round the clock, so that I could stay with Alva. Visiting hours didn't apply to me any more. I didn't want to leave her alone, not at night, either.

From time to time we'd listen to music on the CD player I'd brought her; Nick Drake albums, or her beloved George Gershwin. Usually she would fall asleep; then I'd lie down beside her, and sometimes I'd talk quietly about my fears of what it was going to be like without her.

If she was conscious, though, I'd tell her about how I'd only joined the athletics club back then because she admired athletes, or about those months of absolute freedom when we moved in together in Munich. About how we would often watch the children as they slept. And of course I told her again and again how much I loved her and how important she was for me and that I would write about her one day.

Alva just lay there and listened.

'Oh no,' she said quietly one day.

'What is it?'

'I just thought about the frozen fox, exactly as you said I would.'

And a glimmer of her former smile appeared on her thin face.

On her last day I scarcely let go of her hand. I didn't want her to go feeling that she was alone, because I sensed it was still hard for her. The monstrousness of the fact that she could die at any moment, that she had to let go of everything and allow herself to fall into the unknown, was palpable. It was sunny outside; I'd drawn down the blinds, but the light penetrated the slats and fell in thin strips onto the floor. Alva kept her eyes closed most of the time now, but whenever I squeezed her hand she squeezed back. And whenever I went to fetch myself a coffee I ran as fast as I could so I could come back and hold her hand again. And she would squeeze again once, briefly, and then I would do the same, and she was still there.

The last time she opened her eyes was in the afternoon. She looked at me, and when she saw that I was weeping silently she seemed troubled, as if she blamed herself. And she squeezed my hand again, and then she closed her eyes once more. I could almost feel her thoughts racing through space and time, looking for one last treasure, one last beautiful moment she could hold on to. Perhaps she thought of the children and me, or of her sister and her parents, the past and the future. One last great explosion of thoughts and feelings, tangled fear and trust, and already it was flying away with her, astonishingly fast and strange and immeasurably far away.

Another Life

What if there's no such thing as time? If everything we experience is eternal, and it's not time that passes us by, but we ourselves that pass by the things we experience? I often ask myself this. It would mean that while our perspective would change and we would distance ourselves from treasured memories, they would still be there, and if we could go back we would still find them in the same place. Like leafing through a book backwards, perhaps even back to the beginning. My father would eternally go for evening walks with me in the park, and Alva and I would be perpetually captured on our trip to Italy, sitting in the car at night and driving towards a future full of hope. I try to console myself with this thought, but I can't feel it yet. And I can only believe what I feel.

It's some time before Liz hears about my motorbike accident; she's travelling around India without a mobile phone and doesn't read her e-mails for weeks. The day she gets back we all go together to Munich's Northern Cemetery. Leaning on Romanov's walking stick, I limp along the path between the graves, my brother and sister at my side. Liz on the left, Marty on the right. Because of my accident the funeral took place without me: this is the first time I've stood at my wife's grave. A plain black marble headstone, engraved with her name and the dates of her birth and death. A cipher for her story: *Alva Moreau, 3.1.1973 – 25.8.2014.*

When I have all this in front of me, the pressure in my chest is released. *Death is the opposite of unreality*, I think. I want to be alone for a moment. Marty leads my children away, and Liz also steps aside. Silence lies over the cemetery; the only sound is the gentle whispering of the wind. All of a sudden I'm ashamed that I fled into my dream world these past few weeks, like a child. But it was only there that Alva could still be alive – there, where my parents were also still to be found.

Memory, the last refuge of the dead.

And I see Alva before me again, and talk with her, but this time the picture soon dissolves and is displaced by another: me on the motorbike, riding along a country road. I'm listening to music on headphones, visor open, and I don't know how to go on. That morning I fixed the date for the funeral, and afterwards I talked to my children, and it's become clear to me again that I'm just not ready for all this.

I accelerate, faster and faster, and yes, it's true, it feels a bit like flying, just as Toni always claimed. But I'm sure it's possible to take it to the next level. Soft guitar sounds in my ears, 'Heroin' by the Velvet Underground; then the drums and vocals tentatively come in, the music gets more forceful, more angry, the vocals let rip. I put it on maximum volume. My heart beats faster, the wind presses my face backwards, and suddenly it all wells up, Alva's death, the prospect of not being able to look after the children on my own, anxiety about losing everything, and I see Romanov before me saying, with fear in his eyes, that he can't let go, but that isn't going to happen to me.

And in that instant I let go.

The motorbike doesn't head into the curve; it keeps going straight on, and leaves the road, and I think that this *really* feels like flying. For one second I am freer than I've ever been in my life, nothing is in my hands, I can't control anything any more, what's happening will happen.

And then, for a fraction of a second, I see my children before me. At the last moment I wrench the bike to the left after all, just scraping the side of the tree, and it all goes dark until I come round in a hospital room.

*

A few days after the visit to the grave I am discharged from hospital. Liz is living with me for the time being; my brother and Elena are often here as well. They can't have children, and now they're looking after mine. While I take the dog for a walk, Elena makes lunch; while I lie in bed, numb, calling Alva's mailbox just to hear her voice, Marty plays with the children in the courtyard. A leaden time in which I simply can't get back on my feet. Years before her death, Alva told me she didn't want to know when she was doing something for the last time, and now I'm thinking of things she did for the last time and when and where. The last kiss, at her bedside. The last sex, quick and perfunctory, at home, firmly believing we'd soon sleep with each other again. The last time she played with the children was in her hospital room: Concentration, and Luise won by four whole pairs. Yes, you remember that, I think; you note something useless like that.

The children have understood that I need help; they do as they're told when I put them to bed, or they want me to help them with their homework. Just like me and my siblings all those years ago, they too will lead different lives now. Their true life with their mother is over; it's gone off down a different track. And they need someone who will guide them through everything on this new and difficult track, and that someone is going to be me. And I realise that perhaps I am the right person for this after all, because I've been through it before.

This thought is enough to give me hope. Enough for me to function, at least. I can laugh again if I have to, read to the children if they want me to, cook for them and cope with the day-to-day. Once, though, a song comes on the radio, a song about the Eighties, a time when I was a child and carefree. I hear this simple line in the chorus and for a moment I am thrown off course:

> *Things are better when they start*
> *That's how the Eighties broke my heart*

213

Our life gradually returns to something approaching normal. It'll never be completely normal again, though, not least because the children and I are moving in with Marty and Elena in the house by the Englischer Garten. They've always had too many empty rooms, and now they won't be alone any more, and nor will my children and I.

The day we finally leave our old, now empty home, I survey the bare rooms and think about what else Alva and I would have changed over the years. Imagine how the children's rooms would have become teenagers' dens, mentally rip out walls or repaint the kitchen.

Marty, standing outside by the removal van, calls me.

'Jules, are you coming?'

I glance around one last time, look down at the inner courtyard, the swing and the treehouse. Then I turn and go to him.

Luise was opposed to the move at first, but Vincent loves his uncle and is pleased to be living with him. They often sit together in the nursery, and just like in the old days Marty spends hours tinkering with a petrol-fired toy car or dispensing drops of liquid into petri dishes. The little sports car and the microscope were a present from him to Vincent. And a bit to himself as well. All in all, it's a time of fulfilling wishes: every couple of weeks we take the children to the football stadium or the zoo; we visit the Deutsches Museum and see an exhibition about ships. On Sundays I put the TV in their room, make them hot chocolate with whipped cream and bacon on toast, and we watch their favourite cartoons together.

Luise often mourns her mother desperately, and then is cheerful again a moment later, whereas Vincent's feelings blossom in secret. You never see him smile, which is a shame, because I think my son has a very beautiful smile; it instantly chases all the introspection from his face. For months he loved drawing; now he's given it up, and recently he started to be afraid of the dark. We always have to leave the door of the nursery slightly ajar now so the comforting light reaches him from the hall.

One evening he still can't sleep and, clutching his blanket, he comes into the living room where I'm watching television, as I do every night. It's a wordless exchange. Vincent looks at me questioningly for a moment, wondering whether he's allowed; I stroke his head; he understands, and snuggles up to me. The TV is showing a documentary about rock crystals and how some only grow and thrive in the dark and shadows. *Crystallisation.*

Suddenly Vincent starts to cry. He doesn't make a sound, though, and goes on staring at the television as if he doesn't want me to see. I hug him, and it's only then that he really starts to weep.

'I miss her too,' I say, over and over again.

After a while he calms down and falls asleep. I stopped watching television long ago; I'm just watching him. The old images in my mind: *Sitting alone in my dorm room at school after my parents' death, snow still in my hair. Standing uncertainly in the school-yard watching the other children play. Drifting away – far, far, far away.*

I carry Vincent back to bed, tuck him in, feel a deep connection with him. I see myself in this boy so clearly it hurts.

In late autumn I visit Liz in Berlin. She's resigned from her teaching post in order to write and illustrate children's books. I think it's a good idea, especially when I see the first drafts and sketches. In any case, Marty and I have pledged to support her financially.

'Do you regret giving up your job?' I ask her.

'Not for a second. The pupils weren't writing me love letters any more. That's when I knew I had to stop.'

Liz has moved into an apartment in Kreuzberg; she's given most of her old things away. All the little boxes and chests of drawers, the dolls and figurines, the Asian cups and African pitchers. Her new apartment is clear and bright and empty. There's just one old photo on the wall in the kitchen, from boarding-school days. In it I'm not quite fourteen, tiny, daydreaming; Marty is sixteen, a long-haired giant in a leather coat, Liz seventeen. She's staring rebelliously into the camera from beneath the hood of her green parka, fag in mouth, invincible in her youth.

'I'm sorry I just ran away,' I hear her say. 'I'd like to be the older sister who always looks after her brothers; instead, I've let you down twice now, and that's twice too often. I just can't escape myself.'

I look away from the photo. 'It's okay.'

'You always say *It's okay*. You can complain sometimes too, you know. Nothing is okay, if you stop and think about it.'

'Maybe. But that doesn't help anyone.'

She nods. 'I'm sleeping with him, by the way.'

'With who?'

'Who do you think?'

I honestly can't guess.

'Toni.'

For a moment I'm so surprised that all I can do is give her a mocking look. 'Why now, all of a sudden?'

'Because I want a baby.'

'And apart from that . . .'

'There is no apart from that, it's solely for the purpose of procreation. I know how weird that sounds, because I used to get so worked up about it, all that talk about motherhood; my view was always that sex is something wild and should above all be fun. But now, for once, it's also the thing it's actually intended for.'

I'm about to say something, but she indicates that I should keep my mouth shut.

It's no surprise, then, that Toni is particularly euphoric these days. When I warn him not to hope for too much, he waves at me to be quiet.

'*You can't be wise and in love at the same time.*'

'Says who?'

'Bob Dylan.' A broad grin spreads across his face.

'But you know she doesn't love you.'

'Maybe she will when the baby arrives.' Toni nudges me. 'I think it's great, by the way, that you've all moved in together.'

'The whole thing does remind me a bit of boarding school. I'm starting to believe that everything in life eventually comes full circle.'

'Boarding school . . . What was that little bar called again, the one where we used to play billiards?'

'The Jackpot.'

'Right – the Jackpot. How do you remember all that? It seems to me you never forget anything.' Toni pointed at my forehead. 'All locked up in there.'

You're a rememberer and preserver, you just can't help it, Alva said to me once, years ago, and perhaps it's true. Her sister Josephine and the somersaults at bedtime, my Aunt Helene, our careworn grandmother, old classmates, casual acquaintances, my ex-boss at the record label, and Norah, too, of course: there's a whole realm in my head filled with all these people, some half-forgotten, that I've met along the way. I want to preserve them all, prevent them from disappearing; I have the feeling that otherwise they would never have been here at all.

And so I start reworking and rewriting my novel. Sometimes I'm afraid it could get too dark, and I also know it'll be difficult to do justice to them all; especially *her*. Ultimately, that's what I plan to do with Alva: immortalise her as a character in a novel. But even if I never finish this story, I won't stop writing again. Because I've understood that this is the only place where I can be all of them at once. All the possibilities.

Because the little boy who's afraid of everything: that's me. And so is the child who cycles fearlessly down the hill, breaks his arm, and immediately gets back on the bike. I am the outsider who withdraws after his parents' death and does nothing but daydream thereafter. And I'm also the high-spirited pupil, popular with girls, whose parents are still alive. I am the teenager who doesn't dare confess his love and slides into loneliness. The cheerful, confident pupil who lives life to the full. The drifter who dropped out of university and works for a record label in Berlin. The man who didn't hear about that job and moved abroad, where he still lives. The photographer who really *wanted it* and is now successful. The writer who was able to reconcile with his father and so didn't have to make amends by becoming a photographer. I didn't stand a chance with Alva, because her sister didn't disappear and she didn't need me later on. Alva didn't stand a chance with me, because things went well for me after school and I was able to forget her. I found the love of my life and lost her again too soon. I was able to hold on to her in my youth; we made good use of the time. I never got back together with her, but stayed with Norah; we have a son. And I grew up in Montpellier and am married with no children; I never met Alva.

All these were possible, and for a long time it seemed to me quite random that, out of thousands of variations, this was the one that came about. As a young man I had the feeling that since the death of my parents I'd been leading another life – the wrong life. Even more than my siblings, I wondered to what extent the events of my childhood and adolescence had defined me, and it was only very late that I understood that I myself am the sole architect of my existence. This is what I am when I allow my past to influence me, and, conversely, just as much when I resist it. And all I have to do is think of the moments with Alva and my children in order to understand that this other life, the one in which I have now left such clear traces, cannot be wrong any more.

Because it's mine.

Just like before, Marty reads out interesting newspaper articles to us over breakfast; and these days we even have a billiards table in the basement. 'Isn't it funny that the two of us have become friends?' I say to him one night, while we're playing a game. 'When I was a child I thought I'd hate you.'

Marty responds by potting the green. He pats me briefly on the shoulder, then, seemingly unmoved, starts talking about a particularly talented student. I can tell that he's embarrassed, though.

'Just out of interest,' I say. 'That time they stuck me under the shower. Did you really not hear me?'

'When was this?'

'At school. I was shouting for you, right outside your door. So: did you hear me or not?'

Marty shrugs. 'I don't remember.'

I laugh. 'You bastard. Of course you remember.'

A guilty smile flashes across his face, then Marty pots another ball with an artful shot off the cushion.

'Stop showing off,' I say.

Later on we're upstairs in the kitchen; my brother is making chicken sandwiches with salad and mayonnaise, his speciality. He hands me the plate, then puts a saucepan of milk on the stove.

'What's that for? Are you making cocoa for me now as well?'

He just grins. We sit ourselves down in front of the television with our plates.

'I have to admit, this sandwich is absolutely outstanding.' I lean back contentedly and take another bite. There's a black-and-white film on TV: Charles Foster Kane enters the sleepy editorial offices of the *New York Daily Inquirer* and shakes the whole place up.

'Jules, do you remember when we were lying in your old bedroom? It was the day you found out Alva wasn't going to make it. I wanted to say something comforting to you, but I couldn't think of anything.'

I nod; I haven't forgotten.

'That really bothered me,' says Marty. 'I'm your elder brother – that doesn't really mean much any more at our age, but still. These past few weeks I've thought a lot about what I could have said to you back then. Then something occurred to me, while we were at the shipping exhibition. A comparison. It's a bit silly.'

I sip my cocoa. 'Fire away.'

'It's . . . From the moment we're born we're on the *Titanic*.' My brother shakes his head; he's uncomfortable giving speeches like this. 'What I'm trying to say is: we're going down, we won't survive this, it's already been decided. Nothing can change that. But we can choose whether we're going to run around screaming in panic, or whether we're like the musicians who play on, bravely and with dignity, although the ship is sinking. The way . . .' He looks down. 'The way Alva did.' My brother is about to say something else, then shakes his head again. 'Sorry; I'm just not good at this stuff.'

I am only slowly growing into Alva's death. In the meantime I've enrolled at the university and am going to philosophy and English lectures, while at night I often go for walks. Insomnia is my new companion, so now I often roam the neighbourhood on my own after midnight. My ramblings always end with a visit to a particular café, one of the few that are still open at this late hour. It's stylish and unpretentious, with an elderly gentleman improvising at the piano. 'Ah, the Gershwin fan,' he says when he spots me, because last time I was in I asked him if he could play something by George Gershwin. I nod to him, then once again I watch the few customers who come here night after night, and ask myself why they're in this café and not at home. All of them have their stories, their reasons, and I like to guess at them quietly, for myself.

I don't visit Elena as much in her practice these days; instead, we occasionally go for walks in the Englischer Garten.

'How often do you think of her?' she asks me one day.

'Often,' I say immediately. I consider. 'But not as often as a few months ago. There are moments when I realise I've forgotten her, and then I feel bad.'

'You shouldn't,' she says. 'It's important now that you start to look ahead. Vincent and Luise will need you in the coming years. They'll have friends, enter adolescence, fall in love; they'll have problems and will need help. You've got all that ahead of you. And you're going to be good at it.'

As she keeps talking, I realise that, as so often, Elena is right. The past is noticeably fading, but the future is still a long way off. I can think only of the moment, the children, their worries at school or the task of bringing them both up. Their needs loom so large before me that I can barely see what lies beyond; my own descent into old age, for example. Reassuring, somehow.

I stop and take Elena's hand. 'I don't think I've ever told you how glad I am that we have you,' I say. 'I wish I knew how I could thank you, for everything. You saved my brother, and my children love you.'

Elena stops too, and brushes her dark hair off her forehead. 'When I found out that I couldn't have children, something inside me broke. I accepted it, of course, but I believed something would always be lacking. A constant, silent feeling of regret. You and your children have made that feeling gradually disappear.'

It's a rather formal exchange, I realise with amusement, as if each of us has handed the other an important certificate. I nod to her, and we walk on. I notice that I'm feeling better.

We spend Christmas in Munich; as well as Liz and Toni, Alva's father joins us. When he sees his grandchildren he comes alive. He helps them decorate the tree and cheerfully recounts a spectacular climbing trip on Mont Blanc, but shortly afterwards I see him sitting on the sofa in silence, lost in thought. I'm just about to go over to him when Elena sits down beside him and they start talking.

I make a grand announcement that I'm cooking for everybody, then retreat to the kitchen. My children are allowed to keep me company. Vincent is soon bored and runs out again, but Luise watches me with interest.

'What are you doing?'

'I'm stuffing the turkey. This is going to be the stuffing.'

'What do you put in it?'

'Dates, peppers, onions, a bit of sage and seasoning . . . Do you want to help?'

I show her how it's done, and because she enjoys it I show her a few other things, too. We spend half the day in the kitchen;

she helps me with the herb sauce, the potatoes *au gratin*, and also, later on, with the 'Irresistible Cake'. Watching her, I get quite sentimental, but she doesn't seem to notice, scurries to the fridge, darts back again, and keeps a close eye on the saucepan as she melts chocolate. I remember how my mother used to bake this cake, and again I think: everything comes full circle.

It doesn't happen as often any more that images of the past reach out and clutch at me, but when they do I'm always surprised by how the light of memory makes particular moments shine brightly. An ordinary evening at boarding school is transformed, in retrospect, into a beautiful experience. I see myself sitting with my classmates by the lake; we're having a drink, teasing one of our number, picturing what the future holds. Now, though, my memory moves me closer to the others than was in fact the case, lovingly placing me right at the heart of the action. Suddenly I am laughing lightheartedly with my classmates. I know that there were very different moments, too, yet I can feel that, back then, I must have been content. Memory is a patient gardener, and over the years the tiny seed I planted in my head that evening at school has grown into a marvellous memory.

There's singing before the opening of presents – self-mocking looks among the grown-ups, the children innocent and cheerful – and after dinner, as we're sitting round the table, pleasantly full, Toni does a few tricks for us. He turns playing cards into banknotes, then picks a fork up off the table – mine – and rubs it until it lets itself be knotted like a piece of string. As we're staring in astonishment, Toni's gaze drops to his left shoe, the laces of which have come undone. He casually shakes his ankle and the shoelaces tie themselves as if by an invisible hand, even doing a double bow.

'You lunatic,' cries Marty. 'Tell us right away how you did that.'

Later, as we're putting the children to bed, Alva's father also takes his leave. He gives his grandchildren a quick but affectionate hug, then I walk him to the door. 'Thank you for inviting me,' he says, and starts to head out to his car.

'I'm not sure whether you know, but when Alva was little the thing she liked best of all was skating with you on the frozen pond.'

He stops.

Embarrassed, I continue, head bowed: 'And every time you came to visit us these last few years she was excited for hours beforehand, and was really happy. Alva understood your pain, and why you were so seldom here, and couldn't come to the hospital any more at the end. She always understood everything, and she loved you, I know that . . .'

I feel Alva's father's hand on my arm and look up in surprise. He's looking straight at me for the first time this evening. His eyes are green; not as bright as his daughter's, but very gentle, and melancholy. He seems to want to say something, but eventually he just nods at me.

After he's driven away my gaze falls on the Italian chest of drawers in the hall, which came from my former apartment. Alva particularly liked to sit on this chest of drawers, like a strange animal, knees drawn up close to her chest, engrossed in a book, listening to music or discussing something with me. And although it's been a really lovely Christmas, everything inside me suddenly collapses and my vision blurs. I bite my lip and find myself thinking of the ward where Alva spent her final days. At this moment I miss her *so much*, and instead of going back to the others I step onto the veranda and stare out into the night. Glittering hoarfrost on the twigs and branches of the trees, the stone paving coated in a delicate layer of crystals. It's cold, but that doesn't bother me.

After a while Liz comes out to join me. She puts a red envelope in my hand. 'Your other present. I hope it brings you more luck than it did me.'

In the envelope I find a little white wooden counter. The kind you use to play Barricade. Touched, I put an arm around my sister.

'Don't think it's just you who sees us.' – Liz leans against me.

– 'You're seen, too. I often think of my Jules and wonder what he's brooding about and how he's doing.'

We contemplate the star-spangled sky. I am filled with a profound sense of security: for the first time, I find the indifference of space comforting.

Liz, however, is looking at me sideways, her mouth curled up at the corners.

'What is it?' I ask.

I don't get a reply.

'Come on, tell me, what's the matter?'

But she just goes back inside.

Later, when all the others are asleep and I'm about to set off for my nightly walk to the café, I see Liz sitting on the living-room sofa in her pyjamas, with the guitar on her lap. She doesn't notice me, and strums away randomly at first; then she starts to play a song familiar to me since earliest childhood. I can't think what it is to begin with, but when I hear her sing it for the first time, I know.

It was just like Liz to keep her pregnancy secret for weeks. Marty and I tease her that she's going to be the oldest mother in the world, but she says that's just how long it took her.

Toni, of course, is delighted. Only the fact that Liz isn't sleeping with him any more bothers him. 'Mission accomplished,' he says, in his Viennese lilt. 'So that's it for us. But I wouldn't have thought it would upset me this much.'

'Yes, that really is a great surprise.'

'Go ahead and laugh,' he says. 'I'm still convinced she'll come back to me when the baby arrives. Then maybe she'll want another one, and we'll magic that up as well.'

'She'd be forty-six by then.'

'Who cares? Some clocks tick differently to others.'

The amniocentesis shows that everything's fine. It's going to be a girl. Luise is especially pleased, and is determined to 'teach' her cousin something later on, but won't say what exactly. She seems to have more or less got over her mother's death. She goes to an acrobatics course every week (and does cartwheels at home, too, out of sheer exuberance), often brings friends back for meals, and her teacher assures me that she's a cheerful, popular child.

Vincent, on the other hand, is still finding things hard. His grades have nosedived, he hardly talks any more, the other children are starting to avoid him. He only has two friends, who are similarly withdrawn, and he often visits them in the afternoon to play video games. I know I have to do something if he isn't to end up one day being as uncommunicative and fearful as his father once was.

The boy is tough, though. I go to every one of his football games. He usually sits on the reserve bench and is only swapped in just before the end. The other children all seem to be bigger, more robust, more ambitious; he'll often stand there on the pitch daydreaming, which makes his coach furious. He always makes Vincent play defence, which is definitely not his position as he's far too slender and light and just gets pushed aside by the opposition forwards.

On one occasion, though, a bleak, rainy day in late March, he's brought on again near the end of the game. Instead of staying at the back, Vincent keeps attacking. His coach yells at him from the touchline, telling him to get back, but my son just stays out in front. Just before the final whistle, one of his team plays a long, high ball. All four opposition defender skip past it in a slapstick routine, and suddenly Vincent is alone, facing the goal. He shoots, too hastily; the ball bounces off the goalkeeper, comes back to him, he shoots again, and this time it lands in the net. His first ever goal. Vincent turns, wide-eyed; he himself can't believe what's just happened. The other kids run up to him and hug him, the coach offers hesitant praise, and still he stands there glancing around in disbelief. Then he looks over at me, and suddenly he smiles. It's his beautiful, rare smile, enigmatic and almost a little bit wise.

With that smile he can salvage everything.

I wave back, but it seems to embarrass him, because he's already running on and wiping his nose on the sleeve of his jersey.

In the Easter holidays, Liz and Toni come to visit; the plan is to drive to France, according to old tradition. We're already in the car, the luggage has been stowed. Only my brother is dawdling; as so often, he's last. Then I remember that I've forgotten the children's football. I run back to the house, and as I reach the veranda I hear the old, familiar sound.

I see Marty outside the front door, concentrating on pressing the handle down again and again, always the same pattern. Eight fast, eight slow, eight fast. He's so immersed in what he's doing that it's a while before he notices me. At first he feels caught in the act. Then he shrugs, shamefaced: 'Well, I suppose we all have our dark little secrets.'

We look at each other without speaking.

'Please don't tell Elena,' he says eventually.

'How often do you actually do it?'

'Sixty-four times altogether. Eight is my lucky number, so eight times eight is twice as lucky. I used to do it twenty-three times, but it didn't work out. With the luck. So now it's eight times eight. First I press fast, for fast luck, then slow again, for steady contentment.'

I say nothing, then I go indoors and fetch the ball.

'You know I have to do it all again from the beginning now,' says my brother, at the door. 'Sorry.'

'What shall I tell the others, about where you are?'

'Think of something.'

'You do realise you can always talk to Elena about it?'

Marty just shakes his head and grins at me helplessly. A little spark of madness, the price for normality. I go back to the car alone, bouncing the ball on the pavement, and hear my brother press the handle down again.

The spring sun hits the trees with searing force. Lured by Languedoc nature in bloom, I take Vincent and Luise on an outing. On the way, they want to know who the house in Berdillac belonged to, why I almost never speak French, who's the best footballer in the world and whether Uncle Toni really has magic powers and went to Hogwarts, as he claims. I answer patiently, filled with the happiness of having them around.

We come to a hill. 'First to the top,' says Luise, and off she runs. Vincent immediately chases after her, and I follow, at a distance. After a long race to catch up, it seems for a moment that I'm about to win; they both squeal as I push past them, then let them overtake me after all just before the finish.

We stand on the crest of the hill, panting and laughing. Down below is the valley. When we come to the oak tree beside the little bench with the view, my children react much as my siblings and I did all those years ago.

'Someone's lopped off a branch.' Following my gaze, Vincent points to the still-leafless lump protruding from the tree.

'I know,' I say. 'I suspect it was your grandfather who sawed it off, with his own hands.' I don't want to tell my children the tale I heard from my father.

'Your Papa sawed it off?' Luise asks. 'But why?'

I just shrug, but a slight shiver runs through me.

With her hand, Luise keeps tracing the words carved into the tree. *L'arbre d'Eric.* Written into the bark with a knife, by my father, more than fifty years ago.

The two weeks in Berdillac fly by. I often think about how my brother and sister and I lost sight of each other after childhood. How we were compelled, early on, to face up to the finite nature of life, and reacted in completely different ways. My sister greedily enjoying her life to the full, my brother anxiously patrolling his. But after all those years in which each of us went his or her own way, we're actually here, sitting together again round the breakfast table. There are only just enough places; my children are winding each other up, Elena is talking to them, calming them down, Toni's voice echoes cheerfully through the room, Marty rustles the newspaper and talks about an article, Liz contradicts him, a chair falls over, there are shouts, a confusion of voices. I'm the only one at the table who is quiet, who just closes his eyes and listens. I love these sounds. The only way we can overcome the loneliness within us is together.

On the last day we have a picnic in a meadow. The sun points down from a cloudless sky, scorching hot on the grass. My siblings spread out a blanket; the husky sniffs excitedly at Elena's ham sandwiches. Meanwhile the children run away from Toni, who follows them, roaring wildly and bellowing that he's a forest monster who's going to catch and eat them.

Liz, now heavily pregnant, sighs. 'He's such a child.' But a little smile steals across her face.

I watch my son, running away from Toni with a serious face; as always, he's good at concealing his amusement. And my daughter, who's making squeaking noises. This morning we had quite a long argument, as – to her horror – she's supposed to get a brace after the holidays. She ran up to her room, crying. It was one of those moments when I missed Alva and wondered how she would have dealt with the situation. And as I did so I wondered whether I really am all that different from my own father.

Luise, however, has long since forgotten this morning's row; she's hiding behind my back and shouting at me to protect her from the forest monster.

Toni walks up to us and points his finger at me.

'Out of my way,' he growls in a deep, disguised voice.

'Buzz off, loser,' I say.

I hear my daughter laughing behind me.

Toni steps closer, looking menacing. 'One more wisecrack like that and you die.'

I'm about to answer when I see Vincent, alone, skulking at the edge of the wood. I mumble that I'll be right back and head over to him.

'Hurry up, though,' says Toni. 'We want to play football.'

I run into the wood, where my son snaps a twig and flings it away, irresolute. I put my hand on his shoulder, and we walk together for a while. Eventually we come to the stony river with the tree-trunk lying across it, and I immediately hear my father's warning that it's too dangerous.

My son is staring at the tree-trunk, intrigued.

'Look how high that drop is,' he says.

'More than two metres.'

'Do you think anyone's ever walked across it?'

'I'm sure they have,' I say.

'Don't believe you.'

'Well, my friend, when I was your age I often walked across it.' I do a quick calculation, and have to laugh. 'That was thirty-four years ago.'

Vincent looks at me in surprise. 'Don't believe you,' he repeats. 'You could really hurt yourself.'

I think of a saying of Wordsworth's: *The child is father of the man.* I look into Vincent's eyes, so full of fear, and I decide. He tries to stop me, but I step onto the tree-trunk. Vincent is shouting at me not to do it, but I keep putting one foot in front of the other. The trunk wobbles; I start to feel dizzy, and sense fear coalescing into a lump in my chest. I remember how Alva, many years ago, on her first visit to Berdillac, tiptoed across the trunk with outstretched arms. I have to do this for her as well.

About halfway across Vincent realises there's no point in trying to hold me back any more, and starts to cheer me on. I glance down once, quickly, at the big rocks sticking up out of the river, worn smooth by the water, and picture another stay in hospital.

But all goes well. When I reach the far side I see my son standing on the other bank. Vincent's eyes are wide and incredulous once more; he seems momentarily speechless. The return crossing proves more difficult; I walk slowly along the slippery trunk again, and at one point almost lose my footing. But I know that there's no going back, because this moment is a seed. I will plant this scene in my son, and hopefully in a few years it will germinate, and he will lose a little piece of his fear forever.

Just after reaching the other side I do slip, briefly; I fall to the ground and get my shirt dirty. Vincent stares at me in alarm, but I pick myself up, grinning.

'No harm done.' I point at the tree-trunk. 'See, it was easy,' I say, though in fact my heart is pounding. I need to catch my breath and recover from this act of daring.

But Vincent is already running back to the others, who are calling to us from the meadow because they want to get on with the game.

'Are you playing with us?' he asks.

'In a sec.'

I stand under a couple of shady trees at the edge of the wood and watch them for a while. Toni is standing in a goal consisting of two pullovers. My daughter kicks the ball in his direction; my son snatches it. He plays a technically elegant double pass with Marty, then dances past Elena and shoots: the ball smacks into Toni's shin. Liz, who's watching the action, tunes her guitar; my brother's dog is also sitting on the sidelines. From time to time he lets out a bark, but he doesn't move. In previous years he would have been sure to run after the ball, but he's grown old now, and calm. If he's lucky, he'll have one or two more summers, and at the end he'll have had a fulfilled life, whereas many years ago another dog drowned in the river not far from here. Things come and go. For a very long time I couldn't accept this. Now, suddenly, I find it easy.

Eventually the children spot me and call out, asking if I'm ready to play at last.

I step out of the forest.

'Yes,' I say, brushing down my shirt. 'I'm ready.'

Acknowledgements

With this book I would like first and foremost to thank my parents. My father for his humour and all the loving, inspiring conversations. My mother for her irrepressible cheerfulness in difficult times and for her belief in me.

Ursula Baumhauer has also been a great support. I'm very lucky to have her as an editor. Thanks also to Thomas Hölzl, Anna Galizia and Georg Grimm, to Roger Eberhard, Tanja Graf, Clara Jung, Daniel Kampa, Ronald Reng, Muriel Siegwart, Veronika Vilgis, Daniel Wichmann, Anne Wiebung, Frieder Wittich and Klaus Cäsar Zehrer.

Philipp Keel gave me as much time as I wanted for this book. His trust and his tireless dedication mean a great deal to me. A loud '¡Muchas gracias!' to everyone else at Diogenes, too, especially Mario Schmuki, and Ruth Geiger, who was always there for me.

In memory of Daniel Keel, who brought me to his publishing house and thus became a major guiding force in my life. So many beautiful things have happened to me since then. For this I can never, and will never, forget him.